W9-AHA-989

Dec '14

# Don't Look for Me

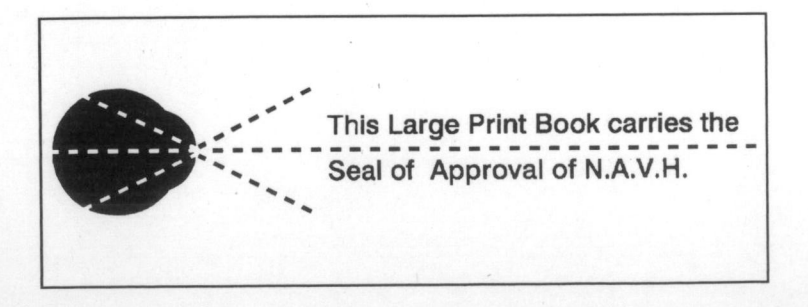

This Large Print Book carries the
Seal of Approval of N.A.V.H.

AN AMOS WALKER NOVEL

# DON'T LOOK FOR ME

# LOREN D. ESTLEMAN

**THORNDIKE PRESS**
*A part of Gale, Cengage Learning*

GALE
CENGAGE Learning·

Farmington Hills, Mich • San Francisco • New York • Waterville, Maine
Meriden, Conn • Mason, Ohio • Chicago

**GALE**
CENGAGE Learning®

Thorndike Press® Large Print Mystery.
The text of this Large Print edition is unabridged.
Other aspects of the book may vary from the original edition.
Set in 16 pt. Plantin.

**LIBRARY OF CONGRESS CATALOGING-IN-PUBLICATION DATA**

Estleman, Loren D.
 Don't look for me : an Amos Walker novel / by Loren D. Estleman. —
Large print edition.
  pages ; cm. — (Thorndike Press large print mystery)
  ISBN 978-1-4104-6853-6 (hardcover) — ISBN 1-4104-6853-4 (hardcover)
  1. Walker, Amos (Fictitious character)—Fiction. 2. Private investigators—
Michigan—Detroit—Fiction. 3. Large type books. 4. Detroit (Mich.)—Fiction.
I. Title.
PS3555.S84D66 2014b
813'.54—dc23                                        2014004472

Published in 2014 by arrangement with Tom Doherty Associates, LLC.

Printed in the United States of America
1 2 3 4 5 6 7 18 17 16 15 14

In memory of Stuart Kaminsky,
who was as good as he wrote;
which was going some

# ONE

I couldn't see the building at first. It looked like a gap in the skyline and one more empty lot. Then a traffic helicopter passed in front of it, dragging its reflection across slate-colored glass standing nineteen stories tall against slate-colored sky. The architect must have hated birds.

WYN-WYN read the plate on a glossy black Porsche in a reserved space, the new model that got seventy-eight miles to the gallon; as if anyone who'd drop $800,000 on an automobile cared about the price of gas. A white-enameled sign with raised black letters said W. HOWARD belonged to the space next to it. I parked there. I figured if Howard hadn't shown up by 10:00 A.M. he was either so important it would be someone else's responsibility to have me towed, or too chronically late to risk attracting attention. Either way it gave me time to finish my business and skedaddle.

I'm often wrong about these things; but there are people in Stationary Traffic who owe me favors.

In the gray-and-silver lobby a Morlock in a formfitting uniform found my name on an electronic clipboard and poked a pass across his lectern. "Hang it on your pocket. Keep it in full view at all times."

It had an aluminum clip and bore only the number 14 in bold black. "Thirteenth floor?"

"Fourteen. Can't you read?"

"You should go outside sometime and count. Thirteen's always fourteen in the plan, and a six-sixty-seven address is really six-six-six. There's a jump for the superstitious."

"You superstitious?"

"Of course not." I knocked my knuckles against the top of his station.

"Well, don't get off on any others, whatever the number."

"You under a bomb threat or what?"

His tiny eyes straddled an icebreaker nose with white hairs twisting out of the nostrils. They looked like fiber-optic wires. "Standard operating procedure. Some people don't like bankers for some reason."

I was confident he didn't include me among the anarchists. The suit was relatively new and I'd stood closer to the razor than usual that morning.

I rode a silent elevator to 14. The pass rode in an inside pocket. No one ever asked to see it. I still have it, a souvenir of a case I'd rather have gone to someone else.

When I got in to see Alec Wynn of Reiner, Switz, Galsworthy, and Wynn, the sun was well clear of the cityscape on the Detroit River. The Hiram Walker distillery glistened in Canada across the way; Walkertown, the neighborhood is called. I can't claim ownership, although I'm one of its most loyal customers. Some daredevils were piloting sailboats among the ice floes, their sharkfin sails striped in bright bikini colors. Wynn sat with his back to the view and never turned to look at it. Why bother? On the wall across from him hung a big framed Monte Nagler photograph of bright-striped boats sailing the choppy surface of the Detroit River.

Wynn, when he got up to shake my hand, turned out to be a big neat man with a black widow's peak trimmed tight to his skull. The graphite frame of his aviator's glasses matched the gray haze where he shaved his temples and he wore a suit the color and approximate weight of ground fog. He had deep lines in his Miami-brown face and bonded teeth with incisors that came almost to a point. It was a predator's face. He was an investment banker, and whatever that was, he seemed all of a piece with the way he kept up his payments on the Porsche. All that gray made sense with the blue walls and yellow-green carpet, like a shark cruising through the bright waters of the Gulf Stream.

"Walker, Amos," he said, as if he were reading roll call. "Is it a nom de guerre?"

"I don't know what that is, but it's on my birth certificate."

"I like it. It has a certain smoky strength."

"So does bacon."

"Speaking of that, have you had breakfast?"

"Not in years."

"I can't manage without it. I missed mine. Would you mind if we took this to the executive dining room? My treat, of course."

So I rode the elevator again, two more floors, directly into a gray-shaded room that took up the entire length and breadth of the building. A well-seasoned party in a red jacket with gold buttons greeted him by name and sat us in a booth upholstered in blue leather looking directly across at the city of Windsor. It was late for breakfast but

10

too early for brunch. We had the place to ourselves along with the waitstaff and four men in their twenties seated at a far table in their shirtsleeves and suspenders. Each had an ear-mounted cell phone, and the way they were conversing without looking at their companions made me wonder if they were talking to each other over the things.

"Conquering the world by microwave." Wynn snapped the creases out of his linen napkin. "When I was their age, we did it on the golf course."

"You have to wonder why the overhead."

"This barn? It's our answer to the Roman Forum. Those senators and philosophers didn't need those Ionic columns to talk about taxes and whether animals have souls. It's all set decoration."

A young waiter in a red jacket with silver buttons arrived with our menus, each the size of a Shakespeare First Folio. He asked if we cared for coffee.

"Tea, please, Jason. The chef knows my preference."

I asked for regular coffee and Jason drifted away. I browsed the light morning fare, decided on eggs Benedict, sausage links, and tomato juice, which Wynn wrote down on a blank piece of pasteboard with an onyx fountain pen, added some fruit and bran

11

cereal for himself, and handed it to the waiter when he came with the tea and coffee. The setup was like the dining car of a train.

When we were alone again, Wynn folded his strong brown hands on the edge of the tablecloth. "I keep seeing your name on reports. The Reliance people employ your services often."

"Only when the job involves people. Those big-box agencies are a whiz with computers and blood diamonds and those teeny little cameras you can hide in your belly button. When it comes to stroking old ladies who see things and leaning on supermarket stock boys who smuggle sides of beef out the back door, they remember us little shows."

"How big is your agency?"

"About six-one and one-eighty."

"Better and better. It means you're in a good position to keep secrets."

"Honest, too; eventually. I lied about my weight."

"The humor I can take or let alone." He refolded his hands the other way. On one he wore a gold wedding band with a respectable diamond, matched closely to the watch on that wrist, heavy, with a diver's dial. The shark resemblance increased by the minute. "I don't like going behind Reliance's back

12

like this. Ernest Krell is an old friend — emphasis on old — and like many men who should have retired long ago, he's sensitive about what he perceives as disloyalty among his shrinking circle. I'm being candid with you for a reason. If what I said gets back to him, I'll know you're not someone I can trust with my situation."

I sipped from my cup. I missed smoking over my morning coffee. State law says you can only light up in a public place if it's a casino. "Krell's a dinosaur with a J. Edgar Hoover complex. If this meeting is a test, you owe me the five hundred dollars I could've earned working a real case, minus the cost of the eggs Benedict. I'd have had to eat one way or the other. If you trusted Reliance in the past, you trust what they said about me."

Wynn pressed his lips together, deciding whether to get mad. The jury was still out when our food came. He dismissed the waiter's obsequious inquiries, and the waiter himself, with a slashing movement of one hand. I'd thought of asking for ketchup, but he'd forgotten all about breakfast. Finally he jerked out a nod. "Fair enough. I take it this meeting is confidential, whether or not I decide to make use of your services."

"That comes with the price of the meal."

13

I dug in. The eggs were perfect, even without ketchup. The tomato juice tasted like can, but the links were good. "Who's missing, your wife or your daughter?"

He shot me a look he probably would have kept hooded in a meeting with competitors. "I suppose it's not all that uncommon, although I don't consider myself a common man."

"No one does. Someone has to be, or the word doesn't mean anything. I do other work, but my specialty is tracing missing persons. I have to think that came up when you were reading those reports. You aren't the kind of man who takes his car to a veterinarian for service. I saw what you drive."

"The thing's a damned embarrassment. There are parking lots in this city I can't use. I'm either barred outright or a Ford assembly worker takes out his key and —"

"We're straining the metaphor, Mr. Wynn." I poked at my hash browns, which I hadn't ordered. In Michigan they're like grits in Tennessee; they come with the territory. If I'm going to eat fried potatoes before noon I ought to be wearing deer-hunter orange.

"It's my wife," he said. "She's left me. Not for the first time, it pains me to say."

14

I laid down my fork and sat back with my coffee. Said nothing.

"Last time, it was with one of the apprentices here, Lloyd Debner. I fired him, naturally."

"Naturally."

He showed his incisors briefly. "Seems awfully Old Testament, I know. I tried to be modern about it. There's really no sense in blaming the other man. We all wake up with hard-ons for a reason. But I saw myself hiding out in my ridiculously palatial office to avoid running into him in the hall, as if I were the one at fault. Grotesque. I gave him excellent references. One of our competitors snapped him up right away.

"Thing is," he added, twitching another smile, "he wasn't that good. I overcompensated on the side of forgiveness. In a perverted way, I guess you can say he slept his way to the top."

"What happened this time? With your wife."

"She left the usual note."

"The usual note?"

"She left one the first time. I tore it up. She said again she was going away and I was not to look for her. I called Debner — a no-brainer, don't you think? Also wishful thinking — but he assured me he hadn't

15

seen Cecelia since their first fling."

"He said fling?"

"Something on that order. I don't suppose this generation has any interest in the argot of ours. I'm assuming you and I are contemporaries."

"I may have a head start on you."

"What did Cicero say? 'Not to have knowledge of what happened before you were born is to live forever as a child'?"

I didn't swing at that pitch. He had a fixation on classical literature.

"However Debner put it, I believed him. But it's been almost a week now and I'm concerned for her safety."

"What about the police?"

His seamed face crumpled like butcher's wrap. "I believe we covered that when we were discussing keeping secrets."

"You've been married how long?"

"Six years. And, yes, she's younger than I, by fourteen years. That was your next question, wasn't it?"

"It was in there. Do you think that had anything to do with her leaving?"

"I think it had everything to do with it. She has appetites that I've been increasingly unable to fulfill. Why is it the fantasies of our adolescence only come true when we' too old and worn out to do them justi

His cheeks rusted orange under their tan. "I'm spilling my guts here, Walker. I —"

Poor Jason chose that moment to materialize, asking if there was anything else we wanted. Wynn swung on him like a great white. "Young man, I believe I made myself clear before that you weren't to approach this table until I summoned you. Must I ask the maître d' here to translate?"

"No, sir." The waiter paled to transparency.

"Good."

"You didn't, you know," I said, when Jason had stumbled away. "Make yourself clear, I mean. You just moved your hand. Not everyone understands sign language."

"I'll tip him a month's wages. Satisfactory?"

"Until the revolution. You'd better hope they don't make him a general. Let's get back to Cecelia. You quarreled?"

"The normal amount. Never about sex. Which I suppose is revealing. I'm pretty sure she's found a new boyfriend, but I'm damned if I can say who."

"Do you have the note with you?"

He extracted a fold of paper from an inside breast pocket and passed it across the table. "I'm afraid I got my fingerprints

17

all over it before I thought over all the angles."

"That's okay. I never have worked on anything where prints were any use."

It was written on common drugstore stationery, tinted blue with a spray of flowers in the upper right-hand corner. A hasty hand full of sharp points and closed loops. It actually said, "Don't look for me." Signed with a C.

A melancholy melody drifted through my brain as I read the line. I couldn't place it.

"There's no date."

"She knew I'd read it the day she wrote it. It was last Tuesday."

"Reason I bring it up, if anything happens to her, even a dull prosecutor could make the case it was the same note she left the first time. He'd tell the jury you used it to cover her disappearance this time."

He'd speared a square of pineapple while I was reading the note. It stalled halfway to his mouth. "Jury? You're getting ahead of yourself, Walker. I said I was concerned about her. I said nothing about foul play."

I pushed away my plate. "That never set well with me, 'foul play.' Sounds like a foot-fault at cricket."

"I know a little something about the game. There are no foot-faults."

"Murder's something I know a little about. I'm trying not to become an expert."

# Two

He topped off his cup from the little steel container the waiter had brought and dandled his tea bag, watching the water darken. The color of his face lightened in inverse proportion to it.

"What can I say? She didn't date the note. People often don't, these days. They're so accustomed to sending them electronically and letting the computer do it for them. Can we agree not to charge me with homicide in the absence of a corpus delecti?"

"Sure. Getting a client's goat in the first session is a trick I invented to clear away the crap. It helps keep from wasting your money. Any ideas where she might go to be alone? Favorite vacation spot, her hometown, a summer house, anything like that? Do wives still run home to their mothers?"

"Her mother died when she was young. We sublet the place in Florida in the off-season. Cecelia grew up locally and has

20

universally disliked every place we've visited on vacation. Do you seriously believe I didn't think of those things, or are you still testing me?"

"I finished. Now I'm groping for a handle. What hobbies does she have?"

"Spending my money."

"Are you sure you want her found?"

He sat back. He hadn't touched his tea or his breakfast since refilling his cup. "I apologize for my shortness. This latest — abandonment — has me on a roller coaster. I'm furious with her, hurt, but I do want to talk with her face to face, ask her if she wants out. If she does, I don't intend to be ungenerous. Just to leave without a word —" He shook his head.

I drank the rest of my coffee. "It seems to me you don't know your wife too well after six years, Mr. Wynn. When I find her, if I find her, I can tell you where she is, but I can't make her come back, and from the sound of things she may not want to come back. I wouldn't be representing your best interests if I didn't advise you to save your money and set the cops loose on it. I can't give guarantees they won't give."

"Are you saying you don't want the job?"

"Not me. I don't have any practice at that. Just being straight with a client I'd like to use as a reference next time I meet someone in a snazzy restaurant."

"No police. I said that."

"Okay. I'll need a picture. And what was her maiden name? She may go back to it." I shook loose my notebook.

"Collier." He spelled it. "And here." He took a three-by-five photo printed on glossy stock from an inside breast pocket and sailed it across the table.

I caught it. She was a redhead, and the top of that line, athletically built in a sleeveless top with one arm raised to smooth back her hair. She looked like someone who would wind up married to a full partner in an investment company with gray temples and an office with a view of two countries. It would be in her high school yearbook under Predictions.

She knew how to work a camera from the supply side. Smiles can make you popular; pouts can make you rich. I stuck the picture in my notebook and asked him where I could find Lloyd Debner.

"He's with Paxton and Ring on West Michigan. But I told you he doesn't know where Cecelia is."

"Maybe he should be asked a different way."

■ ■ ■ ■

The sun was as pale as if it had been dug up from the ground. Our January thaw had come right on time in mid-February, followed by another Arctic episode broken up by two days in the seventies, which were capped off by the biggest blizzard in years. We were three weeks short of Easter, and where the earth had turned to snot under the pavement, stalagmites of ice had formed in the potholes like miniature tiger traps. Everywhere else it's called climate change. Here we call it Michigan.

For once I'd been on top of the season, getting the radiator flushed of antifreeze during one of the warm days. Now I could smoke a cigarette in the time it took to start the motor.

An Asian accent at Paxton & Ring told me over my cell that Lloyd Debner would be tied up in a meeting the rest of the morning. Since his building was a short hop from mine, I bribed the vagrant who lived in the grown-over parking area in front of the abandoned coffee shop across the street not to vandalize the Cutlass and went upstairs to throw away my mail. When I'd done that I called Barry Stackpole.

"Who's working the cop house since you kicked yourself upstairs to cyberspace?" I asked when we were through maligning each other's family tree.

"When you read the *News,* you know." As always he sounded like a kid whose testicles had just dropped. We were born only a couple of months apart; but he hadn't spent the time since then curing his vocal cords with tobacco.

"I never know when to look for it on my doorstep. Is it Thursday and Sunday, or Tuesday and Saturday? I remember when news meant new."

"Also when 'cyberspace' was still in the dictionary. Who's dead this time?"

"Most of my cases don't involve murder."

"Only the ones I read about."

"It's a wandering wife job. I'm trying to find out if the cops pulled in any Jane Does in the past week, either horizontal or in the upright and locked position."

"Why ask the squirrels? Go straight to the tree."

"Officer Krupke answers questions with questions. The client wants it OTR."

"If clients didn't, you wouldn't have clients. FYI, I don't gather most of my information from the Net just to put it back on the Net: That'd be like jerking off in front of a mirror. I still get it the old-fashioned way."

"You're getting too old to B-and-E the FBI building."

"OMG, you're dense. I hie myself down to Thirteen Hundred, or wherever the department's outsourcing its officers these days, and read it off the blotter, just like Jimmy Olsen. GMD?"

"I just ran out of alphabet. I don't know that last one."

"Get My Drift?"

"OK. F.U."

"What's this Jane look like?"

"I'll fax you her picture."

"Bullshit. You notice I didn't say BS."

"Shows how much you know, smart guy. There's a chain drugstore down the street. They won't sell me Vicodin anymore, but their fax service is for everybody. What's your number?"

"Hang on, I have to look it up."

*"You?"*

"Shows how much *you* know. I only keep the machine for historical value. When the e-file came in, fax went to live with the crank-up phonograph."

I said he'd have it within a half hour, hung up, and sat looking at the wallpaper across from the desk. The butterfly wings had faded since I'd put it up, but the paste still held. Meanwhile a dozen technologies had hatched, fluttered for a while, and died. Some butterflies are born without mouth parts. They aren't expected to live long enough to get hungry.

Paxton & Ring occupied two floors of a respectable-looking building that had harbored a string of local banks dating back to Jesse James, with nonfunctional columns in front. It was coming on lunchtime, and a lobby the size of Carlsbad Caverns was a riot of men and women in knee-length coats and leather gloves breaking for the feed-lot; but I had a hunch Lloyd Debner was the type of upwardly mobile junior executive who ate at his desk. There was no guard to direct me this time, just a square black menu with white snap-letters on the wall by the elevators. I listened to "Sweet Caroline" on the way up and for the rest of the day.

On my way to the reception area I swept past a pair of men conversing in the hallway, almost missing it when one said, "I hear what you're saying, Lloyd, but the Dow Jones is speaking louder."

I braked and spun about. A man in his early thirties with a fashionable five-o'clock shadow was listening to his grayhead companion with an elaborate show of patience, his hands in the pockets of his suit pants; I could see they were balled into fists.

"Tim, the market's a nervous old lady. When a coolie sneezes in China, it drops below ten thousand. Then he blows his nose, gets back to raking the rice, and it shoots up to fifteen. You can't set your watch by a clock without an hour hand."

"Rice is grown underwater. I'm not sure you rake it."

I nosed in. "Lloyd Debner? Amos Walker. I'm —"

"Second," he said, without taking his eyes off the other man. "We're talking a million, tops. Your firm spends more than that in a year on paper clips. This one will bring in a billion that same year. You know the difference between a million and a billion?"

"I think I do. In first grade, when the other chaps were counting marbles, I was counting dollars." I couldn't figure out if his West End accent was real; that *chaps* stuck out like a monocle on a frog.

"I wonder. A million dollars in singles would stack three feet high. A *billion* would reach the top of the Penobscot Building."

"Why would anyone ever want to stack them at all? Especially in the street, and in Detroit."

I said, "This won't take long."

"Make an appointment. Tim, you can joke all you —"

"It's about Cecelia Wynn," I said. "We can talk about her out here in the hall if you like. Tim won't mind, will you, Tim?"

Debner looked at me for the first time. His eyes were set close in a narrow face atop a body that looked as if he'd sprouted in an orchard with trees planted too close on either side, his shoulders pinched into peaks alongside his stalk of a neck. In that situation there's no way to grow but up, but he hadn't the material to reach beyond six feet. I couldn't see what Cecelia saw; but I wasn't married to Alec Wynn.

He brushed a well-kept hand over his stubble. "Tim, I'll catch you later."

"Maybe then we can guess the number of beans in a jar." The grayhead chuckled as he went down the hall.

"Who'd you say you were?" Debner's earnest tenor became a spaniel's bark when no billions were involved.

"Amos Walker. I still am, but a little older. I'm conducting a private investigation on behalf of Alec Wynn."

"You came to the wrong place — and incidentally may have destroyed a deal I've been working on for months, that will involve thousands of jobs. What happened

28

between Mrs. Wynn and myself is all over."

"I'm interested in when it wasn't."

He glanced up and down the hall, like a spy in a bad movie. There were a few people in it, men in suits, women in the same suits cut to exhibit their narrow waists and treadmill calves, hair plugs, tennis bracelets, and exposed elbows galore with cell phones clamped in place. "Come on. I can give you a couple of minutes."

"I might need more."

He led me into a men's room two doors down, upholstered in white marble, with mahogany stalls and urinals you could walk into without ducking your head: GENTLE-MEN was lettered in flecked black on a frosted glass panel in the door. We stared at a guy combing what was left of his hair in front of the long mirror over the sinks until he put away his comb and picked up a maroon leather briefcase and left for his loan appointment.

Debner evidently was a fan of bad spy movies. He bent down to see if there were any feet in the stalls, flung open two at random to make sure no one was crouching with his feet on a toilet lid, straightened, and brushed again at his baby whiskers. Either shave or grow a beard; but mine had grown too gray for display just as the fashion came in, so I may be prejudiced.

"Credentials," he said.

I unshipped the leather folder with the state ID and county sheriff's star. He pointed at the bling. "Is that legitimate?"

"Clap if you believe." I put it away. "You can confirm it with Wynn, if you like. I put him on speed-dial." I brought out the cell.

He shook his head. "I believe you. I haven't risen far enough in this profession to become the target of blackmail." He looked in the mirror and moved his silver necktie a centimeter to the right. "I don't see Cecilia when we pass on the street. I had all my phone numbers changed, my e-mail address, after we got back from Jamaica so she couldn't contact me."

"Jamaica, that's where you went?"

"I rented a bungalow outside Kingston. Quaint word, bungalow: Sounds charming and inexpensive. Take my word, it's much more the second than the first. They don't mention poisonous snakes in the brochure.

"Worst mistake I ever made," he went on, "and I'm not talking about the vipers. I was headed for a junior partnership at Reiner when I happened to fall for the boss's wife. Now I'm back to arranging back-door deals with corrupt Third World bureaucrats for pennies on the Euro."

"Who isn't? How'd you and Cecelia get on?"

"Like a couple of doves. So good we crammed a two-week reservation into three days and came back home."

"What went wrong?"

"Different drummers." He found a stray hair in an eyebrow and plucked at it between finger and thumb. He kept missing it. Everyone does, in a mirror.

"Not good enough."

He grinned; boyishly, if he was that stuck on himself. "I didn't think so. To begin with, she's a health nut. I run and take a little wheat germ myself sometimes — you don't even have to point a gun at me — but I draw the line at dropping vitamins and herb pills at every meal. She must've taken sixteen capsules every time we sat down to eat. It can drive you blinkers."

"Blinkers?"

"Sorry. Tim went to London once. His pseudo-Brit's contagious. Batshit. People in restaurants probably thought she was a drug addict."

"Sure she wasn't?"

"She was pretty open about taking them if she was. She filled the capsules herself from plastic bags. Her purse rattled like a used car."

A fat character in a blue suit, pink shirt with a white collar, and lemon-colored tie came in, hesitated when he saw us standing near the sinks, and nodded at Debner. "Lloyd."

"Mr. Zinzser."

He looked at me, politely not moving his gaze below my chin to take in my ready-made suit, glanced toward the stalls, then washed his hands. Debner used the time to inspect his stubble for lint.

"Owns the old Kern block," he told me after the fat man waddled out.

"You don't have to be rich not to want to use the toilet in front of an audience."

"Look, I'm late for a meeting."

"Not at half-past noon. Your story's leaky. You don't cut a vacation short just because your bed partner does wild garlic."

"It just didn't work out, okay?"

"You were sleeping with the boss's wife, a man who could come down on you so hard your great-grandchildren would be born midgets. It had to work out just to stop her from going to Wynn with her tale of scorn."

"Scorn. Seriously?"

"The old sayings are always the best." I waited.

He finished grooming his pelt and grinned at his reflection. I bet that melted the widows looking for a place to stash the life insurance. "If this gets around I'm washed up. Not just with women. Don't be fooled by all the marble and Armani; we're in the jungle. Virility's the real coin of the realm."

"Whether or not you can get it up doesn't have to get around. I'm just looking for Cecelia Wynn."

"It wasn't that," he said; but he said it too fast. "Not the way you think. There's not a thing wrong with the throttle."

"Yeah?"

"Yeah. She said she wasn't satisfied."

"Yeah?"

"Why do you keep saying that?"

"You mean, 'Yeah'?"

"Yeah."

"I've never had to pitch to a roomful of investors. In my line of work you don't get much chance to expand your vocabulary."

"Yeah. Well, no one's ever told me that before. I'm not used to complaints."

"So why take this one so hard? Excuse the expression."

"Damn it, I said it wasn't that! Look, we never had this conversation, okay?"

"As far as I'm concerned we never met. Except I have to report to Alec Wynn."

"I guess it's okay if you tell him. He might give me a break down the line. One rejected lover to another, you know?"

"Yeah."

We shook hands. He squeezed a little harder than I figured he did normally.

# THREE

I couldn't get a signal through all the polished stone in the downstairs lobby. I dropped two quarters into a pay telephone in a bank of five, without any other customers, bombed out on Wynn's cell, recycled the coins, and fought my way through two executive assistants before Alec Wynn came on the land line at Reiner, Switz, Galsworthy, and Wynn. His voice was a full octave deeper than it had been in person. I guessed it was that way in front of stockholders, too.

"I had the damned thing turned off," he said. "What news?"

"If it was my wife missing I'd keep it on, but that's just me. How come when I asked you about hobbies you didn't tell me your wife was into herbs?"

"Who's Herb? She with him?"

"Herbs; silent *H*." I told her what Debner had said about the capsules.

"I haven't dined with my wife in months.

35

Most of my business these days is conducted in restaurants, and she gobbles down Cobb salads or whatnot with the women she's disposed to call her girlfriends. Really, what married couple eats at the same table now?"

"I wouldn't know. The last time I was married there was only one telephone company. I guess you can't tell me the name of her herbalist."

"Herbalist?"

"Sort of an oregano guru. Most people, when they get into the health jag, get into it up to their eyebrows. There's no GPS yet to direct them to active old age, so they go to professionals."

"How do you know this?"

"I work this job, Mr. Wynn; it's not a fantasy football league. A lot of the runaways I trace go to religion before they go off the radar. Some of them go to politics and sign up as volunteers. Others go to drugs. The rest take their restlessness to whatever quack promises to improve their lives with branch water and underbrush served up in expensive containers."

"Well, I wouldn't know about that. I improve my life with single-malt Scotch."

My respect for him went up a degree. "What about her girlfriends?"

"Possibly. All told I suspect she's logged

in more time with them than her husband of six years. Try Patti Lochner. That's Patti with an *i*. I suppose you might call her the ring-leader of their litter of cats."

I scribbled it in my book. "Not a friend of yours, I'm thinking."

"Nor of Cecelia's. In every cadre of women, there's one who's poison to all the rest. The best poisons taste sweet the first time."

"I'm liking Patti. I'm just wondering why she wasn't already in my book."

Air blew out on his end. "She should've been. This is like being burglarized. In the first shock of the event, when you report to the police, you overlook some of the most important things that were taken. You miss them only when something brings them to mind. Not that anyone would object to Patti's absence; it's a rotten metaphor.

"Now that I think of it," he went on, "I should have mentioned her first off. If anyone was born to cause trouble in a happy marriage, her name is Patti Lochner."

I turned to a crisp new page. "Tell me about Patti."

The house in Grosse Pointe Woods was tucked just off the U of a cul-de-sac lined with baby grand mansions on wedge-shaped lots, a geometrical miracle: Local ordinances prohibited contractors from building too close to neighboring property lines. Dwarf trees squatted like Oompa-Loompas in tidy rows and there wasn't a tiny windmill or whimsical mailbox in sight; the local property owners' association would see to that.

It was a doll's house on steroids, at first glance a cute little construction of red brick with glass inserts on either side of the front door, reinforced with filigreed iron to discourage smashing and entering. Decorative rocks bordered flower beds dozing under straw pallets, with red cedar boxes under the windows.

With the leaves not yet on the trees, the miniature effect turned out to be an illusion. The house had been added onto in the rear, going back and back until it crowded four thousand square feet, and it wasn't the biggest on the street. My house and office would fit snugly between the broad curved sidewalk and the front steps.

The neighborhood had a bright plastic smell, like a new toy. Not so long ago it had belonged to the estate of an auto pioneer who had drunk himself to death during the Depression, leaving a widow to wallow into centenarian old age in a bin full of greenbacks and stock certificates. The new houses had sprung up like lichens on the stump of a demolished mansion built of Florentine marble and half the Brazilian rain forest.

A Vietnamese housekeeper in a gray uniform answered the bell. The eyes in the crumpled rice-paper face were small and sharp. I'd called ahead, and Mrs. Lochner was expecting me. I followed a pair of sore feet in broad deck shoes through a series of rooms done in pearl-gray and mauve into a solarium with a retractable roof — locked in place that day — and bumped-out glass panels all around. Normally such rooms are wasted that time of year, when the dismal sunlight skulks in with its tail between its legs, but the curved glass warped it into something almost virile. It fell directly onto a rattan sofa where the lady of the house lounged in a yellow sundress and pink prescription lenses, jingling ice cubes in a tall narrow glass.

I've stopped expecting anything when I knock on a door, but if I'd formed a picture of Patti Lochner based on what Alec Wynn had told me, I'd have been disappointed. She didn't look like anyone's idea of Lucrezia Borgia. She was a plump little thing in her late thirties who wore her black hair in bangs and a lot of copper-and-turquoise jewelry that clanked when she moved her head, gestured with her hands, or recrossed her ankles. The ankles were too thick for any runway, but her bare feet were well-shaped, with high arches and a French pedicure with tiny crystal inlays that glittered like shattered glass at the scene of an accident. A distinct roll pressed out the fabric between the bra built into the dress and the waist of the skirt. Her cheeks dimpled deeply when she turned up her red-red lips in a smile and her long eyelashes glittered also. She had a start on a double chin and probably cookies in the oven.

"Like the place?" she said. "We put it in last fall. Got me through the winter with only two trips to Miami."

I looked at the glass blisters. "Nice. Now I know how pus feels."

She hesitated, then reacted. She had a tinkly laugh, like vampire women in a movie. "You look thirsty. Long Island iced tea?" Her underarm jiggled when she waved a hand full of copper rings at a cloudy pitcher on the table at her elbow.

"No, thanks."

"Something stronger? Nha's gotten to be a good little bartender."

"It's a little early for me."

Her smile shut down like a bank window. "Meaning it isn't for me. A polite phrase with a venomous sting."

"Diplomacy. I come down with a bad case of it every time I cross Eight Mile Road."

"You should lay off judging people until you get to know them. It happens I played a round of golf yesterday and got a little enthusiastic putting away the chill at the nineteenth hole. Stoli, no ice. I recommend it. Today I had Nha put in just enough vodka and plenty enough caffeine to settle my head. What's *your* remedy?"

"My father said the best way to avoid a hangover is to stay drunk. I wasn't judging you, Mrs. Lochner. I was giving myself a pep talk. I'm still coming down from a spell of too many prescription drugs, and I'm too old to move all my bags from one habit to another. I'm no stranger to that one either."

She swirled her glass again. Ice jingled, copper clanked; and while we're at it, she had a tinkly speaking voice too. A living set of wind chimes. "Is that how private detectives work it? Open up with a bunch of personal stuff and expect the suspects to follow their lead?"

"I don't know. Maybe. I've been at it so long I don't think it out that far. What is it I'm supposed to suspect you of?"

"Talking Cecelia into leaving that shirt stuffed full of money she married. I'm sure he told you all about how I've been poisoning her mind against him for years."

"That would fall under the category of client confidence. Yeah, he tore you up, down, and across: A shredder should be so efficient. Female dogs would have a hell of a class-action suit against the entire married male human race if they could just dial a phone."

She laughed again. I'd need to tone down my shining wit to keep my skin from crawling away from the bone.

"I've been called worse," she said. "I wouldn't give a shit for any woman who hasn't. If I shock you with my language, fuck you. My father blew out his heart working quality control at Dodge Main."

"Whose didn't? Chrysler made rotten cars for years."

She changed direction. "What did you think when he told you all these things about me?"

"I came here first thing to see for myself."

"Sit down, Mr. —" A pair of strong eyebrows lifted helplessly above the pink glasses.

"Wolfe. Nero Wolfe. I'll send you a case of black orchids later so you won't forget again." I drew up a chair with palm-frond upholstery to match the sofa and sat.

She rattled her fingernails, bedazzled also, against her glass. Just picking her nose would cause a hemorrhage. "I think you're just about the rudest man I've ever met on first acquaintance."

"Everyone says that, but I keep working. What've you got against Wynn, apart from his shirt stuffed with money? I liked that image, by the way. He wasn't nearly as lyrical on your subject."

"Proving my point. But being married to one of those myself gives me the advantage of clear observation. Trouble is, my Harold isn't stuffed as tightly."

"Ah."

"What does 'Ah' mean?"

"It's just a space filler. I get nervous when there's a lull in the conversation."

"That's the first time you've been less than candid. I doubt you've ever been nervous."

"Wrong. I have a carry permit for a reason."

She played another concert with her ice cubes, caught a sour note, and addressed the problem with another hit from the pitcher. She took a deep gulp. "I'd admire to make a run at Alec. He's quite a good-looking man, you know, and clean in his habits. I doubt a pair of his undershorts has ever made contact with the floor of his bedroom; unlike those of some other men I could name."

"So Mr. Lochner's a slob. Even slobs have their good qualities. Anyway, you married him."

"Everyone makes mistakes. They put a delete key on computers for a reason." She sucked in a lozenge of half-melted ice and crunched it between her teeth; it put my own on edge. "But Cecelia's too good a friend for me to go behind her back. It would be so much more convenient if she surrendered the field."

I got out a cigarette and juggled it, hoisting my brows. She lifted a slim black remote off the table, pointed it skyward, and pressed a button. The retractable roof hummed and slid open, exposing a rectangle of sky the color of a ripe cataract. I lit up and blew smoke that direction. It drifted up through the opening and shot away on a trade wind. "You're some kind of friend, Mrs. Lochner."

"I'm a bitch. Alec wasn't wrong about that. It isn't his fault the language hasn't come up with something less stale. The truth?"

"I thought we'd stopped lying after I said this is a nice room." At that point I'd have

44

welcomed a comfortable lie. You can trust someone experienced in B.S. to run you around the block; but no one can trust the completely honest person to be what she seems to be.

"He deserves better than Cecelia," she said. "The worst bastard who ever lived should have someone to come home to after he's screwed the world who doesn't loathe him just for having a penis."

I burned a quarter-inch of tobacco in the silence of wisdom.

"On second thought —"

"Nha!" She bellowed.

The Vietnamese maid hobbled in, her face wrinkled and bleak.

"What time is it, please?"

"A little past two, missus." It was the first time I'd heard her speak; if a poker face ever had a tongue, it was hers.

"Late enough. The drink cart, please. Detroit isn't Long Island."

45

# FOUR

Nha came in trundling a butler's caddy loaded with bottles, including a leaded-crystal seltzer dispenser you could use for a baseball bat, glasses, siphons, and a brass ice bucket, jangling like a belly dancer, and threw a brake that locked it inside her mistress's reach.

"What can she mix you?" Patti Lochner asked me. "She makes a lethal mai tai, but you don't seem the type."

"I keep sticking my eye with the umbrella. Bourbon on the rocks will hold me till teatime. This time of day I get a sweet tooth."

"We'll take it from here, dear."

The housekeeper left us, hobbling on the outside edges of her feet. Patti caught me looking after her.

"The Cong used old-fashioned flatirons, heated over charcoal. Either it was the Cong or the American Rangers; her English is better than my Vietnamese, but we don't communicate well beyond the basics. Gentleman Jack?" She lifted a tombstone-shaped bottle from the upper deck.

I took it from her gently, as I would Poe's "Tamerlane" in octavo, if there was such a thing; something very fragile and very valuable, anyway, and selected a heavy Old-Fashioned glass. "Yourself?"

"Kahlúa, neat. I feel like a bit of candy myself."

I browsed among the glasses until I found a narrow-stemmed cordial, etched with climbing vines on the outside. She touched the back of my hand with a set of glittery nails.

"My fault. I should have said a glass."

I poured three fat fingers of brown liqueur into the tumbler.

"Second," she said. I stood holding it out like the faithful old family retainer while she gulped down the last of her vodka. We traded glasses. I put her exhausted one in the spot where the Old-Fashioned I took for myself had stood, scooped ice out of the bucket with a pair of silver tongs, and poured in just enough to float the cubes.

"Toast?" I asked.

"No, thanks. I already had breakfast." She laughed the tinkly laugh that played up my

47

spine like bones on bones and took a healthy draft. I sipped mine. No sense confusing a stomach trained on synthetic Scotch with too big a dose of the genuine Tennessee.

When I was back in my seat, she pressed her knees together and swung her legs to the floor in a gesture choreographed by Early Woman. She hadn't the legs for it, not with those ankles, but she managed to pull it off without looking like a scrubwoman standing up. "Why the long distance? I don't bite." She patted the cushion beside hers.

I had a whole category of quick responses to that one, but the eggs Benedict on the floor of my stomach trumped the initial effect of the bourbon. "Thanks, but I'm farsighted."

"Don't know what you're missing." She sent another deposit down on top of the first. "Where were we?"

"Alec Wynn's penis."

"Yes, of course. He might as well not have one for all the workout it got from dear Cecelia."

"You know this how?"

"Girl talk. Over afternoon cocktails. It's not all about hemlines and Brad Pitt, dear."

"I'm shocked. Go on."

"She has a big bag of tricks for avoiding

what we'll call her wifely duties. Headache, of course, but that's only when she's too tired to exercise her imagination. Men don't count the days in the calendar, she said once; that one's always good in a pinch. Early day tomorrow, and he never asks why or what. She puts so much time and energy into coming up with ways to avoid sex she might as well flop down and get it over with. It's what I do with Harold."

"Lucky man, Harold." I drank some more Jack. "What you're saying in your delicate way is Cecelia's frigid."

"Honey, when she does spread her legs I wouldn't be surprised if a little light goes on."

"Not bad. I think I heard it somewhere."

"Everywhere, probably. Apart from the golf course and the mall I don't get out. So you see, I'm not the serpent in Alec's Eden. If dear little wifey decided to go trolling for a better tallywacker, she got that idea all by herself. Frankly, I was surprised he took her back the first time. Some people enjoy being miserable. It's a poor substitute for happiness, but when it's the only real feeling they have, they're afraid to let go of it."

"Are you talking about Alec or Cecelia?"

"Alec, of course. He's the one who stayed behind, and the one who's wasting his money trying to reel in the same cold-blooded slut all over again, just when he should be congratulating himself for getting off cheap."

"Why spend time with her if you dislike her so much?"

She arched her strong brows. "Cecelia? She's my best friend."

"Any idea where she is?"

"No. I haven't seen her in a week. She doesn't drive, so she'd have taken a taxi."

"I called all the companies in the area. No record of a pickup at the Wynn address, but she might have taken a walk and hailed one, or used an independent. Economy being what it is, every laid-off assembly-line worker with a crate that still rolls seems to be running a gypsy operation. It's illegal without a license, but the cops are too busy investigating their mayors to spare them the time. What do you know about the pills she took?"

"Drugs? I don't —"

"Herbs in homemade capsules. Vitamin supplements. If I can find out where she got them in the past it would give me a place to start looking for her."

"Can't help you, I'm afraid. I never saw her take a pill or capsule of any kind and she never talked about taking them."

"I was told she takes them at every meal."

"Oh. Mystery solved. We never ate when we were together. We drank our lunch like good respectable wealthy suburban house-wives."

I drank off my glass and rolled the contents around my mouth. I was reluctant to swallow. I wasn't likely to taste anything like it again for a while. Finally I let go, got out a card, and laid it on the drink cart. "Thanks, Mrs. Lochner. If you hear from her, or if anything occurs to you about where she might have gone, I'd appreciate a call."

"So would I." Her dimples deepened into knife creases. "Harold's going to St. Louis tomorrow on business."

"Like I said, lucky man." I showed myself out.

I'd parked on the street. What the weather folk call a "wintry mix" pricked my face with rain and sharp bits of ice like steel shavings. I started the car to get the heater going and called Wynn on the cell. Outside, the bits of ice bounced on the broad side-walk and rattled on the roof.

"What'd you get from Patti?"

"Not much, but she gave me the impression I could get a lot more. She needs another hobby outside golf."

"What'd she tell you about my wife?"

"I'd better leave that till I can report in person. Anyway it's nothing I can use. When can I drop by your house? There may be something in a drawer or somewhere that will tell me who her herbalist was."

"And what would you know once you knew that?" He sounded testy.

"If she's as gung ho as Debner says, she'll go back to whoever supplies her when she needs refills. If she was preparing for a long trip, she might have stopped there on her way out. Maybe she said something. People tell their barbers and mailmen things they'd never share with friends and relatives."

"Aren't you grasping at straws?"

"At this point I'd kill for a straw. All I've gotten so far is fistfuls of air."

"Trina might know," he said after a moment.

"Trina?"

"Our maid. She's at the house now."

The windshield was fogging. I adjusted the blower that direction and caught sight of an exasperated face in the rearview mirror. If I'd known about Trina I might have put off my tea party with Patti Lochner, at least until I had better questions to ask. The trouble with clients of private investigators is they expect the investigators to draw information out of the atmosphere, like the condensation process.

The phone rang a half second after I broke the connection. It was Barry Stackpole. "Zilch at all the police stations in Metro, ditto the morgues. Your redhead hasn't shown up."

"By now she might not be a redhead."

"I never thought of that. Neither did any of the experienced cops and attendants I talked to. As a matter of fact, no one connected with professional law enforcement considered the fact she might have changed her hair or anything else about the way she looked. We're all stumped here at the Yard, Mr. Holmes. How did we ever manage before you came along?"

"That's flattering, but I can't help thinking you're being ironic."

"Well, a looker like her would stand out regardless. When and where do I collect?"

"Tonight, bar at the MGM Grand."

"Since when do you like gambling?"

"Since I applied for my license, but if you mean slot machines and roulette, never. They let you smoke there."

"Make it the restaurant. They make a good steak."

We settled on seven. When I rang off, the

windshield was clear. I threw open the throttle and crossed into Grosse Pointe proper.

There are four Pointes, not counting East- pointe, which used to be called East Detroit and is actually west of the original Pointes and north of Detroit: Compasses are lost on city planners. The first four are inter- changeable, although Grosse Pointe itself has the advantage of Lake St. Clair, where the Detroit River stops to take a breather and fills the floodplain with turquoise- colored water — more like cotton wool under April overcast — and the grand old- auto-money mansions slumber in their well- kept greensward lawns.

I noticed a few wrought-iron fences this trip. An earlier generation of residents had donated theirs to the Second World War and are still too proud of the sacrifice to replace them. Until recently, it was the last four square miles in the United States with penny parking meters downtown, another common touch that had fallen before the transfusion of New Money.

They'll tell you the real wealth now is in Birmingham and Bloomfield Hills; but those places smell of crisp greenbacks and not the soft old bills of the aristocrats whose great-grandfathers put the world on the gasoline standard. Their men wear French cuffs on weekends and their women clank their bracelets and talk too loud over trick martinis built of colored liqueurs and bobbing bits of fruit. In Grosse Pointe they go out in open-neck sports shirts, plug the holes in their earlobes with tasteful star-cut diamonds, and hoist boilermakers in honor of their ancestors lying with their bagged livers in marble vaults. They haven't a thing to prove until you ask them just where their money is invested at present.

The Wynn house, located on the less-desirable side of Lake Shore Drive across from the cul-de-sacs on the lake, was a nice place if you like washing windows; which wasn't a problem even on that side, because the servant pool is always deep when unemployment tops 10 percent, a chronic situation in southeastern Michigan. There must have been fifty on the street side alone, with ivy — rusty-brown now, but showing optimistic dots of green among the shriveled leaves — crawling up the fieldstone walls. That was a lot of fieldstone; it had to have been trucked in from someplace like Washtenaw County, where they grow rocks like Kansas grows wheat. But the owners of some of the older houses across the street had gone as far as Florence and Greece. There was a courtyard with a chalky Cupid urinating into a round trough in the center and a black chauffeur in his shirtsleeves polishing the chrome on last year's Mercedes in the brick-paved drive that encircled it. The car would be Alec Wynn's beater when slush and road salt threatened the Porsche. The chauffeur was young and angular, and so tall he had to stoop to buff the hood: There but for an ounce of athletic skill went the next captain of the Pistons.

Maybe that was racist. Maybe it had been his life's dream to drive a rich white couple wherever they wanted to go. A job is what you make it.

So why hadn't he driven Cecelia Wynn where she wanted to go, when she went? Or had he? Another thing I would've asked Alec, if it had occurred to me they had a driver. Or if he'd thought to mention it. If he was so rich, why wasn't he smart?

A white-haired woman with dull eyes and a faint moustache answered my ring. The serving-class demographic was growing old. If Silicon Valley didn't ramp up its robotics soon, people were going to have to start dusting their own knickknacks.

"Trina?"

"Yes. You are Mr. Walker? Mr. Wynn told

me to expect you."

She wore a starched white apron over a charcoal pant-suit, walking shoes on her feet, strong hands folded at her waist. Wynn had said she was Brazilian. A little space before she responded to my question. She spoke in careful English but did her thinking in Portuguese.

She took me through a room big enough for badminton, but that was designed just for following maids through, and down a hall lined with dark paintings to a morning room of some kind. There was a small neat white-painted writing desk with a shallow chair drawn up in front of it that would accommodate an average-size woman comfortably. Among men, a jockey might stand it as long as five minutes. There were sprays of fresh flowers in painted porcelain vases and a Mary Cassatt print on a wall. A feminine sort of room, but no pink flourishes or unicorns. A glass doorwall was ajar and a strong chlorine stench floated in from a crescent-shaped swimming pool. She slid the door shut.

"The pool man says alkali is leaking into the water from an underground spring," she said. "The chlorine controls the smell."

"Being rich is a bitch. Excuse my French."

"French?" Her smooth brown brow broke

into horizontal lines.

"An expression. Your English is swell, but you can live here a long time before you get a handle on American."

The lines smoothed out. "Swell. I know this word. It means good, yes?"

"Yes; but don't bother working it into your vocabulary. It's out of date, like me. Did Mr. Wynn tell you what I wanted?"

"Capsules." She nodded gravely, her hands still folded in front of her apron. "Many, many capsules. In my country, it is only the sick who swallow so many things from little bottles. Mrs. Wynn, she seems healthy. I have been in this country ten years and I don't understand it."

"Congratulations. You've assimilated. I was born here, and I know less about it than I knew ten years ago. Can you tell me where she got them?"

"She has many bottles of capsules in her room. There is a name on the bottles, I think. Understand, I do not pry. Pry, this is correct?"

I nodded. I wondered if she was the Innocent Abroad she made herself out as. You know you've been on the job too long when you question the motives of everyone you meet.

On the other hand, that's the job description.

"Can I see one?"

"You mean, may you see one?"

"Yeah." Right back in Mrs. Stevens' fifth-grade English class, and the old bat twenty years in the ground.

"I will get one." She unfolded her hands.

"No hurry. What sort of woman is Mrs. Wynn to work for?"

A pair of pleated lips pursed. "I don't know that this is a good question to answer."

"Not your place. We don't have places here, Trina. You can call me Amos if you like."

"Oh, no."

"You're a good maid, Trina." I wound a five-dollar bill around my right index finger. She made no move to take it. I shook my head. "Not a bribe. You know bribe?"

"I know this word. I am born in Rio de Janeiro." The pleated lips sealed tight.

I didn't know what that meant, but my history is spotty. "I'd be honored if you'd consider it a gift in return for your patience in speaking with an American." I slid it from my finger, still in a tube, took one of her hands gently, and laid it in the calloused palm.

She flattened the tube and tucked it inside

her apron pocket. I got the impression she was doing me a favor.

Just what I was after. It made me want to scrub myself all over and join the seminary.

# FIVE

Trina refolded her hands. She was as placid as an eel skin drying in the sun. "I do not say anything against Mrs. Wynn."

"I'm not asking you to," I said. "That isn't what the money was for. This isn't a divorce case. Mr. Wynn just wants to know where she went and if she's all right."

"She is a good employer. She says please and thank you and does not run her fingers over the furniture after I dust, like the last woman I worked for. She does not offer me her old clothes as if they are —" She stumbled over the word.

"A bonus. I get you. To hell with employers like that. Is that all you can tell me about her, she's polite?"

"I have not worked here long. Only five weeks."

"Who was the maid before that?"

"A girl named Ann Foster, at my agency. Multi-Urban Services. She was fired." Her

61

voice dropped to a whisper on the last part. We were alone, no one within earshot; but it's a scary word to say out loud.

"Fired why?"

"William the chauffeur told me she was — let go. I did not ask for what. In my country we have a saying."

"English, please. My Portuguese is worse than my Mandarin."

"I was going to say it in English. 'The less you know, the more you work.' "

"Ah. We have a saying like that here, too. Where can I find Ann Foster?"

"Through the agency, maybe. But I think she does not work there now."

"Tough place. One fumble and you're off the team."

"Fumble?"

"Mistake."

"I think maybe it was not her first. The bottles are in her bedroom. I will get them."

"One will do, thanks."

When she'd left I caught my reflection in the glass over the Cassatt print. "Pushed it," I said.

While she was away I went through the little writing desk. A shallow belly drawer contained a sheet of first-class stamps with three gone, a pad of the same drugstore stationery she'd used to write her brush-off note to her husband, some nice ballpoint pens, and a block of yellow Post-its. Neither the top sheet on the pad nor the one on the block showed any legible depressions when I turned them toward the light, but then they hardly ever do outside the portals of the Doubleday Mystery Book Club. The pigeonholes on top of the desk were empty.

I was back on my mark when Trina returned. She handed me a brown glass container the size of a small pickle jar with a broad cork in the top. I pulled the cork and looked inside. It was half full of clear gelatin capsules. I took one out and held it up to the light coming in from the direction of the pool. A fine brown powder shifted around inside when I tipped it. I held it to my nose and sniffed. A sharp, spicy scent, vaguely familiar. Cinnamon: but not the kind generally available at the supermarket. I remembered it then, from a long time ago. It was an Asian variety, the genuine article, made from the bark of a tree found only in and around Saigon. Well, Ho Chi Minh City, but that one wasn't my fault. It was after my time.

The label had been printed out by computer:

There was an 800 number and an e-mail address, but I didn't pay them any attention. I don't have a computer and I wanted to talk to Mr. or Mrs. Olympic in person.

I restopped the container and slipped it into the side pocket of my coat. "How many of these does Mrs. Wynn have in her bedroom?"

"Many, as I said."

"I meant how many bottles."

"Ten or twelve, I think. More, maybe." Her brow cracked across again for a second. Then she nodded. "More."

"As full as this?"

"I don't know. I don't look inside. When one is empty she throws it away. An easy woman to clean up after, Mrs. Wynn. Everything is always back in its place."

"I understand she fills some of the capsules herself?"

"Yes. She says it is less expensive if she buys them empty and fills them. Also she knows she is not being cheated on the amounts."

"That's a lot of capsules to go to all the trouble to fill and then leave behind. Did

64

she take her clothes with her? A suitcase?"

"No, sir. Her closets and drawers are full."

"May I take a look?" When she started to furrow a third time I took out my cell. "You can ask Mr. Wynn if it's okay."

"No. I would like to help." Still she hesitated. "Mr. Wynn said not to disturb anything in her room. I do not leave a place in that condition naturally."

"Normally."

"Normally. Thank you."

I showed her my palms. "No white gloves."

She conducted me into a biggish room decorated in silver-gray with rose accents, not very busy. The rose bedding on the queen mattress was rumpled, the pillow showing the clear depression of a head. A drawer of the silver-gray bureau hung open and some items of feminine apparel were strewn about the rose carpet. More plastic bottles rattled around the inside of the next drawer down when I tugged it out. A pair of double-louvered doors opened onto a closet containing dresses and suits cut to a woman's waist and a lot of shoes on a mahogany rack on the floor. It looked like a complete set of paints, powder, and brushes on the dressing table, but after a hundred years on the job I'm still no judge of that kind of thing. I asked the maid if anything appeared to be missing.

"No, sir. Mr. Wynn asked me the same thing."

The room was untidy, but not so bad it looked as if it had been ransacked or the person who slept there had left in a hurry. A smoky scent of violets lingered; a woodsy variant, unique to the individual who wore it, a chemical anomaly: a clue, if I had any talents in that direction.

It was shaping up to be the damnedest disappearing act I'd covered in a long, long time.

The tall black chauffeur was leaning backward against the roof of the glistening Mercedes, smoking a cigarette, when I came out of the house. The rain and sleet had stopped, and the disgusted expression on his strong-boned face read out as three more hours of nothing to do till quitting time. The expression changed as I kept walking his way without stopping by my Cutlass. Blank now: The shields were up. Following that shift of his facial muscles, nothing moved, not even his crossed ankles in high-topped shoes with the laces crossed over metal hooks. The toes would be steel. You can tell a lot about a man by what he puts on his feet.

"Are you William?"

"You ought to take better care of your automobile. It's a damn shame to abuse a fine instrument like the 1970 four-fifty-five." His voice was deep and resonant. The words plunked one by one into an empty steel drum.

"If I bumped it out and got a paint job, a trooper might want to take a look under the hood. I dummied up the emissions system to improve performance. Sorry about the dumb question. Of course you're William. Complete strangers don't just walk in off the street with a can of Turtle Wax under one arm. Not in this neighborhood."

"Yourself?"

I showed him my ID folder.

He pointed a finger as long as a fondue fork at the honorary sheriff's star. "That a gag?"

"It's pure milk chocolate under the foil." I put it away and handed him a card.

He read it, then bent it into a cantilever between the thumb and forefinger of the hand not involved with his cigarette and held it like that, as if he was thinking of letting it go to see how far it sprang. "Same information, bigger print. I don't need two forms of identification. I'm not a bank."

"I believe you. Who'd lie about that? Can

I piggyback a light?" I shook one out of the pack and poked it between my lips.

He took the half-smoked stub out of his mouth and gave it to me. I lit mine off the end; didn't need it, I always carry a second book of matches in case I drop the first in a puddle of blood or something. I gave him back his stub. The inhaling end was dry.

"Now we got us a bond," he said.

I blew a jet of smoke down the driveway. "Hasn't worked yet. But a man can hope."

Nothing. Not even a grunt to indicate my audio was working. This was going to be like pulling nails with my toes.

I stood a folded ten-spot on the Mercedes' trunk, just inside his long reach. He looked at it, then at the low fieldstone wall that separated the lot from the one next door. The wall looked back. Whatever passed between them wasn't my business. My card remained bent between his fingers, a little tighter now. It was like watching the ash grow on the end of a cigar and wondering when it would fall.

"Your boss hired me," I said.

"Did he."

"He did. You knew that. He'd have asked you if you drove Mrs. Wynn away the other day, or if she left on her own. Whether or not he told you about me, you had to know why I'm here with my cards and Roy Rogers badge. So let's waive the pissing contest. My day's a long way from finished."

"Who's this Rogers?"

"You wouldn't like him. He rode a horse." I waited.

I don't know how much longer we'd have gone on, because just then a little breeze came up and the folded bill lifted away from the hood. My business card sproinged loose from between his fingers and he swept up the bill in a looping left. Whatever his shortcomings on the court, reflexes weren't among them. He stretched it between his hands and held it up to count the threads. Then he folded it square and poked it into the watch pocket of his chinos.

"I didn't drive her. It was my day off. She always called a cab when Mr. Wynn and I were both gone. She doesn't drive. I think she was from New York City or somewhere where they don't."

"I figured she made other arrangements, or you'd have told Wynn where she had you drop her off. It's Ann Foster I'm interested in."

He grinned for the first time, big white well-kept teeth in a face blasted from volcanic rock. "Lots of folks were interested in Ann. I took a run at her myself, but she was born out of bounds."

"That good, huh?"

"No one around here's seen anything like her since the governor cut out the tax breaks for Hollywood. Skinny little thing, but long on looks."

"And aloof."

"I don't know what that is."

"Bullshit. Wayne State?"

"Oakland. Two years, till I blew out my knee and lost my scholarship."

"Tough break."

"I wasn't that good. Just tall."

"Who was Ann closer to, Alec or Cecelia?"

"I wouldn't know. I work outside."

"Which one fired her?"

The cigarette was short enough to scorch his lips. He spat it out, plucked another out of a pack of Old Golds in his shirt pocket, and fired it off a disposable butane lighter. By the time he drew in an egg of smoke and spewed it out his nostrils I got the hint. I always do when they're as subtle as an earthquake in Japan. This time I put the ten in his hand. It rested flat on his palm for a moment, like a butterfly. Then he stuck it back at me. "I wasn't fishing. Not worth the risk. These jobs don't float in on the tide. Even rich people learn to do for themselves when the dividends slow down."

"So drive a bus." But I took back the bill. You could have knocked me over with a dump truck. "Wynn knows I'm here, and if this house means anything he's figured out what sort of questions I'm asking. But you can check with him yourself." I unshipped the cell again.

Again it was refused. But I was still holding the bill in my other hand and he helped himself to it. Into his pocket it went.

"It was her fired Ann," he said. "Mrs. Wynn."

"Why?"

"She didn't run it past me, can't think why."

"For ten bucks you can guess."

He glanced toward his watch pocket, scowled. Digging it out to give it back again was too silly. He took a deep drag on his Old Gold. This time no smoke came back out. "They had a fight the day Ann left, her and Mrs. Wynn. I could hear them screaming at each other out here. I don't know what it was about. I was changing the oil, had the radio on."

"Hip-hop?"

"Classical. WKAR-FM."

"Beethoven?"

"Mozart."

"Beethoven's better. He could drown out

an armored assault."

"Mister, I didn't hear the words, and if I could, I'd've turned up the sound. In this line —"

"Yeah. The less you know the more you work. Any idea where she went?"

"Who? Mrs. Wynn or Ann?"

"Both."

"Nope. No reason Mrs. Wynn would tell me even if I asked, and Ann didn't like me any too much after I tried to get acquainted. It wasn't as if I went to bend her backwards over the bumper. All I did was smile. You know the smile?"

"I know the smile. I've had better luck with the cigarette trick."

"Just between us and this fine piece of German engineering, I think Ann was cut out to be a gym coach, if you get my drift."

"So she shook off your pitch. That doesn't make her a lesbian."

"I guess not. How much you give the Portagee?" He tilted his monolithic head toward the house.

"Five."

He smoked, nodding. "Damn place has too many windows. Better give her ten. Man makes enemies of two maids back-to-back, it starts to look like he's the problem."

# SIX

I drove past the place the first time, turned around in the parking lot of a flat-roofed professional building with the address 97180 posted on a sign next to the driveway, and drove back doing twenty, slow enough to read *Ninety-seven thousand one hundred seventy-two* written in script above the doorway of a small old frame house with a card in a window identifying it as the Elysian Fields Health & Wellness Centre. Stopping in a pocket-size parking area, I fished the squat plastic bottle out of my coat pocket and looked at the label. Yep, it said "Olympic Gardens." Between that and the way they posted the address, I figured the owners were in Witness Protection.

The window in the front door, behind which hung a brittle-looking lace curtain, was decorated with rows of faded and chipped decals belonging to Greenpeace, the World Health Organization, Amnesty

International, People for the Ethical Treatment of Animals, and two or three symbols I couldn't put a name to; testimonials that no monkeys or Rwandans had been harmed in the manufacture of the goods available inside. At first glance it looked like the cluster of lodge seals stuck in front of a Korean massage parlor.

The door struck a copper bell mounted above it when I pushed it open. Someone had pulled down all the walls that had cut the ground floor into separate rooms, clearing space for a lot of plants hanging in pots and freestanding shelves with bottles and jars and sealed brown paper sacks crowded onto them. The floor was made of twelve-inch planks joined tongue-in-groove, too broad to have been hewn from second- or third-growth Michigan pine. The house was old, but not that old: Probably the same someone who'd knocked down the walls had reclaimed them from one of the historic buildings the city demolished on a rotating basis. Fluorescent tubes, mounted in troughs between the open stacks, struggled to stay lit with the hopeless buzzing and flickering of a beetle caught in a spiderweb. The air was a confusion of sharp spices, thick-smelling herbs, and cow manure. There were sacks of that, too, and no doubt

74

in the soil the hanging plants were using.

As I shut the door behind me, a tall creature dressed all in white wafted through a curtained doorway behind the antique oak counter without appearing to disturb the curtains. She was just drinking age, with blond hair pulled behind her head and, from the way she carried herself, probably spilling most of the way down her back. The dress she wore might have been made from two bedsheets fastened at the shoulders. It was designed to hang straight down, but parts of it clung to her curves and hollows through a combination of static electricity and pure sex. She had high cheekbones, a straight nose, full unpainted lips, and eyes that changed from smoky green to stormy gray to light brown: living mood rings. I know, because I put them to the test.

She asked if she could help me. Her voice was mezzo and a little scratchy, like a grazing pass from an emery board.

"You can tell me I'm in the right place." I took the bottle of capsules from my pocket and showed her the label.

The eyes turned stormy. "We had to change the name. A thug lawyer from the Olympics Committee paid us a visit last month with a cease-and-desist order. Apparently the committee has the exclusive right to the name."

"I'm surprised they let the ancient Greeks get away with it."

"Anyway, I've got a hundred labels printed, and I intend to use them up before I order any under Elysian Fields."

"You're the owner?"

"No, it's a corporation. I just run the place when the manager's out. He's out a lot. You know, you look pretty healthy to me. Are you running an errand for Cecelia?"

"Cecelia. You're friends?"

"I'm friends with all the customers. Especially when their checks stay put when they land." Her smile was as cool as the hazy green haze that had eclipsed the gray. "I seem to be answering all the questions. Are you Mr. Wynn?"

I showed her my license with the deputy's star folded back out of sight. I had a feeling it would have ended the conversation. Maybe it was the state-of-the-art computerized cash register that didn't go with the battered old counter it sat on and the big stainless-steel safe next to the curtained doorway, with an electronic lock. If an operation like that had enough money left after those investments to require a safe, either the population was sicker than I thought or the place had something in the inventory besides green tea and saffron.

The storm clouds returned. "The only thing I like less than men who spy on their wives is men who hire someone to do it for them. No, come to think of it, I like the men they hire even less."

"We're not all men. And we don't all do divorce work. Mrs. Wynn's gone missing, leaving behind a lot of expensive clothes and a drawer full of pills she bought here. He thinks something may have happened to her. I'm beginning to think so, too. When was the last time you saw her?"

She turned to the computer while her eyes lightened to brown. I could have stood there all day and watched the kaleidoscope, also the way her body moved under the Grecian dress or whatever it was. But I had miles to go before I slept. She crackled the keys, manipulated a mouse built in to the base of the keyboard, and said, "Friday, March twenty-fifth. She bought some fennel seed and clove cigarettes. She's trying to quit smoking."

"You're licensed to sell tobacco?"

"There's no tobacco in them. No license required. Would you like to try one?"

"No need, thanks. I smoke tobacco."

"I know. You have nicotine stains on top of your nicotine stains."

"The twenty-fifth was ten days ago. That was about four days before she dropped off the screen. Did she say anything that might make you think she was planning on changing scenery?"

"Nope. The conversation was dull as normal. How-are-you-I'm-fine-how-are-you-okay. She's a good customer, but not the sort of person I would consider friending."

I caught the verb. "Do you Facebook?"

"It's a good marketing tool."

"Mrs. Wynn doesn't. I asked. If it weren't for holdouts like her I'd be out of a job. Everyone tells everyone everything they're doing and thinking."

"Not this one. I don't even keep a diary. There isn't a thing on my page I wouldn't tell anyone who rang my little copper bell. Why do people think they can splash their secrets all over a global billboard and cut somebody cold when they ask a personal question face-to-face?"

"Why does Aunt Ethel prowl the mall all day in curlers and run for the hills when someone aims a camera at her? How'd she seem that day? Cecelia, not Ethel."

"Actually, I knew someone who had an Aunt Ethel. Not many of those around anymore, and those who are pack their

78

oxygen on their backs. Maybe in fifty years, when the world's full of Tiffanys and Amber Dawns in their eighties, they'll be back." She shook her head, disturbing the straight fall of liquid-gold hair behind her back. I'd been right about that, first time in a long dry spell. "She was edgy, but then she is generally. That's what the flax seed is for. I wish I could be more helpful. Mrs. Wynn is —"

"A good customer. They're hard to come by, with Walmarts springing up all over like third parties."

"Don't I know it. You're the first person in here today didn't have a cell phone hardwired to the side of his head the whole time I was waiting on him. But then, you're not a customer, are you?"

"Maybe. I'd like to try a pack of those clove cigarettes."

"They don't come in packs, but I can tell you're not interested. You smell like the Marlboro Man, and you don't strike me as the kind of person who quits anything."

"I quit the police department, before you were born. I quit Vicodin. I quit on the Lions, along with everyone else. I quit on marriage; or it quit on me. The only thing I can't seem to quit is this lousy job." I realized I was still holding the ID folder and packed it back on my hip. The subject needed changing anyway. "That's quite an olfactory sense you have there. I change my clothes a lot and I kill the tobacco breath with Scotch."

"I smelled that, too, even in this reek."

"If you don't like the air, you can change professions. The auto show's always looking for spokesmodels."

A pair of full lips got pursed. "I can't tell if you're flirting with me or interrogating me. This the good cop or the bad one?"

"A little of both. Like God and the Devil. How'd she pay for her order, check or credit card?"

"Cash. We don't accept anything else."

"I thought that was just for cider mills and antiquarian bookstores."

"It costs us some business — you might have noticed this stuff isn't cheap, even if there is assembly required — but, believe me, it's worth not having to deal with those loan-sharks in gray worsted."

"That's why the safe, I'm thinking."

"That's why the safe. It has a time lock, so I can tell the bandits to settle for what's in the till: for our safety, the manager says. Except you can be shot for twenty and change the same as for twenty grand."

"That much?"

Her eyes turned golden, a new color in the spectrum. "This is Elysian Fields, not Morgan Chase. I was being poetic."

"What's the name of the corporation that owns the place?"

"Haven't a clue. My salary's deposited directly into my account. I never see a check. I suppose it's public record, if you've got the patience to sound it out."

I couldn't think of anything else important. Not that there wasn't. The stench of all that bottled health was pickling my brain. I looked around. "Does all this stuff work?"

"It does if you think it does. Holistics is largely a matter of faith. So far the FDA isn't a convert, but we acknowledge that openly in the literature we hand out to new customers."

I asked to see the literature. She reached under the counter and handed me a glossy pamphlet printed in four colors. She'd had business cards printed with the new name and I took one from a holder shaped like the Acropolis. Next to the name embossed on the card, Diana the Huntress stood in her tennis skirt drawing her bow. I put away my plunder.

"Thank you, Miss — ?"

"Amber Dawn."

"Seriously?"

"No. Smoke." She flicked a hand across her face. "On account of the eyes. You noticed. My parents were hippies."

"I thought babies were born with their eyes closed."

"Myth, like they're all born blue-eyed. They didn't name me until they brought me home and got to know me, like a puppy."

She showed a set of well-polished teeth, with a crooked one up front. These days you either get the orthodontic tour or a gap Hannibal could drive his elephants through. I liked everything about her except for what she was holding back.

# SEVEN

Driving away from there I got the number of Multi-Urban Services from Information and pecked it out. According to the Wynns' new maid, that was the agency that had employed Ann Foster, the previous girl at bat.

"We're not at liberty to give out information about our clients." This was a feminine voice that sounded the way cool mints taste.

I said, "I'm sorry to hear that. I went to a party at the Wynn place in Grosse Pointe about six weeks ago and was very impressed with Miss Foster's efficiency. I'd heard she was free and I was thinking of engaging her services on a full-time basis."

Keys rattled on her end.

"I'm sorry, but Miss Foster is no longer with this agency. However, I can recommend another client every bit as efficient. We screen them closely and have never —"

"Can you tell me where Miss Foster is

currently working?"

"As I said, we don't —"

"Give out information about clients; I heard. But she isn't a client, is she?"

The mints began to melt. "I haven't the —"

"Just tell the one who *has* the authority there's a commission in it for Multi-Urban as well as whatever outfit she's with now." I gave her my name and contact numbers and caught the time just before I flipped the phone shut. If I stepped on it I could get in two drinks at the MGM Grand before Barry showed up.

Where it fronts on the John Lodge expressway it looks like the grille of a 1938 Studebaker, all Art Deco curve with its name stacked vertically in raised letters totaling nine stories. Four hundred rooms, eight hundred million dollars on the hoof, lit up brightly enough to throw a man's shadow clear to Ontario, and the Hope Diamond pinned to a pair of grubby coveralls wouldn't look any more out of place. The address is 1300, same as the old Detroit Police Headquarters on Beaubien, but the plunkety-plunk noise belongs to the slots and not buckets collecting drips from the roof.

A valet got up like Patton on parade, complete with epaulets and ropes of gold, opened my door and slid in behind the wheel without reacting to the dings and rust and handed me off to a doorman in an even more elaborate uniform who grinned at me like a state trooper who'd caught me red-handed trying to use the emergency cross-over on the interstate; once past him, the place had me just as surely.

The great sprawl of ground floor was a racket of jangling one-armed bandits, the trickle of an occasional handful of coins into a metal dish, rumbles of conversation and some laughter, but most of those playing were senior citizens dressed in gaudy Lycra, feeding the machines and pushing buttons with butts smoldering in the corners of their mouths. Few of them used the big chrome handles, which are mainly for nostalgic purposes: Why aggravate bursitis and slow down the stream of cash? Colored lights bounced around and whatever the psychologists on the payroll fed into the ventilation system to keep the customers alert and eager to continue smelled like a crisp new twenty.

With a little imagination, you could convince yourself you're in Las Vegas, but only if you dropped acid and had a recent lobotomy.

It was a weekday, but the place was busy. The only employees sitting on their hands were the poker dealers. All the players of games of skill were busy trying to bluff someone on the other side of the world over the Internet.

The Grand has five restaurants, in case you can't think of another excuse to leave, but knowing Barry when someone else is paying, I went straight to the steakhouse, where you can drop a yard and a half on a meal for two without ordering a drink. He'd order a drink. There was a wait for a table. I left my name, and while I was enjoying a legal cigarette anticipating the Great Event, a barmaid wearing fishnet stockings and a dress that had popped up from a Kleenex box wobbled up on stilts and offered me a complimentary drink from her tray. I selected the one with the least amount of tropical architecture and tipped her a buck. The glass was rounded over with good Scotch that packed a wallop: Two sips and you bet the rent on twenty-two black. All very cold-blooded, and as subtle as a feeding frenzy, but if it's the Salvation Army you're looking for, you're in the wrong part of town.

I tried a quarter machine, just to kill time.

I got two American flags and the Statue of Liberty.

"Wasted two bits. Everybody knows the loose slots are all up front, to rope in the suckers."

I put out my stub in a tray full of sand and turned to smile at the owner of the voice. "Hello, Barry. Just doing my bit to keep Vinnie No Ears off welfare."

We shook hands. He stopped wearing a white glove on the one that was short two fingers years ago. It just called attention to itself, like his limp when he forgot himself and the plate in his skull when he didn't comb his hair right. Aside from the missing parts, he always looked bandbox new. We were close to the same age, but he could pull off a six-hundred-dollar sportcoat over a Metallica T-shirt without drawing a smirk. As an investigative journalist he'd survived the decline of the great newspapers, the brief sad history of cable-access television, and the dot-com bust, leaping from one medium to the next just before the last one collapsed under his feet, and he was still carded every other time he bought alcohol.

"Vinnie's gone straight, didn't you hear? They all have. The best mob lawyer in Vegas is mayor there now. Ran out of clients. What are we standing around for, by the way? I thought you were buying me dinner."

"No place to sit."

"Horseshit. Bobby? We came to eat, not pose for pictures." He rapped a knuckle on the registration desk. The young man behind it, dark-skinned and good-looking in a yellow jacket — his name was probably Roberto — uncurled his lip when he recognized Barry. He looked down at his list, glanced at his watch, and crossed out a name. "Party's five minutes late. Emily? Mr. Stackpole."

A dream in a glittering cocktail dress materialized before us. "This way, please, gentlemen."

Barry grinned as we followed her along the twisting path between crowded tables. "Regular guy from the auto club got sick and the one who took his place showed up stoned. Column he submitted would've closed the joint, and incidentally cracked the guide's legal defense budget when the case went to court. Editor's an old friend. It just happened I'd eaten here earlier in the week. Word got out, as it will. It isn't really a five-star place, but you wouldn't know it when you're dining with me."

"What'd you get from the auto club?"

"Free roadside assistance for five years. Here we are. Just far enough away from the kitchen and not too close to the bandstand. Loud music spoils my appetite." He sat down at a table draped in cloth-of-gold and stuck up a hand without looking. Emily forked a gold-leafed menu between his thumb and forefinger and handed me another.

We ordered single-malt Scotch, a rib eye for me, and duck for Barry. For a while we just ate and drank and talked about spring training. Someone hooted over toward the blackjack tables, an alarm went off indicating that someone else had scored a big jackpot. Over our drinks I filled him in on the job, without the names of the principals. He can be a vault when he wants to be, but he's a reporter through and through and can be an awful pest when he smells an exclusive. I didn't want to find out the hard way if Alec and Cecelia Wynn were good press.

"I've had dealings with Multi-Urban," he said, when I petered out. "The service industry is one of my best sources. Don't know any Ann Fosters. Place is on the up-and-up so far as I know. No escort work on the side, and unlike our local schools they screen their clients beyond last week."

"What about Elysian Fields?"

He turned over a duck breast with his fork

— looking for birdshot, probably. He's the only man I know who can turn a meal into a postmortem. "Nope, nor Olympic Gardens either. But I'm suspicious of cash-only enterprises on principle. Best way to launder money this side of the place we're sitting in."

"I thought you said the Mafia's kaput."

"Yeah, and I miss it, all except that bombing-reporters business; I miss my leg, too. But those paisans had a code of protection. They never went after cops, and when one of the crowd got out of line and threatened the status quo, they recycled him into fish food. These new guys from Mexico and Colombia mow down border guards, kidnap governors, and slaughter tourists just for their motor homes. A whole village can retire on a Winnebago load of Asian heroin. But one in ten deals involves an undercover agent spending marked bills. If Pedro or Pancho wants to spend the profits in this here land of freedom and prosperity, he can't afford to pass a recorded serial number, so he doles it out in change through legitimate fronts and skims the top off every clean dollar that crosses the counter. Out in general circulation, a dirty buck can change hands dozens of times before it shows up on a DEA list."

"But it's only worth it if it's done in volume. I was in the place ten minutes and didn't see a customer."

"These muchachos can afford to run a string of one-horse places and spread it out. It's better that way. A big operation that only accepts cash would draw too much fire. These days even Ma and Pa Kent take Visa."

"The place deals in vitamin pills. Would they be passing drugs?"

"Got a sample?"

I passed him the bottle I'd gotten from Cecelia Wynn's new maid. He opened it and sniffed at the inside, replaced the lid.

"Asian cinnamon. Takes me back."

"It did me, too. It's stronger than the variety they sell in supermarkets. You can cover up a lot of smells with it."

"In theory. I doubt it. They've got a whole industry for distribution. No sense jeopardizing their laundry department with a penny-ante bust that could split the place wide open. But I'll check it out. Keep it?" He rattled the pills.

"Sure. I get my vitamins from barley." I washed down my steak with Scotch.

He slid the bottle into a side pocket. "Any reason to think your Jane Doe's a user?"

"Nothing solid, not even a hunch. I'm just looking for a toehold. Who's your contact at

Multi-Urban Services? I don't expect any-thing from the carrot and the stick I waved over the phone there. I'm jonesing to talk to this Foster person."

He grinned his kid's grin. "You talked to the ice queen in reception?"

"I got frostbite on my ear."

"That's Rosalind. Wouldn't give you the time of day if you were defusing a time bomb. I'll talk to Harry Boston, the owner. Three generations of his family took the hats of visitors to the Dodge mansion. Not a lot of call for butlers after the old lady went to the great charity ball in the sky. He founded Multi-Urban on what she left him in her will."

"How much was it?"

"Just enough to cover his business license. She spent fifty grand on the staircase run-ner and made her great-grandchildren tiptoe up and down the bare ends of the treads to keep from wearing it out. I'll give him your number."

"What's he owe you?"

The grin evaporated. "He's a friend, Amos, not like you. Not everyone I hang out with has his palm up."

I let him have that one. Friendship means never having to say go to hell. "So are the druglords your bread and butter now?"

"God, no. Those animals would blow up a city block just to get one of their own out of a holding cell. All the dons ever did was throw money at the problem. In my line, if you don't have a certain amount of respect for the enemy, you go around all the time breathing through your mouth. I had a longer and warmer relationship with old Sam Lucy than most marriages, including the six years he served in Milan after my five-part series on him ran in the *Wall Street Journal.* Which is where I'm working now, Wall Street. The worst thing those white-collar crooks do when they get nailed is fake their own deaths."

"Not much flash, though."

"I miss the sharkskin suits."

Just then Emily appeared with our bill. He pointed at me.

"Is this Amos Walker?"

I'd been sitting in the uneasy chair in my little living room playing with a drink when the phone rang. The voice in my ear sounded like a mouthful of kippers and kidney pie. I thought my invitation to the royal wedding would come by mail. When I told the owner of the voice he had the right party, he said, "I'm Harry Boston. Barry Stackpole said you wanted to know about

Ann Foster. He wouldn't say why."

"She's not the target of my investigation."

"That isn't an answer."

"Pardon me, but you didn't exactly ask a question. I want to talk to her about a former employer."

"Our people do not disclose clients' information."

"That's not what Barry said."

"My association with Mr. Stackpole is not at issue."

"What does 'not a tissue' mean?"

A throat cleared. "I believe you were informed that Miss Foster is no longer with the firm."

"Yeah. I didn't set up this call for a second opinion. I just wanted to know where she's working now. She can tell me to go climb a rope in person."

"Very well. When she terminated her employment she gave us an address where we could send her final paycheck. Stormy Heat Productions, on Mount Elliott."

"Doesn't sound like a place for a maid."

"Not one that does much dusting, I daresay."

"Well, thanks and cheerio."

That got me a click and a hum. His stiff upper lip had spread like a rash.

I looked up the place in the directory, but

the listing only gave me a telephone number. In the Yellow Pages I found a quarter-page ad under Adult Entertainment among the massage parlors, escort services, and 900 numbers with its name scripted diagonally across a silhouetted couple in a tight embrace, framed by a heart. You could apply for an audition by phone or e-mail.

I almost called, even though it was after six and most businesses were closed; I figured the place put in as many hours after dark as before. But my ear was sore from all the time I'd spent on the airwaves, and anyway a place called Stormy Heat was bound to be more interesting in person.

# EIGHT

Detroit woke to another oatmeal sky. My tires crunched through frozen slush past a clothing consignment shop with a gay yellow SPRING SALE banner slung across its front, hammocked with snow. I cranked my window down and up to scrape away frost and caught a whiff of mothballs and complimentary coffee.

The outfit worked out of an extinct gymnasium across from Mt. Elliott Cemetery, a scorched-brick building as old as the eight-hour day, with factory windows checkered with weathered plywood where panes had fallen out. Its name was painted in cursive on a sign stuck perpendicular to the street in a strip of acid-washed grass.

A little cracked parking lot contained a polyglot assortment of vehicles foreign and domestic. I nosed in between an old bread truck that would carry a lot of equipment for location shooting and a green 1989

Cadillac Eldorado with a brown left front fender. A dozen or so tired-looking pizza boxes stuck out at all angles behind the front seat like fossilized species in a tar pit. That seemed to be what was left of Stormy Heat Productions after it had splurged on its Yellow Pages ad.

The door, beige fire-resistant steel with a thumb latch, was locked. I pushed a sunken button that grated in its socket. No sound issued from within. I was about to knock when a rectangular panel opened in the door at eye level and a scowling black face filled the gap. A beard grew to a point on the end of its chin. It startled a grin out of me.

"Aren't you supposed to be doing your huffing and puffing on this side?"

He looked me up and down, didn't approve of what he saw. I get a lot of that. "We don't do tours." The panel banged shut. I rang again. The panel shot back. He looked surprised to see it was me. "Who're you?"

I showed him the sheriff's star with my ID folded back out of sight.

"We got a license to operate," he said.

"I'm looking for Ann Foster."

"What for?"

"Conversation."

"This ain't a chat room. Come back with paper."

Staring again at the panel I lit a cigarette, smoked a third of it, and crushed it out on the concrete stoop with my foot. Blowing a stuttering plume of smoke I used the button again. When the panel shot back I grabbed a fistful of beard and yanked. His forehead struck the door with a noise like a sledge striking an iron bell. His eyes crossed, then drifted back into position. "You mother —"

I gave the beard a twist. He ground his teeth and his tear ducts squirted.

"Motherfuckers have their place," I said. "Where'd you and I be if they didn't?"

"Leggo! Jesus!"

I hung on. "The goose flies high. Klaatu barada nikto. Have you any Grey Poupon? Pick any password you like, but open the goddamn door."

"Who — ?"

"Jerk Root, the Painless Barber. Open."

"Okay, okay." Metal snapped on his side. Still hanging on to his whiskers, I reached down with my free hand and worked the latch. I let go and opened the door. He was standing just inside the threshold, a big man in jeans wearing through where jeans don't wear through naturally and a white shirt open to the navel Byron-fashion, smoothing his beard with thick fingers. He had a Colt Python in his other hand pointed at my belt buckle.

"Nice. The nickel plate matches your eyes. Got a permit?"

"Gimme another look at that badge."

"One's all you get."

"I don't think you're a cop."

"I'm not here to raid the place. I just want to talk to Ann Foster."

"I said I don't —"

"Stop with the compliments. You're turning my head. Do I have to call for backup, get everybody all in a lather? In this economy, it's cheaper just to send the wagon without waiting for the order."

He bounced the deep-bellied revolver in his hand, the way they do in the movies when it's a prop and won't go off. My innards contracted.

"Okay." He reached back and jammed it in a hip pocket. "Okay. I don't need no beef with the law. You didn't have to get so rough." He stroked his hairy chin.

"You're lucky you didn't meet me a couple of years ago. Back then I wouldn't have waited till you slammed the door the second time."

"Couple of years ago I'da brought out the

piece the first time."

"Just a pair of mellow seniors. Start the tour."

"You don't see nothing on the way, deal?"

"Relax. This isn't an election year."

There was a lot not to see. Films produced by Stormy Heat weren't interested in the Academy Award or even feature billing at the Tomcat Theater downtown, where the patrons supplied their own refreshments in paper sacks. You found them in hourly rate motels and behind saloon doors at the back of the local VideoMart, both institutions endangered by the Web. We passed thin, ferret-faced actors and hollow-eyed actresses standing around in robes, smoking and watching the butt-crack brigade monkeying with lights suspended above foamboard platforms dressed up to look like beds. The cameras and fixtures were strictly surplus, their cables frayed and patched all over like garden hoses. We walked past a couple of scenes in progress, all undulating tattoos and stretch marks, smelling sweat and semen and cannabis. It was like walking through a factory with only a couple of shifts standing between it and termination.

Whiskers jerked open another scuffed steel door, releasing a gust of gym socks and mildew. The showers had been shut off years ago and the lockers sold for scrap, but the smell was as durable as cat pee.

"What's the matter, they don't teach you to knock in the jungle?"

I'd had a flash of a naked youthful brown body, and then it was covered by a red silk kimono that left a pair of long legs bare to the tops of the thighs. She had her hair cut very short and her face, with its upturned nose and full lower lip stuck out, was boyish. I'd seen enough to know she wasn't a boy.

Whiskers twisted his face. "I gonna see nothing I ain't already seen out on the floor? You got a visitor. From the Machine."

Ann Foster looked at me. The whites of her eyes had a bluish tinge against her dark skin. "Cop?"

I stared at the guy with the beard until he left us, letting the heavy door suck itself shut behind him. The room had been converted into a community dressing room, but without much conviction. The walls were a palimpsest of old graffiti under a light application of tan paint. And a row of twisted pipes remained where the urinals had been yanked out. A trestle table littered with combs and brushes and Foundation in a Drum stood in front of a long mirror, but the bench on our side had come with the place, and maybe even the pair of dirty man's underpants that hung on the end. You could catch a bad case of athlete's foot just looking at a picture of the place.

She folded her arms across her breasts and spread her bare feet. The toenails were rounded and painted a frosty pink. "Show me you're a cop."

"I'm private. I let Lothar out there think different. It saved time."

"Well, you're wasting it in here. I don't like rental heat any more than the other kind. I don't even like men."

"You picked a swell business not to like them in."

She smiled, not unpleasantly. Her teeth were bluish white, too, and straight. "I work with an all-female cast."

"It pay better than cleaning house?"

"About as much. But when I get on my knees it's not to scrub floors."

I grinned. "You know, in a couple of years we'll both be exhibits in a museum. Google and CGI win."

"Same thing in the service industry. Jobs aren't going out of style. People are. First species in the history of the world managed to make itself obsolete."

"Quite an education you have there," I said.

"Can't cash a check with just a diploma. What do you want?"

"Cecelia Wynn."

"She's taken, sorry."

"You don't seem surprised it's her I'm here about."

"She's missing, right? She never seemed permanent. Some things you just know about people. Not comfortable in their skins. Mister, I know that feeling."

"Her husband wants her back. You had a fight with her just before you got fired. What started it?"

"I bet you talked to William. Chauffeurs have too much time on their hands when they're not driving. Say what you like about the skin trade, folks in it know how to keep a secret."

"What makes it a secret?"

"What happens if I don't answer?"

"Nothing. Now. But if it turns out she doesn't want to be missing, the cops get it. I could save you a trip downtown."

"Hell, she's probably off with her lawyer boyfriend like last time."

"No, he's accounted for. Also she left almost all her clothes behind, along with the herbs she spent a small country buying and a lot of time stuffing into capsules. It's starting to look like it wasn't her idea, or that where she was going she wouldn't need those things. What was the fight about?"

"I wouldn't do windows."

I stuck out my leg, hooked her behind the ankle, and dumped her off her feet. She sat down hard on the concrete floor and yelled. The door swung open. Whiskers stuck his face inside. Farther down the magnum glittered. "What?"

I looked at him, looked down at the woman, sitting with her hands braced on the floor. Her robe had fallen open to expose her left breast. She saw the angle of his gaze and adjusted the robe to cover it. "Nothing."

"You just got tired, decided to sit down in the dirt?"

"I slipped, okay?"

The man with the beard slid his eyes past mine and took his face and gun out of the way of the door. It drifted shut. I reached down to give the woman a hand. She took it and when she had her feet under her swung her other hand around in a long loop. I moved my head with it, but she caught my ear and a bell rang.

"We're friends now," I said, rubbing the ear.

She wasn't listening. "It was weird. Serving dinner this one night I spilled salad oil down the front of my uniform. I went to my room to change. Mrs. Wynn stepped inside to ask for something. She caught me naked."

"Not hard to do. So?"

"So she excused herself and got out. Half an hour later I was out of a job. For spilling the salad oil. Sure, we fought. After she fired me, not before."

"Sure it was the salad oil?"

"It wasn't."

"Damn right it wasn't. Think she's gay?"

"Takes one to know one, that it?"

"I've been in the bars. I never saw anyone clocked yet for making a mistake."

"Well, it isn't like with men. Some women are just curious. But if you're looking for a reason she left, I'd say she went cruising."

"Why ship out when she had you at home?"

"It's not a decision you make all at once. Uptight woman like her, she'd fight it first, remove temptation. Then, after she's thought it over —" She rolled a shoulder, smoothed the kimono across her pelvis.

"Where does one go cruising around here?"

"Try the Pink Diesel in Centerline. It's a saloon. The place is kind of advanced, though. It could scare a newbie off three feet inside the door."

"Sounds scary. Should I wear body armor?"

"Maybe a cup."

# NINE

I bought coffee at a drive-through and pulled into a slot to scald my tongue and call Information. A recording at the number I got for the Pink Diesel told me the place didn't open till four. The gender of the voice was indeterminate and it came with its own musical score: a rock riff on a combination electric guitar and circular saw that was still zinging in my ear when I finished the coffee and drove away.

The trail was cold at least until late afternoon. I checked into the office, letting myself in the miniature waiting room I leave unlocked during the day for anyone who has nothing better to do than catch up on the Clinton Administration in a magazine. I almost dropped the key to the private office when someone stood up from the uphol- stered bench to greet me.

It was Smoke, the clerk at Elysian Fields. She'd traded the Grecian gown for a loose sweatshirt with a boatneck wide enough to bare one polished shoulder and a classically curved collarbone and black tights. Flip-flops with garnet-colored crystals on the straps set off a pair of slender feet without paint. Her pale yellow hair was pulled back as before and swung near her waist when she turned my way. Her kaleidoscope eyes — frosty green today — were large and startled-looking, as if I'd come on her unexpectedly grazing in a forest glade.

"I looked you up," she said. "Do you remember me?"

"Sure. Amber Dawn."

A straight nose wrinkled. "The joke seemed funnier yesterday. A lot of things have changed since yesterday. Can we go inside?"

I unlocked the door and held it open for her. She went straight in without looking around at what passed for the décor and sat down in the chair on the suckers' side of the desk. She managed to make the rest of the room look even shabbier than always.

"Who's minding the store?"

"There is no store. That's why I'm here."

I adjusted my protuberances into the declensions in the swivel chair behind the desk and broke out a fresh carton of Winstons. When I raised my eyebrows to ask if

108

she didn't mind, she stuck out a hand. "Bum one?"

I wasn't sure whether I was more surprised by the fact she smoked than by the turn of phrase. It had gone out with cigarette commercials. I zipped the top off a pack, thumped the bottom with my thumb, and offered her the one that separated itself from the rest. I took one for myself, lit hers off a match, and used what was left of it getting mine burning. "Isn't that grounds for dismissal from a health store?" I asked.

"Oh, please. If you slam that crap we sell all day every day for the rest of your life, you'll live exactly an hour and a half longer than if you didn't. Or not. I think I told you the FDA hasn't signed on yet." She cocked her head to blow a jet of smoke away from her hair. She was a puffer, not an inhaler. I couldn't see the point. "Do you hire yourself out for all sorts of jobs, or just missing-person cases?"

"I guarded a necklace around the neck of a GM board member's wife once. It got me a night of Wagner in the opera house and a rib eye in the Diamondback. These days you can't be particular. What did you mean when you said there is no store?"

"When I got to work this morning, the parking lot was jammed with squad cars and

109

an armored vehicle of some kind. Cops in vests and helmets standing around talking into mikes. I just kept on driving; borrowed a look at a phone book in a party store and came straight here. Shouldn't you have a receptionist or something?"

"I should have a helicopter to beat rush hour, but I can't afford the fuel either. What kind of cops?"

"Cops cops. How many kinds are there?"

"In Detroit? The FBI maintains a standing army just to keep an eye on all the others."

"Oh. City cops. Blue-and-whites, black-and-golds. The armored job had ERT on it in letters you could read in Windsor."

"Early Response Team. They don't leave home without AK-47s and a couple of dozen shock grenades. Why would Detroit cops raid the place?"

"Your guess is as good as mine. They knocked over a medical-marijuana dispensary two blocks from my apartment last year: Owner had a permit and everything. They like to push in places just for fun."

"Does Elysian Fields sell pot?"

"If it does, I never handled any sales. There's a padlock on the door to the basement. My boss said it's to protect employees from falling down the rickety stairs and suing him for personal injury. If he's growing the plants down there, I wouldn't know. I've never seen it."

"So what makes this your problem?"

"If they had a warrant to search the place, I've got to assume they had one to arrest everyone who works there. Everyone being me. I'd like to know my rights before they show up at my place."

"You don't need me. I can give you the names of some lawyers. A couple of them have never faced disbarment."

She took one last drag, leaned forward in her chair, ditched it in my souvenir tray from Traverse City, and folded her arms on her side of the desk. "I had a lawyer once. He forgot to tell me the date of a hearing was changed, and when I didn't show up and he had to go there and represent me, he charged me for two hours. Ask me again why I didn't call a lawyer."

"Hearing for what?"

She smiled crookedly. "Possession of marijuana: one gram over the limit for personal use. I pulled two hundred hours of community service for possession for sale."

"Guilty?"

"That's what the judge said."

I cupped a hand over the tray until the butt smoldered out. I've never met a woman

111

who finished the job. "I don't sweat over doobies, and I've got nothing against free enterprise. If I'm going to help you, though, I need to know if I'm representing a garden-variety pothead or the Colombian cartel. I can pull up your rap sheet, but I've only got so many chips I can cash in downtown."

She rolled the naked shoulder. "I lived with a small-time dealer for eight months. When DEA decided he was worth squeezing for information on his superiors, I got hauled in alongside. They kicked me after six hours in a crummy hotel room they used for interrogations in Redford. When he didn't cave, they tagged him for statutory rape. I was a child of sixteen. That's the load, swear on a stack of Bibles."

"A stack's no improvement over just one. Are you even a Christian?"

"I was baptized Catholic. For a little while I was a Wiccan, but it's not a real religion, even if it is registered. Say what you like about Christians and Muslims, they buy into the shebang. Nobody who calls herself a witch really thinks she can cast spells. They're just Shriners without the funny hats. If you want to stick me with a label, I guess you could say I'm a recovering believer."

"A very large congregation, bigger than

Hindu. What do you want me to do?"

"Find out what's going on, and tell me I don't have anything to worry about."

"I can deliver on the first part. I can't guarantee the second. If the cops decide to put the screws on you to build a case against your employer, they've got a prior on the possession deal and a person-of-interest card to play on the six hours you spent in Holding. It all depends on how badly they want your boss. Who is he, by the way? You said before it was a he."

She licked her unpainted lips and slid her gaze toward the pack of cigarettes on the desk. I shoved it her way and struck another match. When she had one going, she said, "I'd rather not answer that one until I have to. Is that all right?"

I finished mine and screwed it out in the tray. "It's not all right, but if you're going to be mule headed, I can look into the official investigation and let you know where you stand. If the cops don't care whether you exist, my job's done. If they do, we're going to have this conversation all over again, and if the answer's the same, I'll give you that list of attorneys and wish you good luck."

"That's fair. Now let's talk money."

"Five hundred a day. Three days up front."

That time she inhaled. Very little smoke

came back out. "I knew it would be stiff. I didn't know how stiff. I don't guess you haggle."

"I never alter my fees except when I omit them entirely."

"That sounds familiar. Did I read it somewhere?"

"Sherlock Holmes. My role model, except when it comes to deduction."

"Isn't that all he did?"

"Well, he dressed funny; but I can't pull it off."

She got rid of the butt, this time with finality. I had the strange suspicion she was picturing my face in the bottom of the tray. I took pity on her then, I didn't know why. Probably it was her exposed collarbone. I'm a connoisseur. Breast and leg men have nothing in common with me.

"I'll look into it for a hundred. It shouldn't take all day to find out what the cops have in mind. If I'm wrong, we'll have to renegotiate."

"Done." She slid a hand inside the neckband of her sweatshirt and came up with a fold of bills. The crooked smile came out with it when she saw my reaction. "Case dough; that's what they call it on TCM, right? I'm an old-movie geek. Ever since that first bust I never go out without a

114

getaway stake." She peeled off a hundred in twenties and two well-traveled tens and smoothed them out in a stack on the desk. I broke out a receipt pad, wrote out the amount.

"Last name?"

"Wygonik." She spelled it.

"Polish?"

"Fourth generation. My great-grandfather shook the dust of Crakow off his heels a week after he found out Mr. Ford was paying five dollars a day at the River Rouge plant."

"Doesn't go with Smoke."

"I went back to it in a fit of ethnic pride. My parents had it legally changed to Free."

"Smoke Free?"

"Maybe the pride wasn't entirely ethnic."

I entered the name, handed her the original, and kept the carbon. "I live by Hamtramck. Not many of the old guard left."

"I know. I looked up your home address. Why I'm here."

"Not Polish; sorry."

"There's something to be said for osmosis."

"Science degree?"

"Two years, U of D. My Catholic period.

It's how I got into botany. You have to grow herbs."

"Good grounding for pot production. Sure you never got a peek at that basement?"

She crossed herself, held up her right hand. Her eyes clouded over brown. "I said I was a recovering believer. It's an ongoing process."

I got her address, wrote it on my pad, gave her a card with my office and cell number on it, and got up to see her out. Afterwards I smoked too many cigarettes and reached behind my neck to smooth down the hairs that had stood out on it. No good: They sprang back. A simple missing-persons case had turned into something else, like most things in a bad dream.

# TEN

The nightspots were opening, beginning the bottom half of my double shift. I had a date with a lesbian bar. You can be in this business fifty years and still find something new to add to your memoirs.

A stranger was reading the building directory when I came down the third flight, moving his lips over the white plastic snap-letters arranged according to the imagination of Rosecranz, the super. He was on the tattered outer edge of middle age, wearing a gray corduroy sportcoat over a yellow polo shirt that barely covered his belly fat, tan Dockers bagged at the knees, and sneakers fastened with hook-and-loop straps, the designers' gift to the terminally out-of-shape. He needed a haircut, especially near the collar, where the black and gray coiled over the top, and his face was burned a deep and unhealthy shade of cherry. A surgeon had gouged a deep gully in his left cheek,

117

foraging for a melanoma.

I asked him who he was looking for. He jumped, as if he hadn't seen me coming down a stairwell directly in his line of vision, then pointed a ragged nail at the third line.

"C.E. Challis, but there's no office number."

"Dr. Challis has retired from practice, with the enthusiastic approval of the American Chiropractic Association. I heard he opened a yoga studio in Farmington. You don't need a license for that."

"He didn't say nothing about it when I made the appointment." A hand stole to the small of his back: lumbago, or a belt clip. I'd left my arsenal in the Cutlass.

"When'd you call?"

"Last week, if it's any business of yours."

"Your calendar's running slow. He cleared out in January. The building service here makes Washington look good. I think there's still a phrenologist listed on the board."

"What's that?"

"Something that shouldn't still be listed anywhere. I was making sort of a joke."

He slid the finger down the ragged furrow in his cheek. "I guess I got the wrong Challis."

"It's a common name — in France."

118

"Thanks, brother. You saved me a trip upstairs." He touched his back again.

"You ought to try acupuncture."

"Like the Chinese need the business."

That was the end of the scintillating exchange.

I followed him to the street. He crossed into the unofficial parking lot and got into a green Chevy Malibu with a tailpipe held together by rust. The motor started like a bad orchestra rehearsing the Anvil Chorus. It tried to stall as he cranked it out of its space, then caught with a report like a firecracker and spread a screen of greasy black smoke all the way down the block. I had time to unscrew the license plate and put it in my hip pocket. Instead I just memorized the number. It was a Michigan plate, which did nothing to explain the sunburn and skin cancer. The state's far more prone to sunshine deficiency and frostbite.

Not that the number would do me any good: The car had probably been stolen after he ditched whatever he'd driven from Arizona, where dermatologists go to make their fortunes. Arizona: Home to the Apache Nation, the Diamondbacks, and Mafiosi enjoying their pensions. That was just a guess, but I can smell garlic the way Jim

Bridger claimed he could identify Indian tribes by their scent.

I'd spotted the open tail, as I was supposed to by the very definition of the phrase. It's the one you don't see that counts.

# ELEVEN

You can enter Macomb County without striking any bells or knowing you've gone anywhere other than where you've been. Detroit lies spread-eagle north of downtown, and the City of Warren's more of the same, as flat as the General Motors proving grounds, which is the first and only landmark you come to after you cross Eight Mile Road. In the sprawl of buildings nearby, employees with mechanical pencils approach the daily problem of making cars lighter and safer at the same time. Can't be done, so they're on the payroll for life.

Centerline hasn't appeared in the headlines on a regular basis since the Hudson Motor Company stopped manufacturing navy guns there in 1945, which may be a point in its favor. It has no casinos to foster marital unrest and a fair portion of its populace wouldn't travel the few blocks to Detroit even for free beer. It's one of those suburbs-within-a-suburb, surrounded by Warren on all four sides. Again, there are no border posts or changes in architecture to let you know you've arrived.

The Pink Diesel called as little attention to itself as Elysian Fields. It occupied a flat-roofed yellow brick building that looked as if it had been part of a strip mall before the big-box stores had moved in and turned most of them into pawn shops and cash-for-gold emporia, with tinting over the plate glass to cut down on light from outside and no sign to identify it, just a pink neon tube bent like a balloon sculpture into the silhouette of a tractor-trailer rig in the window next to the door. An impressive display of Jeeps, Hummers, and classic pickups with bulbous fenders occupied the parking lot among more conventional vehicles.

Before leaving the car I reached for the cubby under the glove compartment where I keep the artillery: When someone tells you to wear a cup, it never hurts to adjust upward. In the end I went in armed only with the will of the righteous. I was overdue for a mistake and might as well get it out of the way.

Inside was bar twilight, something with a steady beat thrumming low over the sound system, parties seated around tables and at

122

the bar. Except for the prevailing gender, you wouldn't have known it wasn't the usual sort of saloon. There were tattoos and cutoff sleeves, some crew cuts and piercing, but these days you can find those even in a business hangout. Just as many of the clientele had on skirts and blouses and tailored suits. A variety of scents, drugstore and fashion counter, mingled with the hops and fermented grain. Amelia Earhart, Babe Didrikson, Hillary Clinton, Sally Ride in her flight suit, Billie Jean King, Gloria Steinem, and women I didn't recognize hung in frames on the walls. Whoever had done the place had erred on the side of subtlety.

Less subtle was the path of silence I towed through the room as I made my way to the bar. The original murmur of conversation closed back in behind me, but I felt a little like a cattle baron's gunslinger entering a saloon full of small-time ranchers. Eyes watched me under the corners of lashes from the seats on either side as I rested a hand on the bar top. A tall slender party in a starched white blouse placed a drink on a fresh napkin at the end and drifted my way. "What's your pleasure?"

"I'm open to suggestions," I said. "Hemlock, or a strychnine spritzer? Whatever makes me popular."

"It isn't that bad. It's just the name of the place. Thirty-two weeks without a single castration." She dyed her collar-length hair a bright shade of copper, which went well with her pale coloring and a band of freckles across her cheeks. She was either a mature thirty or a well-maintained forty. Her eyes smiled even though her mouth didn't. "Whiskey sour? You don't look like a man with a sweet tooth."

"Hold the syrup." I watched her mix the bourbon and lemon juice in a tumbler. She reached for the sugar, thought better of it, left it where it was, and gave the swizzle a couple of turns. When she set the glass in front of me I slid a ten-spot her way.

"Run a tab?"

"Maybe. Anyway, don't make change just yet."

A pug-nose blonde two seats down touched her glass. I waited while the bartender replaced it with a full one and caught her eye at the register. She brought the blonde her change and came back, brows raised. "Trouble with your drink?"

"It's okay. I watched you fix it. This woman been in lately?" I gave her one of the prints I'd had made of Cecelia Wynn's picture.

She whistled low. "Looker. Police?"

"Private." I gave her a card. "She's been missing about a week."

"Don't know her, but I'm just part-time. Putting my way through community college."

"Recent split?" She had a pale spot on her ring finger.

"Recent, and unofficial. It wasn't legal to begin with, thanks to the good ole boys in Lansing. The rest of the time I model for art classes. Shocked?"

"To the heels. Get many complaints about the freckles?"

She decided to laugh at that. "It pays better than slinging drinks, but the work's harder. I can always tell when the instructor never modeled. They think we're made of pipe cleaners, and their watches run slow: A twenty-minute pose can run a half hour."

"What's your major?"

"Engineering. What was yours?"

"Sleuthing. Okay if I work the room?"

She sucked in a cheek, chewing.

"I'll be gentle. Client just wants to know she's healthy."

"I'd steer clear of the corner booth."

I had a view of it in the mirror behind the bottles. A hefty woman in a sweatshirt sat alone there, both hands wrapped around a glass the size of a burial urn, reading the tea

125

leaves in the bottom. "Dumped?"

"For a pair of pants. I'd like that no-castration record to stand a little longer."

"What's she drinking?"

"She started on Harvey Wallbangers. Had me hold the orange juice the last three hits."

"People who drink straight vodka aren't drinking for laughs. She got a ride home?"

"Takes the bus."

"Set her up again on me." I pushed another ten after the first.

"Mister —"

"Walker. Don't worry. I'll work my way around, come in downwind. Keep the rest. We need engineers more than we need bartenders."

"Her name's Loretta."

"What's yours?"

This time she smiled with her mouth. "Single malt." She rang up the bills and poured herself three inches from a bottle of Glenfiddich.

I wet my lips on my glass — I didn't have the heart to tell her it was too sour — and salted the room with Cecelia Wynn's picture. I found out who was bi and who was committed, got away from under one bedroom gaze while her partner was burning slowly, bought a drink for a party of four that couldn't decide whether they'd seen her around, bypassed a two-top when the woman saw me coming and transferred her Coach handbag from the back of her chair to the seat of the one vacant. By the time I got to Loretta's booth, she was almost finished with the drink I'd sent over. She had an unlit cigarette in the corner of her mouth and she was swaying in place, but the pair of eyes that moved my way were as steady and solid as gray stones.

"Thanks for the booze," she said. "I'm not changing sides."

"I'm not recruiting. Okay if I join you? I'm working."

"That's what Dixie said."

"Dixie?"

"The bar girl. What's the matter, not detective enough to find out who you're talking to?"

"I asked. She doesn't draw out her vowels enough for a Dixie."

"Maybe her old lady named her after a paper cup." She tilted her football-size head toward the seat opposite. I slid in, got the redhead's eye, and twirled my finger.

Loretta waited until after the drinks were brought and we were alone again, then wrapped her hands around her fresh glass. "This like a piece of raw meat wrapped around a tranquilizer pill?"

"Dixie got me a little scared."

"I don't bite," she said, "men. Why blame the guy? You get tired of packing those things around, you have to stick it someplace. Where you do that's up to the stickee."

I drank, said nothing. I was getting used to the puckery taste.

The woman in the sweatshirt took a healthy sip without taking the cigarette from her mouth. The sleeves were short. She had a tiny heart tattooed on the underside of her thick upper arm with a ribbon wrapped around it. It was blank. She saw me see it.

"Keeping my options open; or I was. I had it in mind to have her name put on it next week.

"I've known what I am since I was twelve," she went on. "Suzie said she was full-throttle, too. Men don't have the corner on lying their way into a woman's pants. I was just an interesting detour along the way. A story to share with her friends in the book club over a dirty martini when hubby's on the links and the brats are in day care."

A teardrop the size of a pearl onion rolled out over her lower left lid and followed the crease from the corner of her nose to the corner of her mouth, where it quivered before evaporating.

"Mine left me, too," I said when she didn't continue.

"Man? Woman? Never mind. Doesn't matter. A lot of people think it does, but it's the same plot with different characters. I bet you thought it was your fault."

"Thing is, it was."

"Unfaithful?"

I laid Cecelia Wynn's picture in front of her. She went on watching me for fifteen seconds, then scraped it up from the table and turned it over to look at it, like a playing card. That gave her a view of the back, which was blank. She turned it over again, studied it, shook her head, put it down, and picked up her drink.

"I don't know her. We don't all know each other, you know."

"Facebook will change all that. She's new. She might not be ready for the social scene. For all the evidence I've got, she might not even have changed teams. I'm just playing an angle." I laid my card on top of the photo. "I'd appreciate it if you'd let me know if any of your friends recognize her. She might be in trouble."

"Who isn't?"

I left money for the liquor and was halfway to the door when I turned around and went back. I tore a sheet from my notepad, wrote

129

a number on it, and held it out.

She looked at it without taking it. "Who answers if I call?"

"An actress named Foster. She does girl-on-girl at a place called Stormy Heat Productions."

"I know Stormy Heat. Their straight porn's the same old shit, but whoever does the gay stuff knows his business. Or hers. This a fix up?"

"That's up to you. I wouldn't use my name. We had us a little dustup before we parted. But she's committed, if that's what you're looking for."

"Keep it. I'm depressed, not desperate."

I stuck the sheet in a pocket. "Memorized it, didn't you?"

"Thanks for the drinks."

The stoplight at Ten Mile Road had a NO TURN ON RED sign. I slid up to the crosswalk, tapped the brake, then punched the accelerator before my brake light could come on and swung into the outside lane. Behind me the driver of a Smart Car crossing with the light screeched his brakes and leaned on his nasal little horn for the benefit of a gray Lincoln Town Car turning behind me against the light.

I turned left at Van Dyke and stayed below the limit the rest of the way into Detroit. I didn't want to lose my shadow, just find out what it looked like.

# TWELVE

I tried a drop-behind, as much to find out how good the tail was as to get a glimpse of the plate. I slowed, after which the Town Car did the same, falling back half a block and letting a dilapidated station wagon pass him on the inside lane and slide back into the outside, separating us. A point in his favor: An inexperienced shadow gets nervous when open road isn't available. Town Car closed in on the wagon, increasing speed comfortably while leaving enough room to slide around the obstacle when necessary. I swung right onto the broken pavement of a lot belonging to a check-cashing emporium with bars in the windows, goosed the pedal, and skinned between the cinder-block building and a chain-link fence on the other side of a constipated alley, then opened all four barrels circling the building. When I came out on the other side there was no sign of the

Lincoln. SOP so far.

Back on the street heading in the same direction I'd been going, I fell back to twenty-five, then lingered at a STOP sign before creeping across the intersection, keeping one eye on the mirror and the other on the street ahead, in case the driver had cruised on past, preferring losing me to the risk of discovery. Even that would be valuable information: Cops in general don't care if you know they're following; criminals almost always do.

I increased speed, looking to catch up with him. I caught a break at a light, but stamped on the brake in the next block to avoid rear-ending a panel truck. When I got around it, all I saw was congealing traffic up ahead and deserted street behind.

I passed a curbside strip mall containing a dry cleaner, an auto-parts store, a grubby little place that advertised yoga instruction and probably ran numbers out the back door, and a Christian Science reading room with curtains in the windows. Out of its parking lot came the Town Car. From then until I got back to the office it stuck to my heel like toilet paper.

The driver was good. I knew, because vehicular tails are one of my special talents; but I'm usually hindered by the lack of a

133

good leg man in the passenger's seat to bail out and continue the surveillance on foot when the mark finds the only parking space on a busy street and takes it on the ankles.

This one wouldn't be operating under such a handicap. The bump I'd spotted atop the right-side seat could have been a head-rest or a head. It would be a head; and so it was two against one.

Not so frightening odds, when I was thirty. But that train had sailed. Waiting for the light to change at Eight Mile Road, I popped open the nifty little hatch under the glove compartment and transferred the Chief's Special in its clip to the belt next to my right kidney.

I wondered who I'd ticked off this time, and if it had anything to do with the case I was working. That's the trouble with a long and colorful career. You never know whether you've made a new enemy or it's just old business.

Rosecranz, the gnarled gnome who represented the one note of consistency in a building that changed tenants as regularly as lightbulbs, was rearranging the same gray city grit in the foyer with a push broom that was nearly as bald as he was. He'd given up actually removing the dirt sometime around the first Gulf War. He claimed his mother had saved him from the Bolsheviks by throwing him out an open window, which if true put him just on the shady side of a hundred: But with each passing year he shriveled and shrank a little bit more, never suppurating, just becoming dryer and more wrinkled. He looked like a potato that had fallen back into the pantry and been overlooked for a year.

When he saw me he shouldered his broom at parade rest. "You have a visitor. The Cossack?"

Which was his not-so-pet name for my bane and salvation, a public fixture every bit as permanent as Rosecranz, but with considerably more influence on my life than a petrified potato.

"Let him in?"

He lowered the broom to the floor, leaning the handle against his shoulder, and spread a pair of hands slabbed with decades of callus. "I should say no? January comes, goes, I am too busy always to register."

I skinned a five-spot from my wallet and held it out. A lot of building superintendents wouldn't bother to tell a tenant there was a cop waiting for him in his private office. The bill went into a pocket of his overalls so fast I wasn't sure it had changed hands at all.

At the first landing I leaned against the scaly wainscoting and lit a cigarette, to flatten my nerves and build me up for battle. After half a dozen puffs I dropped it onto the rubber tread and ground it out with my foot, into the gray compost of its ancestors. I don't know what we'll do when they finish taking tobacco from us. Heroin's too cumbersome, with its spoons and matches and rubber hoses, and coke goes against the grain: Most of the human orifices are designed for exits, not entrances. Mountain goats unwind from the office by butting heads. I didn't see the percentage. I never had; but it was part of my job description.

"I don't know why you waste the rent. You're never here."

John Alderdyce sat behind my desk with my office bottle standing on the blotter and a shot glass hiding out in his fist like a thimble in a catcher's mitt. He's an inspector with the Detroit Police Department — Homicide, to put the fine point on it — and as much as he looks like a grizzly bear carved with a chainsaw from a living oak, he likes to drape himself in fine tailoring. Today he had on a plum-colored suit over a grayish-pink shirt. His necktie was aubergine, held in place with a platinum clip bearing his initials in onyx.

136

"It's Detroit, John," I said. "Real estate's as cheap as life."

"How long have you been holding on to that one?"

"Just since the last time we met. Anything left?" I pointed at the bottle.

"You know, there's a law against advertising Scotch as Scotch that didn't come from Scotland. The label reads like a Japanese instruction manual."

"You think I keep the good stuff out where any flatfoot can lay hands on it?" I went around him, unlocked the cast-iron safe that had come with the office, and stood a fifth of Glenfiddich on top of the desk. It was two-thirds full: I doled the stuff out to myself like penicillin in an epidemic.

He drew the bottle close to him, studied the label, unscrewed the top, sniffed. Finally he tossed what was in his glass into the ossified plant in the corner and poured two inches into the bottom. He found another glass among the paper clips and Past Due bills, measured out the same amount, and pushed it my way.

"Global warming," he toasted.

"Can't come soon enough to suit me." I laid away what was in the glass. "Who's dead?"

"Who isn't? I got two women on an apartment floor on East McNichols who went missing in Flint, a homeless guy with his brains beat out in a tent in Cobb Field, a six-year-old girl on Vernor whose uncle doused her with tiki-torch fuel and touched it off for wetting the bed, and a stiff in a basement on Livernois belonging to the manager of a health-food store, all since I clocked in this a.m."

As he spoke, he held his glass at eye level, pretending to study its machine-cut facets but actually using it as a magnifying lens to watch my face. I rolled a shoulder and sat in the customer's chair bolted beyond halitosis range in front of the desk. "I haven't been to Flint in a year. It isn't on the way to anywhere. You've got the uncle, I'm guessing. Do I look like I hang out in health-food stores?"

"Surveillance camera belonging to the dollar store across the alley says you do. It was time-stamped yesterday afternoon."

"Dollar stores need cameras now?"

"Narcotics raided the place this morning. The corporation that owns it has a medical-marijuana license, entitling it to maintain twelve plants per customer. The officers found seven hundred and ninety-two plants thriving under grow-lights in the basement."

I almost said the basement couldn't be

that big; I caught myself in time. The camera story could be just a dodge to back up a shaky eyewitness. "How much space does that take up?"

"Eight hundred square feet. It's a big old dugout, half of it belonging to a farmhouse next door that was torn down around the time of the Armistice. So almost a plant per square foot, and incidentally the manager, thriving not so much."

"How many pot customers does the place have?"

"Fifteen."

"It wouldn't be the first time a competitor got jealous."

"Narcs say no. No such chatter going around. This was the second unit. First's still tamping out that super-heroin fire from last year before we run clean out of junkies who don't check the dosage. There's not enough money in pot to risk a homicide investigation. Anyway they kicked it over to us, and here I am."

"What's his name?"

"Radu Czenko." He spelled the name. "Age thirty, Romanian, naturalized citizen, emigrated with his parents after the Ceausescu assassination. BS degree in Horticulture from Michigan; as if you need a diploma to water and heap shit on marijuana plants. They don't call 'em weed for nothing. No known living relatives, lived alone in a rented house in Redford. Nobody to report him missing. No priors. Single shot through the bridge of the nose."

"Professional size caliber?"

"What's that? Every copycat's seen *Law and Order.* We'll know what size when the M.E. digs out the slug. Right now the padlock on the outside of the basement door makes a compelling case against suicide."

"Improper disposal of the body, maybe."

"M.E. says no, based on prelim; postmortem lividity in all the right places to suggest he wasn't moved. Dead twelve hours, minimum: Rigor starting to wear off. Those grow-lights can make an unheated cellar right comfortable for the living, so there's no delay due to our celebrated spring climate. What sort of man was he to talk to?" His thick lids hung low over his eyes. He was having trouble staying awake, was Inspector Alderdyce.

I grinned. "Show me the surveillance tape with me on it and we'll continue this conversation."

He didn't pursue that line. He wouldn't chase his hat in a gust of wind, expecting it to come blowing back and land back on his head, at the angle he liked. "We're chiefly interested in his full-time clerk. The only employee on the premises when the drug boys busted in was the janitor, who comes in twice a week to sweep the floor and wax the leaves on the hanging plants, the legitimate ones in the shop. He says the clerk clocks in every morning just in time to open at eight. Not today."

"What time did the raid go down?"

"Seven fifty-six."

"So if they'd held their water four minutes you wouldn't be sitting here drinking my good liquor."

"You don't punish initiative. So the clerk comes around, sees all the activity going on inside, and cruises right on past. I call that guilty conscience. What do you call it?"

"Same thing. Anyplace but Detroit."

"That a crack against the local authorities?"

"What's local? The FBI's watching the PD, the state cops are watching the crime lab, and the governor's watching all three looking for a reason to run the city direct from the capital. A conscientious citizen thinks twice before he jumps into the middle of a three-ring circus. I call that self-protection."

"What makes you think it's a he?" He was

disappointed, not that he showed it; gosh, in another minute he'd fall forward into his glass sound asleep and I'd have to pull him out before he drowned.

"Oh, is the clerk female?"

"You know goddamn well she is. Smoke Wygonik, that's the name in her personnel file. I don't know where the Smoke came from, but she holds down the joint morning to closing, eats her lunch at the counter. She'd have been behind it when you went in looking for whoever it is you're looking for."

"Oh, is it a who?"

"Missing Persons, that's your beat. Says so in the Yellow Pages. I don't give a shit about you, but I want to find out what she knows about her employer and how he came to his untimely passing, which means I need to know what brought you into the place besides your health, which if you cared anything at all about you wouldn't lock up the good stuff in your safe and sit here sucking down piss strained through a kilt."

"Why didn't you say so? Seriously, how do I look on video? I hear the camera adds five pounds."

"Holy shit." He came awake then, as if he'd been any closer to the unconscious state than a politician to the English language. His size-thirteen feet in hand-lasted leather hit the floor with a thud and he thunked his glass down on his side of the desk. Two bits' worth of the Auld Cadenhead slopped out and landed on the corner, playing hell with what finish was left. His eyes were wide open, and as bright as new handcuffs. "She's the client."

# THIRTEEN

"That's against the law," Alderdyce said.

I finished lighting a cigarette, shook out the match, and lobbed it toward the tray on his side of the desk. It teetered on the rim, then fell out. "So's breaking and entering. What do you want to talk to this Smoke person about?"

"If that's what she's paying you to find out, why should I do all the work?"

"If the taxpayers are paying you to find her, why should *I* do all the work?"

"Because obstruction of justice is a hell of a lot more serious than smoking in a place of business."

"That's my loophole. I don't do enough business here to cover the price of a carton. And you make a better obstruction than I ever did."

The rock pile that was his face slid into a scowl. He hadn't been smiling to begin with. I crossed my legs and tapped ash into my pants cuff. "I'm working a missing person, John. That's not the same as working *for* a missing person. If I went to this health-food store and talked to this Smoke girl, it was to develop a lead on something that had nothing to do with your locked-room murder mystery."

"Would you sign a statement to that effect?"

"Nope."

"Why, because it's only legal to lie to a cop until you swear to it in writing?"

"Because my mug on a video isn't enough to drag me in and make a formal statement. If there is a video, and if my mug is on it. If it is, so is the killer's."

"We need your steel-trap mind on the CID. We're checking, but the place has a rear entrance for customers who park in back. No camera there. Who's the missing person?"

"If I could tell you that, you'd be working it already. It doesn't say 'private' on my license just for the rhythm."

"It won't say anything on your license if you don't have it anymore."

"That's state, not local. I'd get a hearing, and the date would still be pending long after you wrapped this one up or stamped it cold."

He got up, making none of the noises big men his age usually make in the process. "Did you ever do the right thing purely on the basis of good citizenship, without being bullied into it?"

I took out my notepad, tore loose a sheet, and held it out. He didn't move to take it. "What is it?"

"It's a license plate number belonging to a character who's been following me around in a beat-up Chevy Malibu, or did until he tagged off to someone driving a gray Lincoln Town Car. That number I didn't get. It could be it has something to do with your homicide. How's that?"

He frowned at the sheet before taking it. "Arizona. Why would those guys mess around in a pitch-penny racket like pot?"

"Maybe the RICO laws backed them into that corner. They've taken away just about everything else."

"What about the Town Car?"

"Two guys. The one behind the wheel's plenty good, so I have to assume the shotgun is too. I only noticed them and the Malibu this morning, so it might have something to do with the raid." I described the driver of the Chevy.

"That surgical scar is promising. Think you can pick him out of the book?"

"He wouldn't be in one of yours. Anyway, what would you haul him in on, loitering in my foyer? But if you can trace the plate, you might know who's paying his 401(k). Probably not, but if you can find out who the car was stolen from, maybe the owner got a peek at the thief and can pick him out of a book in Arizona."

"Right now I'm more interested in the ones in the Lincoln. If they're tailing you for some reason other than you dinged their door in a parking lot. Or if they're tailing you at all. If you look in your mirror long enough, everyone in the world could be on your heel."

"The guy in the foyer had an appointment with a chiropractor who hasn't been in business all year. He could have come up with a hundred better excuses for gathering moss downstairs, but he didn't have to. I was supposed to spot him, so I'd be looking for him instead of his pals in the better set of wheels. Either they think I'm pretty smart or dumber than a string collection. I'll let you know when I know."

"If the mob's interested, this is a whole different kind of investigation."

I nodded. "The black and Mexican gangs crowded them out of Detroit years ago, when they were too banged up by Washington to fight back. The boys in the District ought to have learned the basic theory of vacuums."

"They might be trying to shove their way back in by way of an enterprise nobody else cares about."

"On the other hand, I might've been tagged by someone who has nothing to do with what went down on Livernois."

"That's the trouble with real life versus murder mysteries," he said. "Stuff seeps in from outside."

He locked glances with Custer in the framed print on the wall, not that they had much in common; Alderdyce wouldn't have set foot in the Little Big Horn until Forensics reported on DNA evidence left by the Sioux and Cheyenne Nations and a positive on Sitting Bull based on FBI photo files. He turned his back on the Seventh Cavalry. "I've got a man in front of her place, but so far she hasn't shown up. If she gets in touch with you, call. She isn't a suspect, not even a person of interest. Just someone we want to talk to so we can mark her off the list. I don't hear from you by close of business today, I come back with a court order to search this office and your house. If I were you, I wouldn't do any spring cleaning while I'm waiting. That would rotate you up to the top of the list."

I watched him grip the doorknob. "Last time I waste good Scotch on you."

He wasn't gone five minutes when the phone rang. It was my latest client.

"One moment, please." I laid down the receiver, got up, and stuck my head into the waiting room to make sure Alderdyce hadn't forgotten to leave. I went back and picked up.

"I'm standing across the street," Smoke said. "A big scary-looking man in a nice suit just left your building and drove away in a car that might as well have had UNMARKED on the plate. I'm impressed. How'd you get them to pay a house call?"

"Lady, all I have to do is stand still and they drift in hip deep. Are you stalking me? I'm hauling around a lot of rolling stock as it is."

"I thought I'd drop in, kill some time since I don't have a job. I had a foot off the sidewalk when Shrek came barreling out. What do you mean, rolling stock?"

I didn't go into the Malibu Man or the pair in the Town Car.

"Is the *he* you said you work for named Radu Czenko, by any chance?"

"He's the one I answer to. I've never met

the owner. Is he in jail?"

"Come on up and we'll gab about it."

"Connection's fine out here. What about Radu?"

"Let's not discuss it where any little old lady with a scanner can pick up your signal. I can offer you a smoke, Smoke."

"I'm hanging up now. You can tell me later."

I gave up then. "Your boss is in cold storage in the Wayne County Morgue, waiting for a party with a scalpel to find out what put him there. Somebody left him in the basement at Elysian Fields to fertilize the pot."

You can't judge a silence by its length over a cell. That's one of the things our hit-and-miss technology has taken away from us. I'd wanted to see her face when I told her, but she was elusive, like her name.

"Hello?"

"I'm here," she said. "Radu's dead? How do they know somebody left him there?"

"He was locked in from the outside. Do you have a key to the padlock?"

"No. I told you I've never been in the basement. Are you —"

"I'm a lot of things. Accusing you isn't one of them. Anyway, you don't need a key to lock a padlock that would've been left open by someone who went downstairs. But it's one of the things the cops will ask you. They don't mind being obvious."

"So they think I'm responsible."

"The cop I spoke to says no, but I wouldn't rule it out. He's an inspector with Homicide. If I were you, I'd head straight to his office. It can make the difference between a comfortable seat with a cup of coffee and a couple of sweaty bulls asking you questions with leather throats."

"What about my previous situation?"

"I'd be up front about it. They probably already have it, but if you outdraw them it'll look better for you all around. How come you didn't give me Czenko's name when I asked who you worked for?"

"Because he wasn't a very nice man to work for, and if he found out I was talking about him with a detective, he'd be even less nice."

"Was he a yeller or a hitter?"

"He was a yeller. Might've been a hitter, too, but he yelled so loud nobody let it go beyond yelling."

"Did he yell at you?"

"Every day he didn't was a day on the black side of the ledger. I don't think he had the balls to raise his hand to anybody his size; but I wasn't his size. Bullies are all cowards, right?"

"Some of them. The rest are either on the lam or on Death Row because someone thought all bullies are cowards." I looked at my watch. "You've got my advice, which is free. I just scored a record from hire to final report. I'm feeling guilty about that hundred. Swing by the office after the cops kick you and I'll refund fifty."

"Let's let it ride until we know who killed Radu and why."

"Uh-uh. I don't investigate murder to begin with and to finish with I don't investigate it for fifty bucks and in the middle I don't investigate murder."

"I can raise more if you give me a couple of days. I own a couch Craigslist would love to post."

"What's so important you'd give up having something to sit down on to find out?"

"If he was selling pot and someone thought he was worth killing over it, what's to stop him from killing me, too?"

"Everything, unless you've got an idea who did it."

"If I did, I wouldn't be trying to hire you to find out. Look, why don't I come up? We'll hash it out."

I drummed my fingers on the desk. "This couch you're putting up. Is it a couch or some inventory that found its way out of the basement at Elysian Fields?"

When the dial tone came on I jumped up, scurried through the waiting room into the hall, and looked out the dusty window at the end facing the street. She was gone. Smoke. Parents rarely get it that right when they tag their kids.

I sat back down, burned just enough tobacco to scrape at the place where a cheeseburger belonged, and remembered I hadn't eaten since the USSR fell. I closed up and left. I looked for my Town Car, but either they'd laid off or had changed vehicles, which is what a good closed-tail does when he starts to go stale. An independent pub I'd been in before sat me in a booth that needed a wipe down. That came along just as I sipped my beer and picked up my charred coaster on a bun. I managed to dodge the crumbs and then my cell rang.

The voice in my ear was so low I had to thumb up the volume to hear it above the murmur of voices and crackling of grease in the kitchen. I asked the owner to repeat herself.

"Mr. Walker?"

I'd guessed the gender right, although it was one of those throaty contraltos that can make you wonder, if your senses aren't on edge when you hear it. I confessed to the identification.

"This is Cecelia Wynn," she said. "Alec's wife?"

"Oh, that Cecelia Wynn." I put down the burger and scrubbed my hand on my napkin. "How are you?"

But she wasn't making small talk. She wanted to meet me.

# FOURTEEN

"Hold on," I said. "Show me you're Cecelia Wynn."

"My mother's maiden name was Howard. Mine was Collier. I was born in Effingham, Illinois, April 8, 1984. I married Alec Wynn June 19, 2006. We live — I lived at number three Woodland in Grosse Pointe. I'm five-six and a hundred and fourteen pounds. I'm a natural redhead, although you'd better buy me dinner if you want me to prove it. I had a mole removed —"

"Okay."

"Are you sure? There's so much more."

"Who'd lie about being born in Effingham, Illinois?" I was scribbling what she'd given me onto a pad to check with Wynn. I'd thought her mother's maiden name was Slobotnik, but that was just a guess. I hadn't needed most of it to start looking. "Where can we meet? The office is off-limits at the moment."

"Renovating? Or fumigating? There's a reason I never go downtown."

"We flushed out the rats a while back. Now we're working on the rodents. At the moment I'm someone's object of interest. If your husband's double-teaming me, I don't want another agency stumbling over you and do me out of the rest of my fee."

"That happens?"

"There's no American Sleuths Association to regulate ethics in my work. I can lose the tail, don't worry. I'm the best around at that." You never know when the subject of a case may be a future client, and the advertising was free. The silence on her end was just long enough to make me wonder if I'd been too up-front. It wouldn't be the first time I'd scored a point in my own backfield.

"I'm going to take the chance you're telling the truth," she said then. "You know Downriver?"

"I'm surprised *you* do. Most people think civilization ends on the east bank of the Rouge."

"Do you know it or not? I don't have a whole lot of minutes on this dime-store phone."

"I know it."

"There's a bar in Wyandotte, Little

Roundtop?"

I said I knew it too. "Eight o'clock?"

"Nearer ten. I want the homebound commuters long gone."

"You could wear a false beard. No sense taking the chance one of your husband's cronies'll recognize you anyway."

She addressed that obliquely. "Needless to say, Alec mustn't know we're meeting. Afterwards you can tell him what you like. I won't be in this part of the country much past midnight. I'm counting a lot on the discretion of a complete stranger, Mr. Walker. The background check I did on you was encouraging, but what's more changeable than human nature?"

"The weather, in this state; but you can always throw a raincoat, a bottle of sunscreen, and long johns in the backseat. You get in the same trouble trusting no one as trusting everyone, my father said. I'll pick up the check and put it on Wynn's account. That way, you get a free drink out of the deal." But I was being glib to an empty line. Going back over what I'd said, I didn't think it was such a bad deal.

The caller ID read BLOCKED CALL. I wondered why I wasted money on the feature. Everyone knows star sixty-seven.

The same two words came up when the

phone rang again a minute later. I let out air and picked up. "A. Walker Investigations. Running behind technology since 1979."

"Funny; not." It was Barry Stackpole's voice, still singing about the High School Hop. "What I got on Elysian Fields would burn out every fiber-optic cable in town."

"I know about the pot."

"Pot's for fifth-graders. I don't get out of bed for anything less than Asian heroin."

"Is that what it is?"

"That's what I get out of bed for, I said. When did you get so literal? We need to meet."

"My date card's filling up, and expenses won't stand another trip to the Grand. Drop in here and I'll buy you a drink from the office bottle."

"Three flights on a Dutch leg? No deal. How's about you make the trip? I'm parked next to a fireplug in front of your dump."

"Risky."

"All the arsonists are working the west side this season, haven't you heard? Those HUD houses go up like airfares. Bring that bottle." The connection went away.

I found him behind the wheel of a Sebring convertible with the seat fully reclined and him as well. He had on a pressed flannel shirt, khaki slacks, and hundred-dollar running shoes. Even in broad daylight he could pass for a college freshman. There was a gizmo attached to the steering column that let him operate the brake and gas pedal with his hands; regular driving was just about the only thing he couldn't do with his prosthesis.

"I'd never have pegged you for a ragtop," I said, sliding into the passenger's seat.

"In the old days that was only practical. Now it'd be filed under paranoia. Nobody tries to kill reporters anymore. We stopped counting years ago." He reached over and scooped the bottle in its paper sack off my lap.

"I meant there's nothing to stop you from flying when you run into something in a drunken haze."

"Just a bracer," he said, unscrewing the cap and taking a swig. He put the cap back on and gave me back the bottle.

"That bad."

"Bad enough."

"Guess you know about the stiff in the basement."

"I caught the squeal when it went out." He waved a hand toward the scanner in the dash. "He was just the help. Place belongs to a syndicate with Eurasian connections, meaning high-grade dope. It's a poster child

159

for ethnic diversity: blacks, whites, Italians, Mexicans, Asians, Chaldeans, Netherlanders."

"Chaldeans? Catholic Arabs?"

"New players, operating on the West Coast."

"Last I heard those gangs were all still trying to wipe each other out."

"They got wise. Or somebody did for them, somebody who can mix oil and water."

"Place moving that kind of stuff, how come the cops are only interested in phony medical marijuana?"

"They were just getting set up. First shipment's still sitting on a dock in Singapore."

"What's your source?"

"If I told you that, I'd wind up in the federal pen in Milan, getting butt-fucked by an entirely different class of con than I'm used to."

"This somebody who got wise for them, he have a name?"

"Well; the property's registered to a place called Pacific Rim."

"Never heard of it."

"You weren't supposed to; no one was, especially the FBI, the CIA, the U.S. Marshals, and every other investigative organization in the world. The owner changed the name after all its assets were frozen. Before that it was MacArthur Industries."

I unscrewed the cap and took a long draft. "Christ," I said. "Jesus Christ."

"Not even close," Barry said.

# FIFTEEN

"Are we even sure it's her?" I asked.

"Who's sure about anything where she's concerned? If she's smart, she got out from under. Maybe that's when the name changed."

"She's smart, all right. Also as crazy as a bug in a skillet. You never know what she'll do except be back. Do the Detroit cops have any of this?"

"They should by now. They don't have to hack into my sources."

"It's her," I said. "There isn't another person living who could get all those gangs to march in step."

"It takes a big bankroll. She must have cash hid out where the World Bank can't find it."

"Rackets she's in, it's all cash. She'd've been stashing it away for years against this situation. She's always ten moves ahead of everyone else."

"Step off, Amos."

"I was never on. I'm looking for Cecelia Wynn, not Charlotte Sing."

"Madam Sing always seems to find you."

"Not this time. She has no reason. This case just brushed her territory, that's all."

"Straight dope?"

"Yep."

"Okay, then." He cranked his seat back up and started the motor. With his hands on the wheel he looked at me for the first time since I got into the car. "But just to be safe —"

"I'll sleep with the lights on." I opened the door and got out.

It was dark when I crossed into Wyandotte. The yellow lights of an ore carrier showed on the Canadian side of the river, twinkling like stars when snowflakes drifted between us. Freezing rain had sizzled on and off throughout the day, and when the temperature followed the sun down behind the horizon the needlelike drops changed to little ragged flat floaters that turned like cinders in the air in front of my headlights. When I switched on the high beams, the light glittered off crystal jackets on all the tree branches; beautiful, fragile chandeliers that could break under the weight any time and send two hundred pounds of shattered bough through my windshield. West Jefferson was paved with black ice. It was a treacherous night near the end of a treacherous season in a treacherous life that was more than half over. I was in a sunny mood. I couldn't walk two steps in any direction without tangling my feet in corpses and international criminals.

Nobody knows Wyandotte. I don't think even Wyandites, or whatever they're called, do; they just sleep there. Detroit sure doesn't know it. The slaves who stopped there along the Underground Railroad knew it. For a brief space during the Industrial Age, the world knew it. The city on the river had made most of its steel there, courtesy of Detroit's first millionaire and pioneer of the Bessemer Process. But Eureka Iron and Steel had barely outlived Eber Brock Ward. Prohibition rumrunners knew it: They bought its elected officials and docked their boats in broad daylight. But after Repeal the place joined the rest of Downriver as a blob on the map where sea serpents swim and traffic empties into during the evening rush hour. The big furnace and sprawling foundry are gone, along with 2,200 acres of railway and coke-providing beech forest, barns and basements where fugitives crouched dreaming of freedom, and the slips where young toughs in snap-brim hats and underarm holsters beached their fermented gold. What's left is a horizontal town of bedrooms and widescreen TVs, order-in pizza, indifferent sex when the kids are in bed, and back to work in the morning.

Little Roundtop belonged to a local Civil War reenactor whose great-great uncle or something had taken a ball through a lung in a skirmish while serving with the First Michigan. So far as anyone knew, he was back in overalls pitching hay in South Lyon long before Gettysburg and the battle named for the hillock that had claimed much of the fifty thousand dead; but Cold Harbor sounds like a sushi place, and Midwesterners like their food cooked and their fish made of cow. Georgian columns held up a porch roof as thick as a cracker and parking valets dressed like General Sheridan climbed into cars knocking off their cocked hats and swearing under their breath at the plastic sabers slapping their calves. Six months after I ate there it was a Denny's.

A hostess got up like Scarlett O'Hara shook her sausage curls when I described Cecelia Wynn and conducted me to a two-top under a painting of Pickett's Charge done in toothpaste on terry, with a tag informing me it could be mine for $250. "Nice dress," I said. "I bet you saw it in the window and had to have it." She smiled a vapid smile and drifted out of my life. I was ready for stuffing and mounting.

I was a little early; when Melanie, my waitress, boated over in a hoop skirt, I said I was waiting for someone and ordered a martini. She set down two elephant-folio menus with a steel point engraving of Lee surrendering to Grant at Appomattox on the covers and came back five minutes later carrying a square glass of clear liquor with ice cubes and a pimento olive on a tray full of drinks. I sipped pure gin. When it doesn't have vermouth, and it's not served in a funnel-shaped glass, is it still a martini? Downriver is no place for philosophy.

The music playing over the sound system was cornpone marinated in mint julep: There is no accounting for a modern Yankee's sympathies when it comes to the War Between the States. I swung my foot to "I'm a Good Ole Rebel" and admired the reproduction tattered battle pennants hanging on the walls.

Sugarland was covering "The Night They Drove Old Dixie Down" when she came in.

A lot of people will go to any effort to avoid meeting someone in a crowded restaurant. It takes rare repose to stand in the middle of a noisy room, searching for a familiar face, without looking like you just fell off a flatcar. Cecelia Wynn had repose. She paused inside the entrance, spotted me in an awkward half-crouch with my hand raised, and came over. Tables parted to let her through. She had on a dark gray dress of some plush material that gave off violet highlights as she moved, under a white thigh-length coat whose tails spread behind her like a cape. Her legs were bare but evenly tanned, ending in ankles as delicate as stemware and long narrow feet in open-toed shoes of a shade to match the highlights in her dress. She wore her hair as in her picture, the same length and the same natural shade of red. It should have clashed with the violet but it didn't. It wouldn't dare.

Men watched her, women too. I saw all that and wanted to kick Alec Wynn in the ass for not hiring a more expensive detective.

I got up the rest of the way, but she sat down letting my right hand flap loose. "What's that, a martini?"

"I was just debating that."

167

Melanie pitty-patted up. Cecelia pointed at my glass. "Vodka for me. Straight up, with a twist."

I asked her if she was eating.

She shook her head. Her hair moved freely and fell back into place as smoothly as cards shuffling. The place was dark, lit mostly by electric candles flickering in orange glasses on the tables and the lights above the bar. They cast shadows under her cheekbones. She'd lost weight, but her face hadn't the gaunt look of heroin chic. Alcohol and vitamins were the only vices I could swear to.

"You should eat," I said. "I hate to think what that lemon will do to an empty stomach."

"Go ahead and order for yourself. Alec's paying."

"No appetite, thanks. You left some baggage behind."

"Tell him to give my clothes to Goodwill. They were dead weight. He can throw out the pills. I had a hole I tried to fill. Finally I just walked away from the hole. It has nothing to do with him. I don't know, maybe it has everything to do with him. But he shouldn't feel responsible."

There wasn't anything in that for me. "Elysian Fields got raided, did you hear?"

"I heard something on someone's radio. I didn't know the dead man. I didn't know anything about marijuana. How's Smoke?"

"Lying low. She says she has issues not connected with the operation. Pretty girl." I watched her closely in the rusty light.

"Is she? I suppose so. Those natural earthy types don't make much of an impression on me."

"How about Ann Foster?"

Her eyes did a little jig, I thought; I couldn't be sure because of the damn flickering. "What about her?"

"She got another job. In case you were feeling guilty about giving her the sack. I don't think she was really cut out to clean houses."

Her drink came. When the waitress left she took a sip and relaxed in her chair. The air around her had changed. It might have been the booze but I wasn't counting on it. "I'm glad. Maybe I did her a favor."

"She thinks you're a closet lesbian."

"Then she must be one. Lesbians think every woman's a dyke."

"She came out. Maybe she was never in. Anyway she's shooting girl-on-girl films in a place called Stormy Heat Productions. Her theory is you canned her because you found yourself attracted to her and it freaked you out."

"So *that's* her theory." She took another drink holding the funnel glass in both hands as if she were warming them.

"Anything in it?"

"What's it to you if there is?"

"It'd be something to report to Mr. Wynn. You said maybe it had nothing to do with him. Maybe it would satisfy him. Get him to lay off. 'Don't look for me,' that's what your note said."

She stood her glass precisely in the wet ring it had left on the table and slid a hand inside a pocket of her coat. "What's he owe you?"

"Nothing right now. He's paid up through three days."

A pocketbook came out and flopped open when she unsnapped the strap. Out of that came cash in a tight roll with a rubber band around it, the way some men carry cash and few women. It didn't have to mean anything; I can match my tie to my display handkerchief, and I like girls. "Here's a thousand. Tell him the case is closed. Say I said I'm okay and happy. I hope he takes it the right way, but if he doesn't, I can't do anything about it. It's my life, and it's brand new."

I took it — fifties and hundreds, but it

made a thick package just the same — got out the receipt book I carried next to my notepad, scribbled the particulars and signed it, and pushed it and the carbon across the table along with my pen. "Just sign the carbon and you'll never hear from me again, Mrs. Wynn."

"It isn't Mrs. Wynn. Nor Collier either. You don't start a new life by going backwards." She signed her name and returned the copy and pen. Before she could withdraw her hand, I grabbed her wrist and pinned it to the table.

"What's your name, really?" I grinned at her. "It never was Cecelia Wynn and you were never married to Alec. I don't think you ever met him."

# SIXTEEN

She tried to pull back, but I applied pressure with my thumb on her pulse. Her face paled and she stopped resisting. She had a tiny X-shaped scar on the back of her hand, a childhood injury probably. Wynn had said his wife had no visible scars. I said, "I could be wrong about that last part, but I think my client would've told me if he knew there was a woman running loose who looked enough like his wife to fool an experienced detective."

Her face went stony. "I thought we settled all this over the phone. I gave you —"

"You gave me nothing you couldn't get from official sources. It's a pity they couldn't include the name of a servant, even one she fired. You'd have had to Google Ann Foster, but you'd have to know she existed first. The name caught you by surprise. I watched you dangle a moment, then threw you a line. Once you knew what Ann Foster was to the missing woman, you got your foothold. I don't know if you're a trained actress, but improvisation isn't your strong suit.

"It was a hurry-up job all around," I went on, "and time was lost tracking down someone who resembled Cecelia Wynn in her most recent photo. Otherwise whoever did it might have stopped to consider that a woman who didn't want to be traced would change her makeup and hairstyle and probably the color. But you look like someone who's trying very hard to look like the person I've been hired to find."

I let go and sat back, not so far I couldn't get up if she bolted. Someone was covering "Johnny Yuma" on the stereo but he sounded less like Johnny Cash than the woman across from me looked like my quarry. "You picked a place to meet Downriver — dark — where it was unlikely anyone who knew Cecelia Wynn would see you and come over to say hello and realize they'd made a mistake and say so. I never heard her speak or saw her move, so you didn't have to worry about doing an impression, but you couldn't fool anyone who knew her even casually. You had a sample of her handwriting and did a fair job of forging it, but the note Wynn showed me had a

173

left-hand slant, which if you're right-handed, like you are, you can only duplicate by crabbing your hand the wrong way around the pen, like you did. The angle's only natural if you're a lefty. But there wasn't time to train you to write with the hand you don't normally use."

"I'm Cecelia Wynn. I don't know how I can convince you if you're so set on not believing me."

"The best liars don't give up easy. You're either a pro or a gifted amateur. Amateur's my guess. The time factor's too tight, and you look too much like her. Professional training too would be just blind dumb luck."

"I'm a file clerk."

That shut me up. I hadn't expected her to get calm. She even managed to drink from her glass without spilling it on the couple at the next table, who'd become very interested in their soup once our voices raised. But I'm just detective enough to know when a woman is putting on a show of nerves.

"A file clerk where?"

She ignored the question. "That's the job I'm good at. Don't judge me by this one. I couldn't resist the money. Are you going to call the police?"

"So far you haven't broken any laws I know about. If you have, I'll help you, because you're just a cat's-paw. All I want to know is whose. Then you can go. Here. I don't take money not to investigate." I pushed the stack of bills her way.

But she was smarter than I thought; or dumber. Anyway she had the shrewdness of a trapped animal. She reached for the money and in the same movement shoved the table into my sternum, and when I pushed back my chair and grabbed for her, she screamed.

Not a good, shrill, theatrical scream like in the movies. It was hoarse and ugly, but it was loud enough to turn every head in the room, and then we had company: a broad, middle-aged black with a cropped head and mascara on his lashes. What he was doing working in a joint with an Antebellum theme was between him and the NAACP. He wore a tight T-shirt that showed his muscles, also a roll of fat around his waist, cargo pants, and size-thirteen oxfords. A big steel meat-tenderizer hammer swung at his hip.

"This fellow trouble?" He had a high thin tenor. I wanted to laugh, but that hammer wouldn't let me. My gun was in my glove compartment. I should have left it there and brought the car.

"Private disagreement, partner," I said.

"She wouldn't let me pick up the check."

"So go Dutch."

He fooled me. The hammer was just a prop. His unoccupied hand flashed up, fetching me a tremendous clout on the ear. It still rings when a moth flutters past it.

The file clerk slid out of her seat and ran for the door, still holding the fistful of cash. There wasn't anything I could do about that.

Hammer time came next. I was reeling from the first blow, but I was chewing the scenery a little. When the hammer swung up, I was ready. I scooped my glass off the table and dashed what was left of my drink into his face. The gin ran up his nose and stung his eyes. His mascara ran. I caught the hammer by the head and twisted hard. The strategy was just to disarm him, but he had a grip on it like a man hanging onto a cliff; he howled when his tendons twisted with it. I didn't exactly hear them pop, but he wouldn't be practicing calligraphy for a while.

Still he held on.

I yanked the weapon toward me and with it his arm, pulling him forward and off balance. When his other hand flattened on top of the table to steady himself, I got hold of the edge and hurled it over. He went right along with it. He hit the floor hard enough to raise the South.

I was out of there before he got up, if he got up. There was no sign of the woman in the parking lot. I didn't even know I was still holding the hammer by its head until I heard sirens.

They keep a clean jail in Wyandotte.

The bars of the holding cell had been whitewashed recently, the linoleum-tile floor swept, mopped, and disinfected with turpentine, a smell that brought memories of spring cleaning and hunting for Easter eggs. The sheets on the cot were freshly laundered and treated with fabric softener. I hadn't a thing to complain about.

I wondered where they'd put the bouncer from the restaurant. Maybe they weren't holding him. I was the cause of the disturbance and he was just doing his job. He'd need medical attention. I felt bad about that until I remembered the meat tenderizer. I wasn't that tough.

The patrol cops who took me in were. I'd ditched the hammer by the time they arrived, but when they'd heard what they needed from the manager of Little Round-top, they bent me over the hood of the squad car, patted me down, and cuffed me to last. I could still feel the pinch. All the way downtown they ignored me in the backseat. They were arguing about whether Dale Earnhardt, Jr., was any good behind the wheel or just lucky in his birth.

My head hurt, too, and my left ear felt as thick as a ham but seemed normal size when I touched it. I didn't try touching it again after the first time.

The watch captain's name was Van Buren, but he didn't look like a Netherlander. He was black and ageless in a crisply starched uniform, his shaved head gleaming like an ebony newel post. He had a wide mouth with creases like knife cuts at the corners and always looked as if he was about to smile or had just finished smiling or was thinking about smiling. He never did, though, all the time I was there, and the pewter-colored eyes overlapped by sad-looking flaps of skin were as humorous as a wheelchair with a flat. A birthmark marred the white of his left eye, a stain shaped like a lopsided geranium. I couldn't stop looking at it.

He came to the door of the cell making no noise at all in high-topped shoes as shiny as his head and laced to the ankles.

"Your man Alderdyce is on his way," he said. He had a pleasant rumbling voice with

178

no judgment in it. "He doesn't have any authority here, you know."

"I know. I'm counting on professional courtesy."

"It won't hold if the man you crippled presses charges. Man your age ought to be home watching *American Idol,* not out brawling in no restaurant."

"I work most nights. Anyway, it's just a sprain. He'll be cracking open heads again in no time." I tried to concentrate on something other than the purple stain in his left eye, but I couldn't do it without looking as if I were avoiding contact. I bet his conviction record was A-1 and that was the reason. "You're not fooling anyone with double negatives, Captain," I said. "These days all the police brass went to college."

"Who's the girl?"

"We've been over that. If Inspector Alderdyce wants to share it with you, he will. Meanwhile I'm saving the story for him. He knows part of it, so I won't have to start from scratch."

"I heard there was money involved, quite a bit of money. You know, in this town we put all the pressure on the johns; the girls are what they are, and they don't contribute much to the local economy in jail. If the customer's caught soliciting from his car, he loses it. Then we sell it at auction. In your case, you could get thirty days and a fine that'll rattle your teeth."

"It was her money. I was just giving it back. You saw the receipt. You've got my ID, you know the business I'm in. I aged out of the john demographic years ago."

"Which would be just about the time that excuse went away. That gent who invented Viagra's got a lot to answer for. Those scientists can't cure cancer, but they sure took horny old goats off the Endangered Species list."

"You didn't find any on me, and the way your boys frisked me they know I hadn't swallowed any."

"They're thorough for a fact. I trained 'em myself. I was a jailkeeper at County when this spot opened up."

"I think your boys trained with Michael Jackson."

"Forget what they did to your man business. It stopped being your business when it became my business. You paw women in my town, you get pawed."

"You got me behind bars, you have to poke me with a stick while you're at it?"

"It's a slow night. Basketball's on strike. You play cards?"

"When I've got circulation in my hands."

He leaned in close and gripped the bars. His nails were neat but not professionally manicured. I was more interested in the scar tissue around the knuckles, like joints in an earthworm. You don't get those from just working the heavy bag at the gym.

"This is Downriver, Mr. *De*troit detective. We keep it tough and we keep it tight. There's no FBI breathing down our collars, making sure we're not carrying a couple kilos out of the evidence room under our hats. That wasn't always true, but while you folks were busy trying to keep your mayor out of jail, *we* were cleaning house. If you're delicate, don't come down here intimidating our women and busting up our public places. We bust back."

"Don't waste your time, Captain." This was a new voice. "He's heard the same speech as far up as Iroquois Heights. It never sticks." The big man in the beautiful suit stuck out a hand. "John Alderdyce. I'm investigating a drug-related homicide. My professional opinion is it trumps your disturbing the peace and assault and battery, but if you don't like the way we do things in the big bad city we can take it up at the Murphy Hall of Justice in the morning."

# SEVENTEEN

We were traveling in John's personal automobile, a Cadillac Escalade with seventeen payments left on it. He'd reached that point in life where comfort trumped efficiency, but he was still too much the egalitarian to be seen driving a sedan some benighted souls insisted on calling a pimpmobile. Also he had grandchildren now, with a DVD player in the backseat and a canvas carrier filled with all four *Ice Ages* and every Harry Potter to date. My Cutlass was safe in the impound lot in Wyandotte.

"Close of business day, I said." He drove with his hands at ten-and-two and both eyes on the road. "What part didn't you understand?"

"All of it. Your business day's still in play or you wouldn't have made such good time after Van Buren called."

"*There's* a shoulder chip the size of the Penobscot Building. What're the odds he applied for a spot on the DPD and got his application shitcanned?"

"I'm guessing that birthmark in his left eye spooked the interviewer."

"Human Resources people got no imagination. You can get a lot out of an interrogation with a spooky thing like that."

"What I thought. What happens to the complaint?"

"Not a damn thing. They forgot to Mirandize you, can you believe it?"

"Nope. They read me some rights. I lost concentration after the opening line. Like the National Anthem. Did you know there's a whole other chorus after 'home of the brave'?"

"Seems to me I remember a high school principal fooling us with it when we sat down after the first. Wyandotte needs Detroit more than Detroit needs Wyandotte. At the moment, anyway. I'd've been more diplomatic about it if he hadn't made that crack about the FBI. A good cop ought to know a hundred bad cops don't mean a hundred-and-one. We're our own worst enemy."

"Anything on that Arizona plate I gave you?"

He shook his head a thirty-second of an inch, which considering the density of its features measured 7.5 on the Richter scale. "You don't get questions. I get answers. What are you working on?"

I'd worked it out while I was in Holding. The night had changed all my plans. If the woman I was meeting had turned out to be Cecelia Wynn, I could close that case and give Alderdyce what he wanted. But now I'd have to report to my client before I said anything official. So I gave him Smoke.

"The clerk at Elysian Fields found out Narcotics hit the place and wanted to know what it was all about before she talked to the cops. A long time ago she was in the wrong place at the wrong time and she didn't want to repeat the experience."

"Description I got from the report on Van Buren's desk didn't match the Wygonik woman."

"I've got a personal life, John."

"Bullshit. And if you did you wouldn't be seen in a public place roughing up your date. You've got character flaws the size of the cracks in Hart Plaza, but that isn't one of them. If you had to restrain her by force, it was business."

"If it was business it had nothing to do with the drug operation. The place wound up in my rounds on an unrelated case."

"An unrelated case that brought you to

the attention of the Arizona branch of the Detroit Combination."

"The plate came up?"

"Yeah, damn you. Your open tail ditched that piece of shit in the long-term lot at Metro. It was stolen in Grand Rapids last week — registration in the glove compartment matched the report — but the plate belonged to this year's Trailblazer, which was still tooling around Phoenix until the owner was pulled over for driving without a plate; he hadn't noticed it was missing. No information yet on what your guy put it on or where he dumped it after he got to Grand Rapids. Not important. What *is* is the prints we got off the Malibu at the airport. We didn't even have to go to the FBI: Had 'em on record downtown."

"Would I know him?"

"Only if you hung around with street soldiers before RICO blasted hell out of the Combination. Martin Maxwell Mondadori: 'Yummy,' they call him, on account of his initials. He broke arms for the Lucy and Acardo families, did four years in Jackson for Man One dealt down from first-degree. When the Colombians were muscling in on the drug trade he spent so much time being questioned in homicides he could list Thirteen Hundred as his voting address. After

185

the Colombians won he retired to Arizona. Retired, that's what they call it when you're hauled in only three or four times a year for running illegal gambling operations and credit card fraud. He was also questioned in a laundry list of local heists. None of it stuck, but he's the go-to guy there when the city and county cops investigate anything with a possible connection to the rackets."

"Sounds kind of small-time for something this size."

I was tired, and my bum leg was hurting, or I'd have paid more attention to what I was saying. He went on driving without reacting; but I knew I'd nailed myself and so did he.

"What size'd that be, Walker? All we got on him, *if* we get him, is wandering into the wrong building, which last I checked wasn't even a misdemeanor."

"I meant working out of state."

"Too thin. Everyone knows your pipeline into national cooperative police investigations is Barry Stackpole. Why'd you enlist him if what went down on Livernois had nothing to do with your case?"

"I only picked him up after I visited the place. I wouldn't have thought much about it except he was a stalking horse for the couple of pros in the Lincoln Town Car.

When the stiff surfaced, I figured the more I knew about the operation the better I was fixed."

He checked all his mirrors and leaned the Escalade into a howling U-turn. The right front tire squeaked against the curb just before he straightened out. I had to grip my door handle to keep my head off his lap. "I just remembered," he said: "There *was* something in that report about you getting your Miranda. Maybe a night on the river will clear your head."

I could do the night; I'd done a lot longer. But too much was happening I didn't know about, and too much more was threatening to happen while I played canasta with Captain Van Buren. I asked him to turn around again.

"Where to, Homicide?"

I said my place. His office had bedbugs.

I asked him if it was okay if I smoked.

"Why get permission? It's your house. It is, isn't it? Don't tell me you're still paying on this little place."

"I bought it for cash. I had cash then, from the army, and no wife yet." I missed the cash. "But you're always quitting, and I'm a sensitive guy."

"Once I even quit quitting. But it took

finally. One day I lit up my first over break-fast. Two puffs and I put it out. Tasted like I was using a bedpan for an inhaler. Haven't had the urge since."

"Maybe it's not so hard as everyone says." I lit one and blew a plume at the bluish patch on the ceiling, noticing a new crack in it. Nicotine seemed to be the only thing holding it up.

"It's as hard as you let it be, like everything else. Ever consider quitting?"

"I've only got two vices. If I give it up and something happens to the other one, what've I got?"

"I don't know; five more years, maybe?"

"The crappy ones at the end."

He drank from his glass and shifted the tectonic plates of his face into something even less pleasant than usual. "This isn't a vice, it's a sin. What do you do, take home bar rags and wring them out over a mixing bowl?"

"I buy it in bulk. A tanker comes to the door and sticks a hose through a window into the laundry tub. I invited you to join me in a drink, John. I didn't say Blue Label." I sipped mine between shifting ovals of ice, bracing my elbow in the dent in the arm of the uneasy chair in my living room. Only one light was burning, the floor lamp

I read by. I'd replaced the Edison bulb with one of those screwy mercury jobs that use one-tenth the energy and take ten minutes to shed enough light to read your wrist-watch.

"Only two vices? I seem to recall you were hitting the pills with both fists for a while."

"I took a high-powered slug through my favorite leg up in Grayling, the deer-hunting capital of North America. I wasn't even in the woods. When I finally got used to it I figured what was the point. How's your boy?"

"Which one's that?" But he knew which one. He got along just fine with one, but he'd had to ask my help with the other. He'd never forgive me for it. I'd known John longer than anyone living; but after fifteen million years the Colorado River and the Grand Canyon are just passing acquaintances.

"So much for old times," I said. "Or should I get out the yearbook?"

"We didn't go to the same school. We still don't. Who's your client?"

"Smoke. I told you that."

"You never knew her till you dropped in on her place of employment."

I tipped my glass, just to hear the ice shifting. It sounded like soggy bells tilting in a

189

gale at sea; but I'd never been in a gale at sea, so it just sounded like ice shifting in a glass. "Ever hear someone say, 'I don't trust myself'?"

"Assholes, yeah."

"Maybe not. But it's a hell of a thing to say about yourself. You have to be careful who's listening. Who else is there to trust?"

"God. Says so on money."

"I mean someone you can afford to wait for."

Alderdyce made a noise in his throat. He thought it was a chuckle. " 'Wait a minute.' "

"For what?"

"No, it's a punchline. Tell you the rest if I'm in the mood by the end of this conversation. Go ahead."

"I don't think I ever heard you tell a joke."

"The record isn't in jeopardy, if this conversation goes on as it has."

"It isn't I don't trust cops," I said. "I don't; but my father told me you can trust everyone or no one and it all comes out the same."

"I knew your father. So did mine. I guess maybe you forgot. Thing about fathers is they say just as much horseshit as wisdom, then leave to let us sort it all out on our own."

"Anyway, I trust myself first, because I know what my angle is. With everyone else all I can do is guess. But this job involves someone I can't even begin to guess about. I'm batting T-ball against a major leaguer."

Ice shifted in his glass, but he wasn't philosophizing, just drinking. His brain wasn't geared toward abstract concepts. He swallowed — two separate and distinct actions, the hatch shutting first, a defensive measure, then opening, passing the decision onto the digestive system. His thought process was identical. It was what made him a perfect cop and a flawed husband and father.

"I know who you're talking about," he said. "She's flesh, Amos. Has all the same disgusting bodily functions as the rest of us. And we don't know she's even in the picture. Every government spook and beat cop in every country dreams about bagging her. Every schnook with his mortgage under water has her picture burned into his skull hoping to snatch that six-million-dollar reward. If she's half as smart as she's made out, she's living in a cave or a split-level in some suburb of Malaysia, afraid to go shopping till after midnight when all the clerks in the Sungai Ujong Walmart are too busy yawning and looking at the clock to pay attention to the faces of the customers at checkout."

"Sungai Ujong, seriously?"

"The wife went back to school. I help with the homework."

I shook my head, not at their study group. "Those rewards are like Bigfoot. When it comes time to collect, they vanish. The accountants turn their pockets inside out and say it all went into the investigation. And this woman can outbid whatever bounty they put up. Anyway, she's not wired to be afraid. She's a psychopath with a two hundred IQ and more liquid assets than an emirate."

"Bullshit. Now who's talking Bigfoot?" He leaned forward from the couch and set his glass on the coffee table. "There are monsters enough under the bed here at home. Forget her. You can be sure she's forgotten you."

I hadn't told him I'd heard from her since the last time her subject came up. There wasn't any point in reporting a threat that could have come from the other side of the world, possibly Sungai Ujong; but busy woman that she was, sooner or later she made time for everything, and she never forgot.

"John, what I'm working isn't a homicide,

that I know of. A woman's wandered off. Her husband would like her back, but if it doesn't play out that way he wants to know is she okay and does she need anything."

"Meaning money."

"She doesn't seem to have taken any with her. Or much of anything else."

"You know what they say about not taking it with you."

"I thought of that. I've been on the job as long as you. She left a note, but it was undated, so maybe. Nothing suspicious otherwise, not even that little clunk you hear when a lead slug drops into the slot. It said don't bother looking, and the woman I met in Wyandotte tonight" — I glanced at my great-grandmother's clock groaning and ticking on the shelf — "last night, said the same thing, only she turned out not to be the one I was looking for."

"Whose mistake was that, yours or hers?"

"Not mine. I'm pretty sure it wasn't her idea: I heard the clunk that time. But somebody wants me to stop looking. If the jokers who are dogging me are there to make sure I do, it doesn't hang on your case."

"Unless making sure you stop looking means you stay away from Elysian Fields."

"Why bother? You cops know all about the place."

"Maybe there's something we don't know about it. Some little morsel a big cat might overlook but a little mouse browsing around might not."

"Squeak, squeak." I finished my drink. It tasted bitter as hell.

# EIGHTEEN

After John left, I put my glass in the sink, undressed, and got horizontal in the bedroom. I was wired, didn't expect to sleep, but I surprised myself. When someone tapped on the window, it drew me up from deep bottom like a hook attached to a lead sinker. It was dark out. I couldn't see the features on the blur of face pressed nearly against the glass. The luminous dial on the nightstand told me it was 5:10. I saw these things on my way to retrieve the gun that wasn't in the drawer. Wyandotte still had it.

"Mr. Walker?"

I recognized the voice. Propped up on one elbow, I gestured toward the front of the house. The pale smudge of face vanished.

I tied my robe on the way to the door. Smoke stood on my stoop, wearing a forest-green hoodie, scuffed blue jeans, and ankle-high brown suede boots trimmed with sheepskin, with heels that brought her up to six feet. The hoodie made her eyes moss-colored. She could rob a bank and no two eyewitnesses would be able to agree on their color.

"The cops have been at my place. Can I stay here? I've been walking around all night and I can barely stand up."

"They're going to find you sooner or later. It's what they do, and you're not exactly the type that blends into a crowd. Turn yourself in, and you'll be out in an hour. A little longer if you killed your boss. Then you'll have a place to sleep."

"I'm not sorry he's dead. I've had better bosses. Less grabby ones, anyway. But I was a dodgeball champ in high school, and I'm saving my one shot at a life sentence for somebody I'll enjoy murdering, whoever he or she turns out to be. I'll turn myself in later, I promise. When I'm not exhausted. You can even give me a ride."

"Right now I don't have a ride." But I stepped away from the door.

I got my other set of bedding from the closet and laid it on the couch. "Two pillows. One to put on top of the wonky spring in the middle."

She stood in the middle of the living room hugging herself. It was a dank morning, and I'd turned down the heat before going to

196

bed. "Do you have anything to drink? Something strong? I'm chilled to the bone."

"You came to the right door. How'd you find it, by the way?"

"Internet café. You're on the grid, like it or not."

"Not." I went to the kitchen for the bottle, pausing on the way to crank up the thermostat. The furnace in the little Michigan basement buzzed for a full minute, then the blower kicked in, stirring the hairs on my ankles in front of the baseboard register as I filled two glasses at the counter. My guest was standing in the kitchen doorway when I turned that direction. She'd ditched the hoodie and it was all her under a cobalt-colored T-shirt.

"You weren't kidding about being chilled," I said.

She looked down at herself, but made no effort to cover up. "I had to get out of that thing. It was like wearing a clammy shroud. Offended?"

"Shocked. You want a sweater or something?"

"I'm good. Or will be." She took one of the glasses. "To excess." She drank, shuddered, and grew roses on her cheeks.

I knocked the top off mine. No roses, but I felt a little less groggy. Thirty minutes in the sack don't do as much for me as they used to. "Let's adjourn to the drawing room."

She'd made up the couch already, but I let her have the armchair and turned back the bedding to keep from contaminating it with private eye.

She looked around brightly. "You're neat for a bachelor. Not too neat, if you know what I mean."

"That's the effect I was going for. I'm straight. You?"

"Never tried it any other way. Think we're the only ones left?"

"We're still rounding them up on reservations. I was in a lesbian bar recently."

"I guess your work takes you all sorts of places."

"Yours too. The marijuana was just an illegal front for something a lot worse."

"How much worse?"

"Heroin. International operation."

I was watching her closely. The blossoms faded. She gulped from her glass, but this time it didn't help. That satisfied me. Experienced liars have been trying for hundreds of years to get their circulatory system to go along and so far it's been no dice. She had no idea what had been in that padlocked basement.

"That's something I've never understood," she said after a moment. "Firing up a doobie's one thing; I draw the line there, but I can even see coke. What has to happen to a person to make him stick a needle in his arm and fill up on that crap? You know what it does?"

"Causes drowsiness, severe constipation, vomiting, strangulation —"

"Strangulation?"

"Severe respiratory depression, same result. What else? Really bad acne leading to permanent scars. Your blood pressure drops like a rock, you lose muscle control — at least that takes care of the constipation, but it's sudden and messy. What am I leaving out? Coma. Cardiac arrest. Death.

"Except what this outfit peddles isn't that patient. If you take a dose of what you think is garden-variety horse and it turns out to be their stuff, it's cheaper to put a shotgun in your mouth. Users have been found dead as Cleopatra's cat with the needle still in the vein."

It had become a drinking game on her part: Hear a symptom, take a swig. Her glass was almost empty. Her eyes kept focus, though. There's nothing like a good scare to cure hiccups and prevent inebriation. The color had changed again, to something gray and murky.

"Health food." She might have been talking to herself. "That's what it says in the advertising."

"I didn't want you sitting in the precinct thinking I'd sandbagged you. But you need to go in before they start to think you're playing hard-to-get. When that happens they assume everything that comes from you is a lie. They don't show it right away. The first time through, they keep interrupting to ask if you'd like a cup of coffee or a snack from the machine. The second, they look like they're not paying attention. On the third pass, they act like that's just to make sure it's all down in order, keep the pencil pushers upstairs happy. Along about the fourth, you'll slip on some little thing, everyone does, but they're not even looking at you, so you think you're okay. Seventh time around is when they grin and crack their knuckles and spit on their hands and go to work. Cops like being lied to. It keeps them on their game, and they love playing it. No one pins on a shield because he couldn't get into medical school."

"Is this a ghost story, some kind of initiation thing, first-time suspect bullshit?"

"A little. They don't really crack their knuckles and spit on their hands anymore.

These days they all went to college. Some of them can even work a Rubik's Cube. That doesn't mean they aren't as tough as they used to be. You're young, maybe too green to be afraid. The minute they get that impression, they'll pull every trick they know to make you cry. I don't like to see children bullied."

"I'm not exactly a child."

"I saw that when you took off your sweatshirt."

"You think they'll hold my record against me?"

"They don't hold anything against anyone. Cops don't have feelings. They'll try to use it as leverage, but unless you left something out when you told me about it, it isn't really a record. It isn't enough to tip you over if you don't let them. Compared to what they see every day, it's not even an unpaid parking ticket."

She swirled the yellow stuff in the bottom of her glass, then looked up. "What's a Rubik's Cube?"

"Get some sleep," I snarled.

I had a bughouse dream. I was in Old China, in a room decorated with silk hangings and a couple of muscular celestials in breechclouts and sandals guarding the door with scimitars at parade rest. Someone was stretched naked on a rack, and a satanic grinning face that belonged on the cover of an old-time pulp magazine was bent over him. The owner of the face wore a shimmering green robe and a skullcap with a jade button on top. I felt sorry for the fellow on the rack. No one should have to put up with that and look just like me to boot.

I'd never been to China, old or new, and I bet it had never really looked like that: The sentries' oiled biceps could only have come from steroids. The hangings looked steam-pressed and screen-printed besides, and the character in the mandarin getup bore a close resemblance to Christopher Lee in Oriental makeup. I'd frittered away my childhood reading comic books based on Sax Rohmer stories. It had taken all this time for my bad taste to catch up with me.

It's never a good idea to go to bed on a stomach full of cheap liquor and a head full of Madam Sing.

This time I woke up all on my own. It wasn't the sun, although it was there, and from the strength of it I figured it had been there a while. Air stirred, and I turned my head and saw Smoke Wygonik standing in my bedroom. She'd shucked everything but a pair of pale blue bikini panties. Her long blond hair hung over one shoulder and she held it spread with one hand to cover her breasts.

"Still cold?" I asked.

She shook her head carefully, then frowned and swept her hair back over her shoulder. Her breasts were small but well-shaped. I'm not a mammary man, anyway. I like a good collarbone, and she passed that test; it was shaped like Diana's bow, polished-looking where the sunlight lay across it. She had a deep navel in a flat belly with some definition and her legs were long, ending in high-arched feet with unpainted toenails. No tattoos or piercings.

She frowned again, misreading my silence. "Is it all right?"

"How old are you?"

"Don't worry. I'm street legal."

"That's not what I meant."

"You're not too old, if that's what you're worried about."

"I'm old enough one more regret won't kill me. You have to learn that all by yourself."

"Maybe I'd better start." She paused with her thumbs inside the waistband of her panties. "I'm kind of natural down there. Any objections?"

I'm not into banter in the morning. I

folded back the covers and shoved over. She slid the panties down, stepped out of them, and got in.

# NINETEEN

Black mold and bats had finally driven the Homicide division out of the historic police headquarters at 1300 Beaubien; the budget for routine maintenance had gone into the silk wall coverings in a late longtime mayor's office and onto the broad hip of the fat little mama's boy — currently awaiting federal sentencing — who'd tried to out-corrupt him. But the new digs are clean and well-ventilated, and schoolbus drivers have stopped pulling up in front of it, no longer mistaking it for Murray Wright High.

Inspector Alderdyce was home catching up on sleep, but he was expected anytime. The polite young third-grade detective who told us that offered to take Smoke's statement while we were waiting. She looked at me. I nodded. The kid in the yellow tie and powder-blue shirt fashionably untucked under his suitcoat hadn't looked me in the eye once since he'd spotted the tall blonde in the hoodie. I thought we'd caught a break.

I'm wrong two times out of six. After setting up camp in an interview room with a video camera fixed on a tripod, the file on the Elysian Fields case spread before him on the chipboard table, he shot questions at her rapidly and out of anyone's conception of order, a trick as old as the Praetorian Guard. The object is to disorient the subject into blurting out the truth.

But this particular subject remained cool under fire, pausing just long enough after each question to take it in and frame her response, but not so long she gave the impression of constructing a lie. After a nerve-wracking beginning I settled back in one of those folding metal chairs that destroy parental backs at school band concerts and reflected on the morning. Mostly it was a confusion of writhing muscles and breathing in each other's gasps for air, bordering on violence, but when it came down to cases it had been conventional enough not to frighten an old dog, while various enough to hold interest. That she was holding back was obvious. She was like a singer with natural talent who left the impression there were notes she could reach easily but chose not to for that particular selection.

The old dog, of course, had given it everything he had.

Afterward we'd showered separately, got dressed, and I'd called a cab for the trip downtown. We hadn't talked about the sex, then or just after or during. There are some things you just don't beat to death with language.

I listened to her answers with professional as well as personal interest. She spoke as if she hadn't fielded the same questions three or four times, and her language varied just enough it didn't come off like a speech she'd rehearsed. Either she was telling it straight or she was a better liar than I'd met in a long time; and I'm a connoisseur.

The detective seemed satisfied as well. While we were waiting for her statement to be typed up he asked her where she was from, seemed interested in the fact that they'd attended Wayne State University the same couple of semesters, and volunteered the information that he and his wife were celebrating their second anniversary in June. If it was detective work, it was a kind I wasn't familiar with. I took mental notes.

Alderdyce arrived, wearing lightweight tweeds and a knitted tie and looking as if he'd slept a week instead of about four hours. When the statement came he read it, then asked Smoke a couple of questions the detective hadn't thought of but whose answers didn't alter the essentials. She signed it with a department pen and he gave it to the detective to file. In the hallway outside the interview room, he asked her if she had a ride home.

"No."

He buttonholed a uniform on his way past and told him he had a passenger.

"Just one?" She glanced at me.

"I'm borrowing your detective," Alderdyce said. "Sorry if you've got plans."

She shook her head and stuck a hand my way. "Thank you, Mr. Walker."

I took it and let it go. When she and the uniform were gone, Alderdyce said, "How was she?"

But I didn't tumble. The old tricks I know. "What do you want, John?"

"We found Yummy. An ID from you would give us a reason to hold him till we find something to charge him with."

"Where is he?"

"Northwest side, staying with a cousin couple of times removed: We think. Neighbors say he's been keeping his lights on later than usual. Some of them heard two men talking. Couldn't make out what they were saying, but the cousin lives alone and doesn't entertain. DTE lineman, retired on a disability. Gets a check first of every month for electrocuting himself on a pole a couple of years back."

"And we thought Yummy lived dangerously. Early Response Team in on this?"

"We're leaving the vests and tear gas behind. Not enough for a warrant. If we double-team the cousin, we might smoke him out."

"I thought I was just for ID."

"Times are tough. Everybody's got to pull twice his weight." He reached under his suitcoat, took something from his belt, and thrust it at me, handle first. It was my .38 Chief's Special.

I didn't take it. "How long have you had that?"

"Don't worry, I wasn't holding out on you. I sent a uniform down to Wyandotte this morning before I punched out. It was on my desk when I got in. You'll have to make your own arrangements to spring your wheels. It'll cost you, but your mother should have told you to stay away from strange women in bars."

"That's the only kind I ever get to meet." I took the revolver, checked the cylinder for rounds, and stuck it under my coattail.

The place was on Greenview off McNichols not far from Mercy College, a solemn block of gray-painted brick that looked like a church rectory, which is what it might have been before it was partitioned into smaller rooms for student housing. It was an apartment house now. Alderdyce cruised the Escalade past a tan two-door parked across the street, got a nod from the plainclothesman behind the wheel, and turned into the narrow lot alongside the house. A stern tin sign said it was for residents only. He parked perpendicular to three cars already there, blocking them.

"If I were Yummy, I'd be in Toledo by now," I said. "I wouldn't hang around after the cops started talking to the neighbors."

"One cop, in a polyester suit. They thought they were talking to a city census taker. He only talked to the ground floor. The cousin's apartment is upstairs, and he doesn't socialize."

"The city doesn't take a census."

"And schools don't teach civics anymore." He got out, climbed the front steps, and pushed the buzzer.

A red-faced manager answered. A pair of

wire-rimmed glasses nested in his head of gray curls. Alderdyce flashed his gold shield. The manager flipped down the glasses like a visor to look at it.

"Anthony Pirandello, in two-C," the inspector said. "He's got a houseguest."

"Not if he don't pay."

"You own the place?"

"No, I work for a living."

"You can keep what he slipped you under the table. It's the guest we want."

"Got a warrant?"

I reached past Alderdyce and snatched the spectacles off his nose.

"Hey!"

"My old man told me never to hit a man with glasses," I said.

"Bullshit." But his voice lacked conviction.

Alderdyce put away his shield. "My partner hit the lottery. He's just filling out the month, then he's retiring to Bimini. One reprimand more or less in his jacket doesn't mean anything."

I grinned. The manager's complexion lost some of its ruddiness and he stepped out of the way. I folded his glasses, slid them into his shirt pocket behind a plastic protector full of pens, and patted it.

On the way upstairs I said, "How come I

never get to be Father Duffy, the gruff-but-kind department chaplain? Why am I always Darth Vader?"

"You don't have a pension to protect."

Two-C was at the end of a hallway carpeted with a pattern I recognized from one of the auto shows. Cobo Hall cut it up after the doors closed and sold the pieces cheap. It had been trodden on by half the human race; or that part of it that still cared what the Motor City had to show. We drew our weapons and held them down at our sides while Alderdyce reached over and knocked on the door. A voice that had been put up in tobacco and alcohol asked who it was.

"Police."

"How do I know that? Neighborhood's gone to shit."

Alderdyce winked at me and slid his Miranda card under the door. It was as crisp and shiny as if it had never been used.

A series of locks came undone and the door opened wide enough to expose a bloodshot eye in half a face shot through with broken dreams. A puff of air that had been put down in malt liquor came out from behind it. I saw the family resemblance.

"Anthony Pirandello?"

"What do you want?"

"Yummy."

"Come again?" The eye looked genuinely puzzled; mob nicknames are often a media invention, like health care.

"Martin Maxwell Mondadori. Your cousin."

"I ain't seen Marty in months."

"Then who's staying with you?"

"Nobody. Just me and the bedbugs."

Something crashed inside. The eye blinked but didn't move in its socket, an impressive effort of will.

"Man, you should've called the exterminator before this," I said.

Alderdyce had lost interest in the conversation. He used his shoulder on the door. Pirandello, gripping the knob on his side, swung around with it; he had to, or be trampled. He wore a scuffed leather windbreaker and a golf cap; we must've caught him on his way out. I came in on the inspector's heels, but fear was faster than us both. A floor lamp lay on its side in front of an open window directly opposite the door. We went that way and leaned on the sill, guns in hand. The plainclothes cop from the tan two-door stood in a fenced-in yard filled with clumps of dead grass and filter-tipped butts, snapping a pair of cuffs on the man I'd seen trolling the directory in my building. He had on the same outfit of corduroy sportcoat, yellow polo shirt, and tan Dockers: At least I hoped there wasn't another like it in town. His face was as red as the apartment manager's, swallowing up the surgical scar on his cheek, and he was standing off-balance, favoring a sprained or broken ankle. Just thinking about that one-story leap made my bad leg start throbbing all over again.

"Hold him there." Alderdyce put away his piece.

When we turned from the window, Pirandello had gone. The door hung open the way we'd left it.

I felt a bad tingle. My whole body became the left arm of a man having a heart attack.

It was a small apartment, with a kitchenette opening onto the living room, where all the living seemed to be done on a stained red crushed-velour sofa in front of a seventeen-inch TV on a metal stand, with an end table stocked with the Blue Ruin in forty-ounce bottles and a saucer domed over with more butts. The only other door led to a bedroom, where the woman who'd tried to sell herself to me as Cecelia Wynn lay on ravaged bedding wearing the clothes she'd worn in Wyandotte, soaked through with blood.

I belted the gun then. All the killers had left the building.

# TWENTY

Alderdyce finished describing the cousin and put away his cell. He looked down at the dead woman.

"Shot or stabbed. Shot, probably. And not in here. She didn't bleed enough onto the sheets." He placed the back of a hand against her cheek. "Cold. Couple of hours, anyway. Sure about that ID?"

"There can't be another woman in town who looks that much like Cecelia in her picture. And she's got on the same clothes." I tried to make eye contact with her, a hobby of mine. You never can, quite. They're always looking at something out beyond the Milky Way. Someone let out a gust of air then. It was me. I hadn't realized I was holding my breath.

She was still wearing the white car coat. He went through the slash pockets, came out empty-handed. Even he wasn't ready to search closer to the body. "Help me toss the place. Gently. Don't want the lab monkeys thinking we're out to bust the union."

"Grid or spiral?"

"Just start looking, okay? Shit."

I didn't ask what we were looking for. He wouldn't know any more than I did. In the nightstand I found a half-smoked box of Marlboros, an unopened package of Trojans, and a revolver. It was a Ruger LCP, a nice little concealed-carry piece in a pocket holster that covered the trigger guard and prevented accidental discharge when drawn. I let the inspector examine it with a hand wrapped in a handkerchief: I have another set of manners when I'm frisking a murder scene alone.

"Not it," he said, taking his nose away from the muzzle. He turned the barrel toward the light and looked inside. "Some dust."

"Serial number?"

"Intact. Not that it won't come out virgin at the other end, if it's Yummy's. The bright boys don't buy their ordnance out of car trunks on the street."

I opened the closet door. Blue suit on a hanger, a couple of dress shirts, a bowling shirt, some polos, a pair of brown shoes and a pair of black. They needed polishing. Baseball caps and a fedora with a stingy brim and a yellow feather in the band on the shelf.

Mixed black and gray hairs in a brush on the dresser. More clothing in the drawers. I took a thick envelope from under a nest of rolled-up socks and thumbed through the bills inside. "Three thousand in fifties and hundreds," I said. "Getaway stake."

"Should've had it on their hips. I'm thinking they weren't expecting company."

"Not such bright boys after all. Unless the phony Cecelia was a surprise package somebody left on their doorstep."

"Who're you, their lawyer?"

I put the envelope with the money back where I'd found it. "The mob may be rusty after all those RICO convictions, but they don't collect corpses, not with a river handy and twenty minutes from the Long Term lot at Metro Airport. Pirandello was wearing a cap and jacket. Maybe he and Yummy just got in. They didn't have time to work out a plan."

"We'll ask Tony when we find him. Yummy'll give us squat." He went up on tiptoe to peer at the air vent near the ceiling.

While he was busy wondering if the screws had been loosened recently, I turned back toward the bed. From that angle I saw the corner of something red and shiny sticking out from under a tangle of bedding. I pulled out a pocketbook bound in red imitation alligator with a strap that snapped in place. It was the one she'd had in the restaurant. It must have fallen out of a pocket when she was dumped onto the mattress. I opened it. A folded sheet stuck out above the cash. I glanced at Alderdyce, whose back was still turned, and put the paper in my pocket.

"Alison Garland," I read off the Ohio driver's license in the window.

He turned back. "Where'd you get that?"

I told him. "She would've been twenty-six next month."

"Hope her people kept the gift receipts." He took the pocketbook from me.

"At least they didn't have to go far to find a double."

He riffled through the bills. "Couple of twenties and some singles. If they paid her, she spent it or banked it or somebody swiped it. No reason not to take it all, though; and the Sicilian Social Club doesn't go around leaving IDs on stiffs. I'm starting to think you're right about Yummy and Tony. Somebody wanted her in their laps. But —"

A siren turned into the block.

I said, "I thought I heard you order Code Two."

"You did. I wish *all* my questions could be answered before I ask them. Dollars to dogshit somebody placed an anonymous call to nine-one-one. We just got here a little faster."

The first uniform through the hallway door was a black sergeant built like a professional wrestler gone to seed. His partner was younger, white, and constructed along narrower lines. The apartment manager brought up the rear, puffing and redder than ever. Alderdyce showed his shield and shut the door in the manager's face. The inspector led the way into the bedroom, filling them in on the way.

"Bag this." He gave the sergeant the pocketbook. The white officer tipped back his cap and whistled at the sight of the woman on the bed.

"Louder," said his partner, fishing a Ziploc bag out of a pocket. "They don't wake up easy from a hole in the heart."

The officer's face went stiff. He cast around for a diversion and lit on me. "This guy a suspect, Inspector? He doesn't look like a cop."

I said, "That's the nicest thing anyone's said to me all day."

"Leave the detecting to the detectives, Boyd." The sergeant looked at Alderdyce. "We caught the descriptions on the radio, sir. Want us in?"

"The others have a head start. Who called it in?"

"Dispatcher said he didn't leave a name."

"It was a he?"

"I don't know. I just said he out of hab—"

"It's a bad habit."

I didn't hang around to hear the rest of the lecture. He was still warming up when I took myself out. Down in the little foyer the manager stood shaking his head and wiping his congested face with a sodden tissue. He looked at me as if he wanted to ask something, but I kept walking. I had all the questions I needed.

I let my cabby wait while I hit an ATM, then had him take me to the police station in Wyandotte.

Van Buren wasn't in. That was a break. The day captain, a redhead with a Marine cut, checked me out on the computer and filled in the blanks on a release for my vehicle. How much drag a Detroit detective inspector draws downriver depends on the inspector, and when there is a platinum shield, this one will be the first on his block

221

to own one: If any charges had been filed in my case, they'd dropped off the screen. I was going to be a while repaying that debt, especially after Alderdyce found out I was packing important evidence in a homicide on my hip.

I wasn't entirely clear on why I'd taken the risk, except his back had happened to be turned and I'd been playing things by-guess-and-by-gosh so long my better judgment had dried up.

I showed the garage man the paper signed by the day captain, paid the exorbitant storage fee, and went away in the Cutlass. The officer who'd driven it there from the restaurant hadn't monkeyed with the seat or the mirrors, but when I turned on the radio I got a bellyful of how Congress was blowing its collective nose in the Bill of Rights and snapped it off. Nothing's sacred anymore, not even a man's pre-fixed stations.

The receipt belonged to The Wolverine Hotel on Jefferson, and was the one a guest signed when she checked in. Alison Garland had registered under her own name, probably because it belonged to the Visa card she'd used. In the old days, when the Wolverine was known as the Alamo, clerks weren't so fussy about people paying cash.

The new management was eager to keep its clientele from speed-dating by the hour or shooting up in the rooms. There'd been plenty of that in the old days, and halfway-house convicts staying there on their way toward respectability. One of them had been a client of mine.

The old neon sign had been replaced by brushed-metal letters on granite. Apart from it, a new roof, and some indoor improvements like brighter lightbulbs and johns that worked, the joint hadn't changed so much I wouldn't recognize it from bad times. The zigzag arrangement of outside staircases and walkways remained, with some wire-brushing and a fresh coat of black enamel on the railings, and a shiny ice machine in the tunnel between the north and south wings stood on the same spot where the old one had been removed after a local rapper who'd called himself Man One was found slowly decomposing inside it. They might not have found him even then, except when all the hotels were filled the last time the Tigers were in the Series there'd been a heavy run on ice and the last several highballs had tasted strongly of Dead Gangsta.

The paint smelled fresh, but only because the Hollywood film crew who'd chosen the

223

place for an important scene had spent half a million bucks regentrifying it as agreed after it had spent the first half-million restoring it to its earlier sleaze.

It was comfortable enough for a family traveling on a tight budget. My thought was whoever had farmed in Cecelia Wynn's lookalike had wanted her stashed in an out-of-the-way place where her husband or whoever he hired to find her wouldn't be likely to run into her. The joke was on them, though: I generally start at the bottom and work my way up. The bottom being closer to where I am at the beginning.

Cheery fluorescents in the lobby ceiling had shoved out the dim green banker's lamp on the desk and the Coolidge-era black-and-white floor tiles had made way for cork, a delight to sore feet. Crisp brochures advertising area attractions stood in a Lucite rack. A bright-eyed blonde in a green vest showed me her white veneers from behind the desk.

"Checking in, sir?" A chirpy accent, crisp as fresh pickles.

"Where's Floyd?"

A smooth forehead tried to wrinkle. "Floyd?"

"The old clerk, looked like an extra from a George Romero film. He was grand-

224

fathered in so deep I thought they'd have to blast him loose with Primacord."

"I wouldn't know, sir. I've only been here six months. The man who had this job before me doesn't sound like the one you described."

"I'm not complaining. Floyd took kickbacks from the inmates and picked his teeth with a switchblade. I'm looking for this woman. Is she still registered?" I took out the hotel receipt and spread it on the faux marble on the desk.

She looked at it and rattled keys on her computer. "She is, but I can't give out her room number. I can call her for you."

"That won't do. She's a person of interest in a criminal case." I passed the folder with the honorary deputy's badge pinned to it in front of her face, not fast enough for a hotel clerk.

"Are you a policeman?" She slapped a not-quite unfriendly expression over the bright smile.

I was in too deep with the law that day to say yes. "I'm working with Detroit Homicide. You can send Security up with me if you like."

"I'm sorry."

I put away the folder next to my wallet, lingered with my hand there, then thought better of it. Floyd would've let me up for a fiver. The angles I work don't work on earnest-looking blondes in green vests. I took my hand out empty. "Okay. Thanks for being polite about it. Can I at least ask you not to tell her I asked about her?"

"Is there really a murder?"

"Unfortunately. She's not a suspect" — and how — "just someone who might have seen something. I'm a private investigator. I was telling the truth about working with the police, but I guess I can wait until they show up."

"I won't say anything."

I grinned thanks at her, picked up the receipt, and went out. I sat in the car smoking a cigarette and watching the clock in the dash inch its way toward noon. I was waiting for the shift to change. It was a small chance at best, and if it didn't pan out I'd have to look up Barry Stackpole and see if he could hack his way into hotel records for the room number. That would take time, which was all the cops needed to find out about the Wolverine on their own. The snooper life was so much easier when all you had to do was wait for the clerk to go to the bathroom, then rifle through the registration cards on the desk.

When the magic hour came I gave it

226

another five minutes, then went back in. There was nobody behind the desk now. I clanged the little bell and a door opened from the side of the little alcove and a sullen-looking man crowding middle age came out chewing on something. He had crumbs on his green vest.

This time I didn't bother with the flasher or a story to go with it. I showed him my ID, told him who I wanted to see, and stood a crisp folded fifty on the desk. Two minutes later I was on the way up to Alison Garland's room.

# TWENTY-ONE

A DO NOT DISTURB sign hung on the brass doorknob, which meant no one had been in to clean. That was another break. I figured I'd spent all I had coming on this job and was into the next.

The Wolverine people hadn't gotten around to replacing the old-fashioned locks with an electronic system. I'd found a way around that, too, but I like to keep my hand in with traditional methods of burglary. A housekeeper had parked her cart outside a room down the hall and the door was open with a vacuum cleaner whining inside. I kept an eye turned that direction as I twisted the knob belonging to Alison Garland's room toward the door hinges and slid a Costco card between the latch and the jamb. I'm not a member; I'd found it in a parking lot and had added several coats of laminate to make it extra sturdy. After a little struggle the sloping latch retracted with a snap and I was inside with the door shut behind me before the vacuum switched off.

The room was narrow, made more cramped by a pair of twin beds, one of which was still made. A Starving Artist painting of the Pictured Rocks was bolted to the wall above the beds in a black aluminum frame and a bulbous cathode-ray TV occupied a long three-drawer console with a glossy plastic finish. A sculptured carpet kept the guests downstairs from tracking every movement above their heads and the usual spearmint-flavored disinfectant had been sprayed around with a firehose.

Women are tidier than men as a rule, but not when it comes to hotel life. Dresses and tailored business suits were laid out on the unused bed, four pairs of shoes were flung about as if they'd exploded off four pairs of feet, damp towels littered the floor. The top console drawer was open, spilling unmentionables out over the front, and a semitransparent ivory blouse hung over the metal shades of the twin lamps mounted between the beds.

I wondered about that blouse; I even reached out and stroked it between my thumb and forefinger, fishing for metaphysical vibrations, and found out all over again

I'm not psychic. But I know women, in so far as a man can know them, which is damn little. Some of them like a light on in romantic moments, but hotel lamps can be harsh on skin imperfections, and sheer material makes a handy filter. A man would never think of it. I pulled back the covers on the rumpled bed, but there were no visible signs of an untidy act. The sheets and pillowcases passed the smell test for excessive perspiration. Anyway, I'd forgotten to pack my DNA kit, along with my ten thousand shares of Microsoft.

Detecting is funny work. In what other job would it matter whether Alison Garland got laid?

The bathroom's the best place to look for feminine secrets. It was narrow, with a combination shower-bath and not much counter space. What there had been was cluttered with a half-used tube of travel toothpaste, a tiny bottle of Scope, half-empty also, and smears of flesh-colored powder and nasty-looking traces of eyeliner and mascara. Nothing hidden in the few places you can hide something in a hotel bathroom: toilet tank, the underside of the sink, between the towels folded on a glass shelf. The wastebasket held only crumpled tissues. Nothing under the plastic-bag lining. I didn't neglect to turn over the basket and look for something taped to the bottom. I found a Band-Aid that might have been there since they came in tin boxes.

Back in the bedroom I zipped open a pull-along suitcase and found the inspection tag tucked in the bottom of an inside compartment, nothing else. She'd hung up the clothes she hadn't laid out in a folding-door closet. The pockets contained nothing but lint, and not much of that. Same with the clothes on the bed. Apart from what looked like a hasty departure — possibly to make her appointment with me in Wyandotte — the Garland seemed to have been neat in her habits. It would be something for her eulogy if nothing else about her surfaced.

An empty Diet Coke can shared the bedroom wastebasket with crumbs of chocolate chip cookies in a small cellophane package like the kind that came in vending machines. She had a sweet tooth. That ought to break the case wide open.

The Gideon Bible in the nightstand drawer gave me nothing my early religious education hadn't; nothing came out when I turned it upside down, fanned the pages, and gave them a good shake. The Detroit Metropolitan phone book left me just as ignorant. Nothing taped to the back of the drawer or underneath it. I got down on my belly and looked under the bed. It was a platform job, no room for a chest full of pieces-of-eight or a murderer to hide. Just to be thorough I tore apart the bed and flipped up the mattress. Not so much as a bedbug. The Wolverine should have put that in its advertising.

I saved the skimpy writing pad next to the telephone for last. The top sheet had been torn off, leaving a triangular scrap attached to the gum binding. It bore a piece of spiky script that read "ois."

Old movies are only good for entertainment. I tried the trick with the midget Ikea pencil I carry with my notebook, rubbing the edge of the lead on the next sheet. In Hollywood, people bear down harder when they write down revealing information.

*Ois.*

It didn't have to be anything I could use, in a town originally settled by the French. It could have belonged to Dubois, which is a street downtown, or the name of a descendant of one of the first families. There weren't many of them left, though, and I didn't think it was Dubois Street either. The only other local place I knew that ended in those letters was Livernois, which happened to be the street where Elysian Fields stood.

It was Cecelia Wynn's source of herbal vitamins and also a clearinghouse for controlled substances, but all the police had been able to clear so far was a corpse from its basement. I broke out my notebook and looked up the home address I had for Smoke Wygonik.

# TWENTY-TWO

I'd almost forgotten my companions in the Lincoln Town Car. I kept looking for them, but all I got was the usual midtown traffic: a couple of slow-moving vans, their only speed, a bicyclist got up in the standard gladiator regalia of teardrop helmet and Spandex, and a low-rider with more grill-work behind the wheel than outside.

I felt bereft; it's a word, last I knew. As someone once said — that someone possibly being me — you can get used to getting hit in the head with a hammer if that's how you wake up every morning, and what friends I had weren't always so loyal as my enemies. Maybe my recent unfortunate association with cops had put them off. More likely they'd switched to less familiar transportation and a closed tail. If that was the case, I'd become more important than I cared to be. There's comfort in being nonessential. Ask any Roman emperor after Christ.

In any case, hunger trumped paranoia.

"Peckish" is another good Victorian word for what I felt suddenly. It probably isn't in the dictionary anymore: The Internet is always enriching the vocabulary with terms just as doomed for the scrap heap, and space is always short. But "hungry" didn't nearly serve, and "famished" is for Jane Austen. My stomach was pasted to my spine and I had a skull full of helium. It happens every sixteen hours or so when I forget to eat.

The lunch crowd was clearing out of the Westin at the Renaissance Center. A couple of GM execs were finishing a pot of coffee and divvying up the Western Hemisphere in a corner booth while I ate a cheese sandwich and chased it with a glass of milk. I left them still there fighting over the check and drove the short distance to the warehouse district, where buildings the size of department stores stand empty among others making the transition toward loft apartments. So far the developers were offering spectacular views of the river and the Windsor skyline and space to train troupes of mounted lancers for less than their colleagues were charging for utility flats in Bloomfield Hills. Smoke had said she'd been tough enough to hold out for rent control when she signed her lease. In fifty years, when Detroit is back on its feet, she'd still be paying just eight hundred a month and using a bicycle to travel from the bedroom to the kitchen.

The building, on Orleans off East Jefferson, had been used to store everything from Studebaker wagons to stoves to Upper Peninsula pine to cases of Old Log Cabin. It was a microcosm of the city's history, encompassing pioneer days, the logging boom, the dawn of the Industrial Revolution, and Prohibition. Its brick and concrete block had been sandblasted, repainted a soothing mint-green, and panels had been erected in place of the old multiple-paned windows to diffuse the sunlight and protect the privacy of the residents. One of the original bay doors had been left intact, probably for moving furniture, but another had been bricked in with a door and fanlight installed and a row of buttons next to labels printed out on plastic strips. I pressed the one for S. WYGONIK and waited. When that didn't work I selected another at random. That one released the lock. Somewhere there is always someone expecting a pizza.

The freight elevator had been installed

personally by Otis. The car was large enough to carry coils of industrial steel, and probably had. The present owners had renovated it in compliance with code, but it hadn't been soundproofed: The big gears designed to lift a ton clanked and clattered and the cables squealed around their pulleys. It was designed for durability, not speed; I could have smoked a carton by the time I got to Smoke's floor. It stopped with a clang and the doors let me out into a hallway that wasn't original to the building, paneled with unpainted Sheetrock and pierced with hollow-core doors numbered in brass from the Sears hardware department. I found hers and pressed the bell button. I pressed it a few more times before the door opened and came to a stop at the end of a chain. When she saw it was me she closed it again. The chain rattled and she opened it wide.

She was barefoot and in sweats with her hair twisted into a ponytail. She took a piece of lath off her shoulder with a nail driven through the end and poked it into a wicker basket on the floor that looked as if the cobra had moved out recently.

"Nice weapon," I said by way of greeting. "Was the nail your idea?"

"I found it in the hallway when I moved in. They were still working on the place

237

then. It came with a bunch of nails. I left one in on an inspiration. I don't like guns." She ran fingers through her ponytail. "Did you buzz me from downstairs? I was pounding my ear. I didn't get much sleep last night. Or this morning, either." She grinned sleepily — there was a bedsheet crease on her right cheek — and kissed me. "I'm not sure I thanked you for helping me out with the police."

"I had the impression you did." I stepped around her into a great open room with a ten-foot ceiling, suspended from fourteen. There was a stove and a sink and a refrigerator, bedroom furniture, a couple of mismatched armchairs, and a sofa that looked better than the one in the apartment where Yummy Mondadori had been hiding out with his cousin. It might fetch a piece of change from Craigslist. "I'd've pegged you for a minimalist. How do you heat the place, by burning lath?"

"Utilities are included, as long as I don't abuse the privilege. I'm furnishing the place a piece at a time. Funny, but I didn't think to budget that in when I signed the lease. Can I offer you a drink? Beer's all I've got, sorry."

"No, thanks. I never drink on a full stomach. How did you know Alison Garland?"

"I didn't know I did. Who is she?"

"Last night, for a little while, I thought she was Cecelia Wynn." I told her about Wyandotte.

"Why would someone want to pass herself off as her? And why do you think I know her?"

She didn't slip up on her tenses. I hoped that meant something nice. She smelled a little like soap. I have a soft spot for women who shower before bed.

"She left a note in her hotel room. It wasn't much, but I got the idea it was connected to Elysian Fields."

"You think maybe she posed as Mrs. Wynn at the store? If she looked as much like her as you say, she might have. I only saw the customers a few minutes at a time. We weren't doing land-office business, but there were enough I wouldn't necessarily remember the physical details of any one of them." She started to yawn, cut it off in the middle; looked alert and wary. "But if you thought I knew her as this Alison person, you weren't suggesting I mistook her for Mrs. Wynn, were you? What's going on, Amos? Do you think I seduced you to throw you off the track? If you think she's hiding out here, go check the bathroom. I just wish I'd known you were coming to search the place. I'd've

239

changed the towels."

"No need. I know where she is. Or where she was an hour ago. By now she may be taking up a tray in the county cold room. Someone shot her to death, probably not long after she left me in the restaurant."

Her hand went to her mouth, but not to cover another yawn. "God. And you think I shot her?"

"It occurred to me, but I didn't know yet how you felt about guns."

"I hate them. I hate that you carry one. If I were ever to kill a person, it'd be some other way. Jesus, you think I crawled into your bed fresh from a murder? You *think* that?"

I let out my breath. I was having trouble lately remembering the process of respiration. "I'm not a theater critic, but I'm guessing you're not that good an actress. No, I don't think you shot her. If you did, you had help, because it looks like she was taken from wherever she was killed and carried into the bedroom where she was found, and I think you'd be smart enough not to share the secret."

"Thanks a bunch. I'm too smart to be guilty. That's not the same as innocent."

"Take it in a hitch, Amber Dawn. Anyone can kill; I only quibble about the why. You're my only link to the health store. Livernois doesn't have many sights to attract visitors from out of state. Just the Chord Progression Lounge, and she didn't strike me as the jazz-loving type. I could be wrong about that. They don't all wear Miles Davis T-shirts and snap their fingers as they walk."

"That's all you had to go on? Livernois?"

"Not even that. Just the last three letters. When there isn't a straw around, you grasp at seeds. Also I grew a tail I didn't have before I went to the store the first time, and part of that tail led to Alison Garland dead in a dump she probably never laid eyes on. Everything about this case has to do with your late place of employment. I'll take that beer now if the offer's still good."

"I made it before you accused me of murder. But I'm not a welsher." She opened the refrigerator and twisted the caps off two bottles of Stroh's. Handing me one: "I don't guess it's as good since they blew up the plant, but it was my parents' brand. I don't know a lot about beer, only that it beats water when you're really thirsty."

"You're too young to remember the Stroh's plant." We clinked bottles and I sat on the sofa.

"Not quite that young. But I was too little to know anything about it." She sat on the

241

other end, swung up her legs, and laid them across my lap. "Mind?"

I shook my head and rested a hand on a bare ankle. "So no bells? Maybe Cecelia mentioned a long-lost identical cousin?"

She swigged and stifled a burp. "Like I said, I didn't get to know any of the customers. Some small talk, questions about which capsule does what. You think it has something to do with Mrs. Wynn's disappearance?"

"I'm not sure Mrs. Wynn's disappearance has anything to do with Mrs. Wynn. I mean that it was her idea. I know they both had something to do with Elysian Fields, and I don't even know that. All I've got is three letters on a scrap of paper."

"What do the police say?"

"I don't know. But I know what they'll say when they find out I've got that scrap. First, though, they'll have to find out about the hotel room. I sort of swiped the evidence that led me to it." I took a long pull and let the liquid pool on the floor of my mouth before committing it to my stomach. She was right about beer. Wherever they were brewing the stuff now it was a big improvement over water.

"Is this how you always run your business?"

"I like to make things interesting. The murders in this town need a little seasoning. It's like dropping a quarter and throwing a ten-dollar bill after it to make bending over worth the effort."

"So am I your ten-dollar bill?"

I looked at her. She was wearing a greedy little smile. "No," I said. "Not when you adjust for inflation." I leaned over to set my bottle on the floor and gathered the rest of her into my lap.

# Twenty-Three

"Where to now?"

She was watching me dress. One bare leg lay on top of the twisted sheets. Her eyes were neutral-colored now behind a sleepy veil.

"The office, where I do my best thinking." I knotted my tie, brushed at a crease it had picked up lying on the floor, gave up, and buttoned my coat over it.

"Thinking or drinking?"

"Don't believe I'm the ambidextrous drinker I'm made out to be. It's PR. Customers like their mechanics German, their decorators gay, and their detectives baggy in the liver. I'm starting all over from scratch and that's where I go when it itches."

"Which case are you working, Alison Garland or Cecelia Wynn?"

"Does it matter? Did you ever read the story about the blind men and the elephant?"

"You know my generation only reads blogs."

"Check it out sometime." I turned away from the mirror and looked at her. "What's your day look like?"

"You mean my evening? The Internet café and the online employment postings. It's going to be harder than usual. The only reference I can give for the last six months isn't available, and if he were, it isn't a reference that's likely to get me hired. How about you?"

"A reference from me is only a little better than one from your dead manager."

"I meant I could come to work for you." She turned over, exposing all of a very long back with a mole on the left shoulder blade, and supported her chin on her fist. "So you're not a lush. Some of the standards need supporting. How about hiring a sexy blond secretary? That ought to go over big with the customers."

"Lady, I couldn't afford to hire me for a day, let alone you for a week."

"Well, you can at least kiss me before you go."

I did that, and she turned that long back on me. She was breathing evenly before I got to the door.

■ ■ ■ ■

The sun had made its first appearance in days, dropping through the overcast. The butternut light spreading under that low ceiling made a phony effect, all filters and reflectors: I was too smart for that. I was a smart character all around. At that point I could outwit a Chevy short block. The gutters were going like sixty with melted slush. A cat with one eye, one ear, three legs, and a tail like a used pipe cleaner crouched on the sidewalk with its haunches tight, watching for rats swimming against the current.

Waiting for the traffic to clear so I could turn onto Woodward, I looked up in the rearview mirror and grinned. My Town Car was back, with what looked like the same pair of heads behind the windshield. Lately the shift changes were working in my favor.

No use boring them with another trip to the office. After I made my turn I swung left onto Michigan and led them out past downtown to the Aurora Car Wash. They hung back a little after I bumped up over the cut-down curb. For a moment I was afraid they'd circle the building and wait for me when I came out the other side, but they were wary; there might be a trapdoor inside and a ramp leading to the Bat Cave. They turned in too, giving me twenty feet.

The attendant, a lanky thirty-five or so with prematurely white hair, beamed when he recognized my car. I always gave him a ridiculous tip to make sure the undercarriage was good and clean. I don't care about the finish, but you don't want a stray pebble clawing at a brake rotor when you're trying to keep up with someone doing ninety. He stopped beaming when I told him what I wanted.

"What are they, cops?" He was wise enough not to look their way. I'd pegged him for an ex-con. You start out working in a car wash or you end up there, but you don't spend your middle years in one unless nobody will hire you for anything else. And he hadn't gotten that white hair scraping chewing gum off chrome.

"What I want to find out. Don't worry, I don't intend to shoot first." I handed him a ten-spot on top of the usual. That put him back on his feed.

He stuck the bill in his shirt pocket and picked up a hose wand. "Gonna get wet."

"I was born wet." I guided my tires into the tracks and shifted into neutral.

After he got the surface dirt off with the wand and a push broom, the conveyors pulled the car forward, and the power washers came on, pounding the sheet metal with spray and swaying the chassis on its springs. Multicolored soap made a gay pattern on the windshield. The car passed through it in lockstep. Just before the thick lather blanked out my rear window I saw the Lincoln in the mirror, pulling in behind.

I tensed up at the sight. A large part of me was hoping I wouldn't have to spring the trap: It had one chance of working and ten of putting me in the hospital, and I was spending more time in recovery than I used to.

The rotating scrubbers started in. Then came the swishing fabric strips, licking the hood and then up the windshield and over the roof. I reached into the backseat for the slicker I keep there for sudden downpours on tail jobs. By the time I'd shrugged into it and pulled the hood over my head, the strips were between me and the Town Car, cutting off the occupants' view. I had to shove the door hard to open it against the water pressure during the rinse cycle, and then the handle was torn from my hand and the door slammed shut. Turning, I braced myself against the side of the car and readied myself for the next move. It was like standing on the deck of a ship during a gale, only the water was a lot hotter, almost scalding. I hadn't considered that.

I took the plunge, literally: Two feet of slick concrete separated me from the catwalk that ran alongside the conveyors. If I lost my footing I lost everything; I could see the nose of the Town Car sliding out from under the strips. I leaped, and slapped my palms against the wall to avoid smashing my face into it. They stung. It all took only a half-second. Meanwhile I was drenched from the knees down. I missed the hot water then: Once out from under it I chilled quickly in the early spring air. When I turned to face my retreating rear fender, my feet squelched in their shoes. It hardly seemed worth the time lost putting on the raincoat, but I hadn't rehearsed the maneuver, so the surprises were bound to be unpleasant.

I unholstered the .38, pulled my oilcloth sleeve down over it, and stood with my back against the wall. It was pale unpainted concrete and I wore dark clothes, but I was counting on the pair in the Lincoln looking straight ahead at the Cutlass.

I held my breath anyway and made myself as flat as possible as the gray car crept past. The conveyors seemed to move slower than when I was in my heap; I was sure one of them would turn his head my way, and wished I were a frog. I didn't need the submersive ability so much as that trick they have of flattening themselves when they're about to be stepped on.

Time slows when you're in that kind of situation, and things were moving slow enough as it was. The longer away from the spray the colder I got. My clothes were plastered to my skin like wet leaves. My breath smoked — I was afraid it would be noticed, but it quickly mingled with the steam from the sprayers. My feet had punched out for the day and gone home. I wanted to stamp them to revive the circulation, but I didn't dare move and risk calling attention to myself.

The front half of the Lincoln passed me, and between it and a glacier there was no contest. The driver, who was the only one I could see, was a blurry profile behind a sheet of soap and water, both hands gripping the wheel. The hand clenching the Chief's Special was numb. I realized I was holding it tight, preparing myself to raise it in case the head turned my way. I relaxed my grip and felt the tingling warm my fingers.

The rear door drew abreast. I tilted my torso ever so slightly forward on the axis of the pelvis, shifting my center of gravity for the big move.

I couldn't count on the door being unlocked. If it wasn't, I'd lose the element of surprise tugging at it. Wrapping my hand around the cylinder of the short-barreled .38, I backhanded it hard against the window butt-first. The glass exploded into a million kernels. I reached in with my free hand, jerked the door open by the handle inside, threw myself into the backseat, and border-rolled the revolver so that the butt was in my palm and the barrel pointed toward the front seat.

The driver was surprised. So was I. There was no one in the passenger's seat in front.

I was sluggish in anticipating the next move. I was just turning my attention from the wide-open eyes in the rearview mirror when the rear door on the passenger's side flew open and the missing party bent down from the catwalk and stuck the barrel of a massive semiautomatic pistol inside.

That's the problem with most tricks. The mark can work them just as easily.

"Your ride wasn't all that dirty, Walker." The voice was shallow, sexless, and sounded dryer than it should have; the owner wasn't wearing a raincoat. It had a foreign accent I couldn't place just then. "Throw your weapon into the front seat."

I shifted the muzzle toward the driver's head. "You first. I just got it back."

The conveyors were still pulling the car along. Keeping the pistol steady on me, the newcomer slid into the seat beside me, twisted my way. The suit was cut mannishly, but it had been soaked through, and clung to its wearer in a way no man's ever would. The face was smooth as polished silk, with the features arranged as an afterthought to the eyes, gray-blue and canted slightly, with large pupils. Black hair cut short and shaped to a long skull with plenty of room for gray matter.

She looked twenty. The gun made her older.

With two fingers of her left hand she reached inside her coat, slid out a folder bound in blue leather, and flipped it open. The card in the window looked official, with a gold seal, her picture looking as grim and eager as her cocked pistol, and lettering that belonged on a box of kosher salt.

"Lazara Dorn. I'm a major with Israeli Intelligence." She snapped it shut with the turn of a slender wrist and dropped it back into its pocket. "My partner, Captain Asa Leibowitz. Both of us are trained to take a bullet in the head rather than fail the mission. Are you?"

All the adrenaline went out of me then. I reached across the back of the passenger's seat in front and let the revolver drop onto the cushion.

# TWENTY-FOUR

"Mossad?" I asked.

Lazara Dorn shook her short-cropped head. "GOLEM. Do you understand Hebrew?"

"No. Reading from right to left gives me a headache."

"Then I won't bother with the words behind the acronym. Do you know what a Golem is?"

"A walking statue with a mission."

"That mission being to protect the Jews at all costs. We're an arm of Israeli military intelligence."

"Right or left?"

She smiled, without warmth. "That depends on the mission."

We were in a room at the Book-Cadillac, one of the grand old buildings that have escaped a city charge of dynamite for the time being. It had been redone in figured wallpaper, furnished in maple and brown

Ultrasuede, and a flat-screen television dozed inside a cabinet with louvered doors. Asa Leibowitz stood beside the window in case I got any ideas about rappelling down twelve stories. He was a pudgy forty with Dumbo ears and a five o'clock shadow that looked as if it had gotten its start last night. His suit, tan to match his partner's, had been a good fit before he'd stuffed ten more pounds into it, mostly around the middle; the skinny tie had come from Hughes & Hatcher by way of a time machine. So far he might have left his power of speech back in Tel Aviv.

The woman had just come in from the shower. Her small slender body was buried in a fluffy white robe and her feet wore a pair of plain mules. Sitting opposite me in the ergonomic chair that belonged to the desk, she crossed a pair of ankles that looked delicate for someone who presumably spent a fair amount of time chasing reluctant detainees on foot; but then so did Secretariat's. Her hair was already dry. She'd probably given it a vigorous shake after toweling off the rest of her. She had an athletic look and moved like a cat. Gymnastics was my guess.

We'd come there in the Town Car. Leibowitz had parked my Cutlass outside the car wash. Maybe I'd see it again.

I was sitting in an armchair barefoot with my soaked pants rolled up to midcalf while my shoes and socks baked on the radiator. I felt like Huck Finn in the mitts of Injun Joe.

"You'll get a bill for that shattered window," Dorn said. "My suit, too, if it shrinks. They don't pay all our expenses."

"Way to overcome the stereotype," I said.

Her strong dark brows went up a sixteenth of an inch. They contrasted sharply with her eyes, gray-blue satellites stopped in mid-orbit as if by a force of will. "Are we a bigot?"

"We are not guilty. We have a Jewish great-great grandmother on our mother's side and Italians, Serbs, Croats, Germans, Alsatians, and English on our father's. We're bulletproof."

"Serbs *and* Croats?"

"Family reunions were always lively."

"Why'd you do what you did?"

"I wouldn't have, if I'd known you'd left the doors unlocked."

"You know what I mean."

That androgynous voice, throaty and with her accent, was intoxicating. I took a strong dose of mental caffeine. "You've been tailing me for days. It was the best way to get a look at you. It's okay, now I know you're fuzz. I'm used to attracting cops. I must have some pretty strong pheromones. But I like to keep track of whose list I'm on this week and why."

She lifted my revolver off a lamp table, swung out the cylinder, snapped it back. My wallet was on the table, contents spread, so she knew I was legal. Not that she'd care. Military intelligence agents regardless of nationality have a marked lack of interest in civilian law. She handled the weapon as easily as a compact; easier, maybe. No cosmetics had done any streaking in the car wash, and she hadn't put any on after showering. For my money she didn't need them — her face was a classic oval, with a high forehead, a straight nose, and thin but delicately turned lips, not to mention those eyes — but these days an undecorated young woman is something you notice.

"You can tell a lot about a person by the way he takes care of his sidearm," she said. "So far you get a passing grade. I prefer my Desert Eagle." She returned the .38 to the table.

The big Israeli pistol lay snug in its speed holster on the nightstand, separated from me by one of the double beds. I said, "When you stuck it in my face I thought it was a refrigerator. Forty-four?"

"Three fifty-seven. Forty-four loads are too heavy. They pull my skirts out of line."

It was the first I knew she owned a skirt. I guessed even foreign spooks went out dancing from time to time. Maybe that was when the war paint came out. "When did you folks start working with the Mafia? Golda Meir wouldn't let Meyer Lansky within a hundred miles of Israel."

"I don't know who Meyer Lansky is, but I'm guessing he's one of your American gangsters."

"Was. I thought your schools were better than ours at teaching history."

She let that one coast. "What makes you think we work with the Mafia?" With her accent the word had only two syllables, like the way some people say "piano."

"Okay, be cute. My shoes need another ten minutes anyway."

"Stop trying to change the subject."

"Lady —"

"Major."

"Major lady, you started it, turning my head with sweet talk about how I scrub and powder my gun."

"Revolver." An automatic reaction from someone with recent army training. She was big on correcting people. "You're lucky your trick didn't work. We act on reflex."

"I didn't jump into your car with a chrysanthemum in my hand."

"You might have had time for one shot. *Your* schools should concentrate more on mathematics. There are two of us, and we're equally expendable. When you grow up dodging bombs you don't have time to become sentimental about the people you work with." She seemed to consider something, then shook her head briefly. "I doubt you'd have had time."

"Maybe not. I didn't know I was at war. Who's the enemy?"

"Iran. Iraq. Libya. Syria. Hamas. Now perhaps Egypt again. You're a spoiled people. We've been at war for sixty years. We've lost more citizens during cease-fires than you have in your last three wars. Men, women, children. Babies. Hospitals and schools are primary targets. Our school bus drivers are required to carry Uzis."

"Ours carry Glocks." I fished for a cigarette, but my pack was damp. There's no such thing as a perfect raincoat. "The Arabs in Dearborn are too busy earning a living to tinker with SCUD missiles. Pick a subject. No? Okay, I'll go. You set a tinhorn Capone we affectionately know as Yummy Mondadori on me in my office building, probably

259

as a spotter. He knew me from somewhere, maybe one of those times I got my picture in the paper or hanging around Detroit Police headquarters. He gave you the high sign as I was following him out; I didn't see it, but the minute I hit the road I grew two more heads." I put a cigarette in my mouth anyway. Wet as it was, it kept my chin from shaking. For all I knew Mr. and Ms. GO-LEM had diplomatic immunity and could fix murder like a parking ticket. "Why a Lincoln, by the way? You could've rented a Fiesta and gotten a room upgrade for the difference."

"We needed the space. We might have picked up some passengers."

"What are you using on them these days, bamboo splinters or something you plug in?"

Captain Leibowitz heaved a sigh they heard in Windsor. I thought he was getting ready to break stride, but he turned back toward the window without saying anything.

Lazara Dorn looked as upset as the Wailing Wall at midnight. "You're stalling, Mr. Walker. Why?"

"I don't know. I expected the cavalry before this."

"What cavalry?"

"I guess they don't get American television

in the Middle East."

"We do. I don't own a set. I share an apartment with two families and I go there only to sleep."

"I'm not stalling. I'm tired. It's hard work holding up both ends of the same conversation."

She uncrossed her ankles and recrossed them the other way. She was getting ready for something. When she twitched at the robe to make sure it was shut, I spotted golden stains on her first two fingers. That explained the hungry little gleam in her eye when I'd stuck the wet nail between my lips. I wondered how much longer she'd hold out against the no-smoking law.

Years, if she had to, I decided. I'd faced tougher opponents, but not without air support.

# TWENTY-FIVE

I put away the cigarette. There wasn't much more of her goat to get, and anyway it was like chewing kelp.

"I don't know who this man Mondadori is," she said. "Captain Leibowitz and I were sent here to investigate an international ring of narcotics smugglers. Our sources led us eventually to Elysian Fields. Apparently there are many such establishments in this country. In Israel, we're under the impression Americans are not interested in health and fitness. In Las Vegas, Nevada, I'm told, there is even a restaurant called the Heart Attack Station, where a customer can order a hamburger sandwich containing sufficient calories to feed a neighborhood in the Golan Heights. Of course I do not believe this."

"Believe it. In *my* neighborhood, there's a Tubby's next door to Weight Watchers. We're a nation of contradictions."

"So Asa tells me. He grew up in Chicago."

She pronounced it with a hard *ch*. "Where I was raised, you would never hear a person say, 'I hope you're hungry.' In many places it would be a cruel jest."

"Are we a bigot?"

I didn't know if she caught it. As far as the muscles of her face moved she could have sat for a sculptor who worked in solid diamond. "You were seen visiting Elysian Fields while it was under our surveillance. You were in there thirteen minutes. Pardon me, you seem fit, but you do not strike me as the type who indulges himself in health supplements. What was your business?"

"Not yours. I like to wreck my body the old-fashioned way, by shopping in liquor stores."

"You're being intentionally evasive."

"I wouldn't know how to be evasive by accident. Did you have the place staked out when the manager was murdered?"

"I'm not at liberty to discuss all the details of an investigation. In any case, homicide is irrelevant except where it pertains to the matter at hand, and that hasn't been decided in this case."

"In this country our various branches of investigation share information."

"And now you are being intentionally disingenuous. We know your history of internecine squabbles. But to respond: Once we're satisfied that to confide in the local authorities will not jeopardize our assignment, we are eager to cooperate. The police can be territorial. Nothing can be gained by antagonizing them unnecessarily."

"Major, your country wrote the book on territorial." I got up. Leibowitz spun my way, hands open at his sides. I wouldn't have thought he could displace that much bulk so fast. I'd had him pegged for a regular at the Heart Attack Station. Dorn kept her seat. I had a hunch she was the dangerous one, naked and unarmed as she was under the robe. I picked up one of my socks, felt it. It was still a little damp, but I put on my shoes and socks and unrolled my cuffs, then returned to my chair. I felt like I'd been wading in wet grass. I could live with that. The captain wore thick-soled shoes on his gunboats and he looked like a stomper.

"I'm looking for a missing wife. Not mine. She's the type who indulges herself in health supplements, or she did. She took off from home without her personal pharmacy and I thought she might drop by the place to stock up."

"Is there anyone who can verify that?"

"I suppose you can talk to the clerk, if you

can find her. I forget her name."

"You seem absentminded for a professional detective."

"Her name is irrelevant to my investigation."

She rooted among the objects on the table, paged through my wilted notebook. "I studied stenography before I joined the service," she said. "I worked in Hebrew, French, German, and English; we have many expatriates in intelligence. I'm not familiar with your shorthand."

"It'd be spooky if you were. I made it up. Sometimes I can't read it myself."

"I suppose today would be one of those times."

I changed the subject. I was running out of banter. "It's time you pooled what you've got with the locals. You're duplicating efforts; the man who controls expenses back home won't like that. If you've been watching the pill store you know it was raided. Detroit P.D. knows about the drug ring. What I can't figure out is why Israel cares what a bunch of Mexicans and Chinese are up to."

"We're interested in them only peripherally. It is their partners in the Middle East who concern us. They're harvesting the poppy and coca fields in both hemispheres and selling the refined product in the United States in order to finance terrorist operations throughout the world, specifically in Israel. We've known for some time they're shifting their emphasis from the West in order to carry out their traditional intention of wiping my country from the face of the earth."

"What is it about Detroit that all these thugs want to use it to destroy whole populations? Not long ago a nutjob with a billion dollars tried to flood the city with high-octane heroin, then cut off the supply and turn a couple of thousand hopheads into mass murderers. It's —" I crossed my legs. I had a sudden chill; should've let the footwear dry a little longer.

She cocked her head. If she were a bird of prey, that gesture would be talons in my throat. "It's — ?" she prompted.

"I just thought of a piece of intelligence I can spare, but I need the same thing from you."

"We are not here to bargain, Mr. Walker. I have the authority to shelter you in a remote place for as long as it takes to penetrate your obstinance."

"Queue up, Major. I got the same speech a little while ago, with contractions. You cops need new writers."

"I am not referring to jail. In the place I have in mind, you will be deposited naked on a concrete floor in a room without heat or ventilation with not enough space to lie down. GOLEM is not subject to your progressive regulations regarding incarceration. You will not have the right to remain silent, you will be denied access to an attorney, and anything you do not say can and will be used against you. You will not be in America. No extradition proceedings will be implemented. We don't need them. Are you familiar with the Eichmann case?"

"How is it Meyer Lansky was before your time, but Eichmann wasn't?"

She turned her head, said something to Leibowitz in a language I will never understand. He produced a gadget the size of a pack of cigarettes from a coat pocket, stuck a bud in his ear, worked a key, listened, worked another key, unplugged his ear, and put the thing back in his pocket. Nodded.

"As I thought. We have discussed relevance twice during this conversation. Mr. Lansky is not. Eichmann is, to every Jew on this planet. At the time he was arrested in Argentina and brought to Israel for trial and execution, there was outcry from most of the world powers about violation of international law, but he was hanged anyway. In your case, I severely doubt many voices will be raised. You will be — what is the Orwellian term? — a nonperson?"

We ordered room service. I needed a sandwich and a drink to float it in, and I figured it was time to find out if Leibowitz had vocal cords and if he was supposed to be the good cop. When I made the suggestion, a look passed between them. Maybe he was hungry, too, and maybe he had a blood-sugar problem. Anyway Dorn nodded her head, this movement taking up only a thirty-secondth of an inch, and he picked up the telephone. His broad Chicago accent had Yiddish edging, either inherited or picked up abroad.

She interrupted the order. "And a carton of cigarettes. Camels."

Well, I hadn't figured her for Virginia Slims.

He added it to the list, frowned, took the receiver from his face. "No cigarettes. There's a state law."

I grinned. "Kidnapping's in, smoking's out. The line has to be drawn somewhere."

"What strange people you are," she muttered.

When he got off the line she said, "Go out and find a drugstore. I will look after

Mr. Walker."

He picked up the Desert Eagle in its rig and started to bring it to her.

"No. Leave it." She looked at me. "Do you accept that it is unnecessary?"

I said sure. There wasn't a brick handy to break and I didn't want her proving it on my arm.

"Alone at last," I said, when he'd left. "What do Islamists need with financing? They wash their undies in oil."

"As you know, there have been great disturbances recently among the Arab governments. They're reluctant to cooperate openly with terrorist organizations. The World Bank has frozen the assets of the billionaires who belong, and much of their remaining capital has vanished along with the couriers. Fanaticism and corruption are not mutually exclusive. And so Al-Qaeda, Hamas, the Taliban, and the PLO are forced to seek funding, like your banks and auto companies. To their mind, it is not an absurd analogy. They see themselves as performing a great service to mankind by wiping out a large portion of it. Is this the information you wished?"

"Well, it's all I'm likely to get. I figured you'd open up with Asa out of the room."

"Because I am a woman?"

"Because you're a woman working with a man who's sure if the mission goes bust it'll be your fault because you're a woman. I'm in the intelligence business, don't forget. My expense account won't cover super high-tech recorders that don't depend on tape or discs and can pick up every syllable of a quiet conversation through a layer of worsted, but the commodity's the same, back-scratching-wise. A man can work a swap without being called onto the carpet, but if Leibowitz thinks you're soft he won't be so quick to back you when it counts. If this is too much vernacular, I'll try to put it in English."

"I understood enough of it. I am trying to decide whether to be insulted."

"Not by me. Women have been making a monkey of me all my life, and don't get the idea from that fizzle in the car wash I'm as dumb as I look."

"And now what is your information? The name of your client would be a start."

"That'd tick off the client and waste your time besides. The cases don't connect."

Her eyebrows, the only expressive things on her face, told me she was going to argue the point; but then room service knocked at the door. She got up, went to the night-stand, unholstered the massive semiautomatic, and went to check the peephole with it pointed ceilingward. When she was satisfied we weren't under siege, she let it hang behind her right hip and let in a young waiter with a buzz cut in a red jacket pushing a cart. She stopped him before he could lift the covers off the trays for our approval.

"Thank you." Turning her back to use her body as a shield, she deposited the Desert Eagle in the nightstand drawer, retrieved a square wallet designed to hold foreign bills, signed the receipt he handed her, and gave him five dollars American. She stood with her feet spread just far enough apart to kick his testicles up into his throat if he made an unwaiterlike move.

I was impolite. Without waiting for Leibowitz to return, I stood, twisted the cap off a fifth of Lauder's, poured two fingers into two cut-crystal glasses, and sat back down with my steak sandwich on a plate in my lap. She inspected the whitefish, made a resigned little movement involving the surface of one shoulder, and drew her chair up to the cart to eat. She washed down each bite with bottled water, then sipped Scotch, then forked up another bit of kosher. A methodical type. She would dispose of a body using the same measured movements.

"What have you to offer?" she asked,

halfway through the entrée.

I concentrated another moment on my meal. Hotel chefs hate applying heat to a prime cut of meat, so I'd ordered medium instead of my usual medium-rare. It had arrived beet-colored and bleeding; with a little first aid I could have resuscitated it. Instead I doused it with A.1. "In return for giving me a raincheck on that all-expenses-paid trip to Israel?"

"You keep flexing your price, Mr. Walker. I have already given you something I was not prepared to give."

"Sure you were. Everyone knows what's going on in your part of the world. The droolers are losing steam. Why else would they go into the drug trade if not to raise money for a direct assault? They want to wind the clock back to the palmy days of the Ottoman Empire, when men were men, women were camels, and infidel heads rolled like marbles. Undermining our moral fiber by flooding the market with primo cocaine and heroin is too subtle for their methods. And our countries are supposed to be allies, but the people you answer to wouldn't send two experienced agents halfway around the globe to protect American interests, especially not with our politicians talking about returning your borders

272

to where they were before the Six-Day War."

"As well reduce the United States to the original thirteen colonies," she said. "Among holders of public office, inanity is the universal language."

"Not an original thought. The point I'm making is I'd have put it all together sooner or later. All you gave me was time."

She swallowed a piece of fish and chased it with Scotch, then water, all out of order. It was the equivalent of Lady Macbeth wringing her hands. "Amnesty would require indication in advance that what you have to trade has value."

"That's not much room to wiggle, but I'll take a stab at it." I ate half my sandwich, letting the masticating motion stimulate my brain, but chewing the undercooked meat made my jaws ache. I put it down and reached up to slide the plate onto the cart. There was broccoli, which normally I like, but I ignored it in favor of diverting blood flow north of my neck. "Any operation involving Mexico, Europe, Asia, and the Middle East needs someone at top. It can't be run by a committee. Can we agree on that?"

"Certainly. The inefficacy of the United Nations is evidence in favor of the theory."

"I can give you her name."

# TWENTY-SIX

" 'Her'?"

"You shouldn't be surprised," I said. "Isn't every baby girl and boy in Israel military property from birth?"

"I did not say I was surprised. Continue."

"MacArthur Industries. That name ever pop up?"

"An international conglomerate, based somewhere in Asia. Just where seems to depend upon the calendar date. The Bamboo Curtain is as impenetrable as ever, despite the economic changes there. In many ways it's a feudal system, with much moving around. Manufacturing. Investment. Real estate. Communications. A firm so large and diverse is bound to appear in any investigation regarding financing. I understand there was some question about its former chief operating officer, but there has been a reorganization since."

"Too close to the vest, Major. The cops in

Detroit know what MacArthur was up to, and their budget's a lot tighter than yours."

"Very well. You are speaking of Charlotte Sing. She is wanted in most of the countries of the world for illegal trafficking in human organs, drug dealing, and racketeering."

"You left out murder."

"I should not have to remind you that domestic homicide is a local issue."

"I don't like to give another guy advice about his work, but maybe if you'd spent a little more time in the beginning on piecemeal killing, you could have prevented a couple of hundred in a school or hospital."

"I am sorry you felt compelled to engage in a practice you dislike."

There was a knock. She repeated her actions of fifteen minutes earlier. When she saw it was Leibowitz, she opened up and returned her pistol to the nightstand. As her partner sat on the edge of the bed and drew the cart close to dig into his meal — chicken and potatoes, with coleslaw in a saki cup — Dorn opened a window, used a disposable lighter on a Camel from the carton the captain had brought, and held the pack out to me. I used her lighter and watched the smoke drift out toward Michigan Avenue.

"If Madam Sing is out to pasture, someone who thinks a lot like her is warming her chair. The cops have traced Elysian Fields to MacArthur. Don't feel bad," I said, although I'd gotten no reaction. "While you were thinking globally, Detroit Homicide was working the neighborhood. First order of business is to establish ownership of the place where an employee turns toes up."

Leibowitz left off eating to watch us. He was trying to catch up on what he'd missed while he was out.

"Assuming for the moment you're right," Dorn said, "what interest would an illegal trader have in bringing down Israel?"

"She's an illegal trader the way Stalin was a practicing Marxist. Savvy Stalin?"

" 'One death is a tragedy. A million is a statistic.' The Jew who does not know this is unworthy of his heritage."

"Sing lost interest in turning a profit after she made her first billion. That was capital enough to wipe out the white race, or at least increase the majority of all the others. She's the daughter of a South Korean national and an American GI who bought her a ticket to the U.S. only to turn her into a sex slave in a massage parlor — modern term for a whorehouse. She got out of that by marrying the owner of a chain, turned it into a real-estate business renting property to customers looking to build unauthorized

276

casinos. That allowed her to charge astro-nomical rates without risking arrest; if you can't prove the owner of a piece of ground where laws are broken knows what's going on, you can't prosecute. By the time she was forty, she had enough set aside to cre-ate MacArthur."

"Why MacArthur?"

"She told me she had a warm-and-fuzzy feeling about General MacArthur because he was the first American to leave Korea."

"You've met?"

"Couple of times. No matter how ready you are, though, you always jump when you see a snake. She never got over that slave thing, and she blames everyone who isn't Asian. She isn't alone; anyone who's been through what she has might feel the same way. But just anyone doesn't have her resources. She's rich, brilliant, and as crazy as a Mexican jumping bean. As long as she's loose, the world's on the receiving end of a game of Russian roulette."

"Russian. Asian. Mexican. American English is so much more cosmopolitan than I was led to believe." She was silent for a moment. "The Korean conflict was many years ago. She must be elderly."

"So was Eichmann. Anyway, between modern medical science and the magic of cosmetic surgery, her curdled brain is just about the only body part that's original to her."

"You make her sound supernatural."

"I wish she were. I'd stock up on silver bullets and garlic."

"Such a person, sought all over, would find it difficult to travel. Who are her agents?"

I ground my cigarette out on the glass top of the lamp table, concentrating on the action. "Your guess is as good as mine. She uses every ethnic type, but the only ones she really trusts look like her."

"You've made quite a study."

"More the other way around; not that I'm more than a gnat swimming in her beer, but no one likes that. A microscope is glass on both ends. When you're being watched, you watch back."

Leibowitz struggled through something in Hebrew. He hadn't been speaking it long enough to think in it. I got the impression from Dorn's response in the same language that she was bringing him up to speed. How she handled the part about exchanging sensitive information I couldn't tell and I didn't care. Somewhere in there my fate was being discussed, and from the way the captain pulled a frown whenever he looked at me I had a handle on where he stood. At the end he started to say something, sputtering like a motor looking for a spark, but she cut him off with a single word, without raising her voice. He picked up his fork and poked at his chicken, sulking. The distance between them seemed broader than a single military rank; but I suppose other things were involved. Notches, maybe.

Her head turned my way. "Collect your things, Mr. Walker. At this point I don't consider you a security risk. You will, of course, tell no one about this discussion, or of our presence here."

"Can I write a spy novel? I'll change the names. From now on you're Esther Rosenblatt. I'm still working on Leibowitz. He may wind up a Jack Russell terrier."

"Of course you're joking, but if you were to attempt such a thing, what you wrote would never see print."

"Censorship or murder? I don't want to influence your answer, but over here we take freedom of the press pretty seriously."

"It would depend on when we learned of the manuscript's existence."

I got up, clipped the Chief's Special to my belt, and distributed the rest of my personal property among the assigned pockets. "Okay if I finish what I started? Even if it crosses your trail again?"

"You are asking permission?"

"Doing you a favor. It's just plain silly following me all over town, burning Arab gas, when you know what I'm up to and where I'm going."

"If as you say our trails cross, and you fail to share whatever you learn, we will talk again, and the result will be different. Asa, drive Mr. Walker back to his car."

"Thanks. I'll take a cab. I've got an image to protect. I can't be seen riding around in a car with a broken window."

"Perhaps you're afraid I am not a woman of my word."

"I wouldn't dream of calling a kidnapper and torturer a liar." I went to the door and palmed the knob. "You should switch to filtered. Those straight-ends will kill you someday."

A pair of shallow creases appeared at the corners of her mouth. I wouldn't call them dimples, exactly, and I sure wouldn't say she was smiling. "Are you aware of the life expectancy of a person in my profession?"

"If Leibowitz means anything, you've got twenty years coming."

"I disagree. The captain has been in intelligence five years. I was recruited at sixteen.

Statistically speaking, I have been living on borrowed time for two years."

# Twenty-Seven

The Cutlass sat clean and shining — where the primer didn't show — outside the car wash exit. I paid the cabby, got in, and drove off without looking back. Next visit I'd tip the attendant for the broken glass he'd had to sweep up. You never know when you might need to play the same trick a second time.

I didn't know where else to go, so I pointed the hood toward the river and called Alec Wynn.

"I was thinking of hiring another private detective to look for the private detective I hired," he said.

"Reporting just slows down an investigation, but I admit it's been a spell. I'm in a corn maze. I take it you haven't heard from your wife."

"No. What's a corn maze?"

"I mean a tangle. I grew up in a farming village. Can we meet?"

"Can't you report over the phone?"

"It tells better in person."

"All right. I have an appointment, but I'll move it. The dining room in twenty minutes?"

"Better make it your office, and send your secretary out on an errand."

"Is it that bad?"

"I'd walk out on it if it were a movie, put it that way." I broke the connection.

The fishes had the river to themselves; the rotten spring weather had driven even the diehard modern Phoenicians back indoors. This time the big man in gray sprang up from his seat in front of the window and crossed the yellow-green carpet to intercept me at the halfway point. The lines in the tan face were deeper and he seemed to have lost weight, but it hadn't been long enough since we'd seen each other for that to show. He'd deflated was all. He hung on a second longer than necessary, as if we were fellow skydivers and his rip cord had failed.

"I was worried before," he said. "I don't mind telling you I'm frantic now. I was sure she'd be in touch before this. I only hired you because I never take anything for granted. It's gotten me where I am. Please tell me everything. Wait."

He went back to the desk, pressed a button or flicked a switch, and a section of blue wall slid open opposite the window. Glass shelves filled a recess and a dozen bottles filled the shelves above a stainless-steel sink. A shaker and ice bucket in matching copper stood on the drainboard among an assortment of glasses. He even had one of those leaded-glass jugs that clowns use to spray each other.

"What's your pleasure?"

"Not just now, thanks. I had high tea downtown."

"I wish I knew what you were talking about half the time." He crossed in front of me, dashed a fistful of ice into a highball glass, and filled it to the rim with Jack Daniel's Black Label. He drank it halfway down in one long draft.

I said, "That's no way to treat premium bourbon. It might as well be Old Liver Eater."

"Please resist the temptation to joke. Is Cecelia alive or not?"

"There's no evidence she isn't. I'd better give you the works."

He led the way to a conversation grouping in a corner, where we sank into full-grain leather. Enough had happened that I couldn't remember what I'd told him and what I hadn't, so I gave him all of it, except Israeli military intelligence. Major Dorn had managed to spook me with her concrete cell, but more than that I didn't know where she and Leibowitz fit in, or if they did, and I don't like being asked questions I don't know the answers to. Even without it, the story belonged inside rubber walls. I didn't believe a word of it even as I was talking. It was like making up a lie, embellishing all the way to shore it up.

His glass was empty long before I finished, with the ice returned to its original state. He sat there a half-minute before he got up, dumped the water into the sink, and built another drink, this time with more ice. He waited until he was seated again before drinking, a social sip this time. "She's dead. She must be. Why else would anyone go to the fuss of trying to throw you off with her double?"

"I'm going on the theory someone didn't want me rooting around Elysian Fields. Why they're worried about that, with cops already all over the joint, I don't have a clue, except maybe what the cops find interesting about it isn't what they want so much to cover up."

"Such as what?"

"The woman I told you about, if she's in

the picture, is ten times smarter than I am and twice as insane. Make that three times: I don't think the world's against me, just the authorities, half the underworld, and my ex-wife. Sing's always a dozen moves ahead of anyone else, and I don't know what the game is. If I try looking at it from the other angle, I might end up right next door to her in the loco house."

"She sounds fantastic. Something out of an old serial. A few days ago I'd have accused you of making her up."

"Make it ten years ago, before we started wading hip-deep in criminal masterminds out to bring down Britney Spears and the U.S. Constitution. Now she's just one of the pack."

"Where does this Mafioso fit in?"

" 'Mafioso's' a bit grand for Yummy. He's the one the dons send out for coffee. I think he and his cousin were just as surprised to find Alison Garland in that bed as I was. The cops have him. Pretty soon they'll have the cousin."

"The cousin could be in Canada by now."

"Maybe. It's not as easy as it was before you needed a passport to cross over. In his place in the food chain, arranging a fake that would pass muster with Canadian Customs would take a while. Don't believe what you read in Sherlock Holmes, Mr. Wynn. The police are smart and they run a tight ship. He'll turn up."

"So you're throwing in the towel."

"I don't have much experience with that. I'm giving you the chance to cut your losses. If you don't want to take it, I have a couple of threads I could tug on. That's why I'm here, to make the pitch. I'll have that drink now, if the offer's still good."

"Help yourself."

I got up and took inventory. He had Johnnie Walker Blue, which some people dismiss as the drink of choice of Bigfoot, the Loch Ness Monster, and other fables. I didn't think I'd earned it, though, so I poured three fat fingers of The Glenlivet into a rocks glass and added two cubes for ballast. I went back to my seat and nibbled at the Scotch. It's not good policy to pour high-octane into a motor accustomed to regular unleaded. "I'd rather not say what direction I'll go. If it doesn't work out, I won't look so good. I'd prefer to give you a refund on the time wasted, no questions asked."

"By God, you're honest. I thought your kind went out with three-piece suits."

"And here I have one on order with my tailor."

"Speaking of that, what happened to your suit?"

I reached down and tried to pull the wrinkles out of my pants legs. They sprang back: Polyester blends have memories, like warped wood. "I got caught in a shower. I'd've changed before coming over, but this is the only good decent one I have. I lied about the tailor. I get them at T.J. Maxx."

"I don't know who that is."

"There's no reason you would. I've been hanging out a lot lately with people who don't share my world."

"I'll write you a check for what you need to continue the investigation. Feel free to spend part of it on a good man with a needle. Mine owes me a discount. I order my suits ten at a time."

"Thanks, but it would cost me business in the neighborhoods. I don't need anything just now, Mr. Wynn. We'll settle up when I hand you my final report."

Which was whistling past the graveyard. If I were as honest as he thought I was, I'd have confessed I had no idea where to proceed from there.

My cell rang as I was unlocking my car door: The theme from *Man of La Mancha*. It had come with the phone, and I hadn't figured out how to change it: I'm not as stuck on myself as some might think.

"Billy-Bob's Bait Shop and Fine Dining. Walker speaking."

"Jesus Christ, do you answer like that all the time? No wonder you buy your paper clips on the installment plan."

"I haven't bought a paper clip since Jimmy Carter. I run into traffic to scoop one off the pavement. What's the score, John?" Alderdyce's cell phone number had come up onscreen.

"Not so good, but I'm looking for a full-court press in the third quarter. Yummy's clammed up tight, no surprise there. I got more reaction out of a *Playboy* centerfold when I was fourteen."

"Too much information, John." I waited.

"I didn't call you to revisit my adolescence. The department switchboard got a call twenty minutes ago from Tony Pirandello, Yummy's cousin. He wants to turn himself in."

"So let him. What am I, your spiritual advisor?" But something buzzed in the soles of my feet, and it wasn't the 455 under the hood. I hadn't turned the key.

"Cut the comedy. The offer came with a kicker. You're the man he asked to haul him in."

289

I dealt myself a cigarette and punched in the dash lighter. That was good for two minutes of introspection.

"Nice try," I said, when I had the butt burning. "We're a week short of April Fool's Day. How long since Alison Garland made the evening news?"

"We're still sitting on it. This is legit, Amos: It's Tony, not a nut looking for his fifteen minutes. He thinks you're the only man who'll make sure he gets jail instead of a tray downtown. He's calling us back at six."

I looked at my watch: 5:27. "Where are you, the precinct?"

"Where am I ever? How soon can you get here?"

"That's me going through the metal detector." I twisted the key, yanked the lever into first, and stepped on the pedal. The rumble became a roar and the world tore away from under my tailbone. I scraped the dust off a hundred fenders switching lanes, got the royal fanfare from as many horns. I waved off the one-finger salutes and tore all the teeth off the shifting gears. When Alderdyce called me Amos, I knew I had green lights all the way downtown.

# Twenty-Eight

The old second precinct, where Homicide hangs its holster, looks like a neighborhood high school — red brick, flat roof, and tinted windows — but it has a few more police officers hanging around. None of them paid me much attention as I left security and headed for the inspector's office.

I detoured when I spotted Alderdyce standing in his shirtsleeves in front of a large-scale city map mounted on a wall. The shirtsleeves were heavy linen and dusty pink, the tie clipped to the placket liquid silver. Dressing like a cop only gets you so high on the blue ladder, and he hadn't come out of the training course intending to retire with the rank of sergeant. He held a black coffee mug embossed with the gold seal of the police department.

I said, "If you're looking for a place to spend your vacation, you should look beyond Eight Mile Road."

He pointed the rim of his mug at a cluster of flag magnets west of downtown. "Each one of those is a city bus driver assaulted by passengers for showing up late at the stop. Half the fleet's in the garage waiting for parts, but the mechanics don't have to deal with the public. Yesterday I caught a detective third-grade putting together an office pool on when a driver would fall into Homicide's jurisdiction. Is it just us? Do they race plague bacilli at Henry Ford Hospital to break up the monotony?"

"I wouldn't know. I always take my gunshot wounds to Detroit Receiving."

"Still being tailed?" He turned away from the map, blowing steam off his coffee.

"That turned out to be my imagination. Yummy talking yet?"

"What do you think? He lawyered up five minutes after we booked him."

"Where was Pirandello calling from?"

"It just came up 'cellular call.' Burn phone, probably."

"Does Yummy know?"

"No, and we're going to keep it that way as long as we can. Tony's not connected — kid-stuff priors, no jail time — so maybe he'll cave if there isn't a lawyer waiting when we bring him in. I told him we'll deal if he rolls over on his cousin, but he's got the family allergy when it comes to cops. Figures a civilian witness will keep him from being shot resisting arrest."

"Why me specifically?"

"He didn't say, but if Yummy was shadowing you they must've talked about you. You're not known to spray a lot of information around. That's a virtue in their world."

"Everyone else's, too, except cops. Where am I taking his call?"

"My hole. I shouldn't have to tell you to keep him on the line as long as you can. I've got it set up with the gadget-jockeys at Thirteen Hundred to start triangulating the second you pick up. I'd rather we handled the delivery. He might change his mind later."

His office always looked like someone had tipped it up by one corner and given it a shake, then set it back down. The pictures and citations hung at all angles on the walls and the duty rosters and arrest reports were piled on every flat surface sticking out every which way. Either it was a psychological ploy to put suspects at a disadvantage or he was just a slob.

"Cup of coffee'd be nice," I said as he was closing the door.

"I smelled the liquor before I saw you.

You used to wait till *Sesame Street* came on."

"It was work-related. People get suspicious when they're drinking and you're not. Is it a machine, or do I just toss something into the kitty?"

"Kitty. Over by the windows, between the thumbscrews and the iron maiden." He glanced at the clock. "Six minutes. Don't stop for cream and sugar."

"That stuff just slows down the poison." I went out, stuffed a buck into a jar the medical examiner used to park vital organs, stacked two cardboard cups for insulation, and poured out a stream of black liquid thick enough to spread with a knife. It might have been steeping since the midnight-to-eight shift. Alderdyce's phone was ringing when I let myself back into the office.

"Early," I said.

"Scared. I'm starting to think you're right about somebody setting them up. Otherwise Yummy'd be offering to deal." He picked up.

I cleared a spot in the mare's nest on the desk to set down my cup. There was no place to sit except the inspector's lap, so I remained standing while he established who was on the other end. He put the phone on speaker and laid the receiver on top of a picture of Boris Badenov from the Identi-Kit.

"This Walker?" I recognized the voice from the one time I'd heard it before. It needed more breath.

"Yeah, Tony. Okay if I call you Tony?"

"Who gives a shit? You the guy busted into my place with the cop?"

"We didn't bust in, but yeah."

"Listen, I don't know nothing about that dead woman. We was out all day. We just got in and saw the stiff when you showed up."

"Then you've got nothing to worry about. Come in and sign a statement throwing it all on Yummy's back."

"Listen, Marty almost shit worse'n I did when we saw what was in that bed. He can't fool me. I know him since we was kids. Somebody planted it there."

"Who'd do that, Tony?"

"Forget that. I know the cops are trying to trace this. You know Fort Wayne?"

I rolled my eyes. "I've heard of it."

"The car warehouse. Eleven o'clock to-night. We'll talk, and if I like what I hear, I'll come in with you."

"Is it all right if I come alone?"

"Joker. I see you throwing more than one shadow, I'm out of there." He wanted to bang the receiver in my ear, but cells don't understand drama. There was just a click.

"That was a relief," I said. "I was afraid he'd say midnight."

Alderdyce snatched up the receiver, took it off speaker, dialed. "Yeah, me. Anything? Shit." He got a nice satisfying bang.

"We were talking about two different Fort Waynes," I said. "I don't know anything about a car warehouse."

"Me neither. I thought all they kept there was cannons and busted beer bottles." He picked up again, called 1300 back, identified himself, and asked for the duty sergeant. "Who patrols Fort Wayne? No, not if you can answer the question. Is there a car warehouse on that beat? *Ware*house." He cupped the mouthpiece. "Dumb son of a bitch." He listened and took away his hand. "No shit? I thought I knew everything about this town. Much obliged."

I sipped from my cup while he was getting off the line. "What don't you know about this town, besides where to buy decent coffee?"

"That we got more cars than we know what to do with."

"That? Hell, I knew that."

He told me the rest.

"I didn't know *that*," I said.

# TWENTY-NINE

"It's worked before," I said.

"Track record isn't so good with wise-guys."

"Pirandello's not a wiseguy. He's a cousin, three times removed: Kiddy priors, you said, nothing heavy. He was just Yummy's port in a storm. Ouch!"

"Sorry." The tech taping the wire to my chest had jerked a hair.

Alderdyce watched the operation from the sucker's side of the desk in his office. I had the chair this time. There were shadows in the corners. It was 9:45 P.M. I'd gone home to catch a couple of hours' sleep. The inspector had not, unless he'd put on the same clothes he'd worn earlier, which would have made him someone other than John Alderdyce. When the boy in the Steve Urkel glasses and Sonny Crockett whiskers finished and put away his cutters and extra wire in a tackle box, his superior slid something out of a manila envelope and unfolded it on top of the debris on the desk. When he was through it covered the surface and hung down over the edges like a table-cloth. "Commit this to memory. Try not to touch it. It goes back to the Historical Society in the morning."

I looked at the brown brittle paper. "Is there a treasure map on the back?"

"Just look it over, okay? They don't burn as many security lights as they used to on account of the economy, so you want to know where you're going. If you dent a Hup-mobile, you bought it."

"I've got a flashlight."

"Try not to use it too much. You might spook Tony."

"He's not a bat."

The sheet he'd spread out was the floor plan of a 96,000-square-foot building. It had been a secret from me only that after-noon, and I'd spent most of my life within fifteen minutes of it.

"It's separate from the barracks," he said, "built on the old parade ground. It was used to store weapons and ammo during World War Two. Now the Historical Society parks its antique cars there when they're not on display in the museum on Woodward."

I buttoned my shirt. "I can't believe I

never heard of it."

"No reason you should. It isn't open to the public, and I guess they'd like to keep it a secret because their security's spread thin. They put the cars up in some sort of glorified bubble wrap, rotate 'em in and out of the displays to keep the museum from getting stale. I practically had to threaten the curator with a warrant to get him to admit it's there: Hello, we patrol the block.

"When he finally came through, he found Tony's name in a personnel file. Tony worked maintenance there until they downsized. Either somebody forgot to collect his keys or he had copies made. I had a hell of a time talking the curator out of relocating museum security to the warehouse. He was afraid Tony'd fire up a Packard and drive it out the main gate. He has the impression I'm assigning officers there to protect the inventory while we conduct an investigation."

"I wonder how he got that impression."

Alderdyce arranged his features into a frown. It was like a landslide on one of the faces on Mt. Rushmore. "I wish we had a less cockeyed plan."

"So do I. It's got whiskers, but there's a reason for that. It works sometimes. I could learn hypnosis at home or take a crash course in sodium pentothol, but Tony didn't give us that kind of time. He's got something to trade or he'd still be running. Either he's afraid of something out there or he thinks he's in a frame. The only way to get anything useful out of him is to jack up the fear."

"The Early Response Team's already in place. They're parked five blocks east, around the corner on Summit. Your go word is 'decaffeinated.' Three minutes after they hear it over your wire, you'll be up to your neck in officers, so make sure he's un-armed."

"They know enough not to shoot me?"

"They're pros. You don't make ERT with-out a sharpshooter medal and good fitness reports up the yin-yang."

"Seems to me one of those pros shot a little girl last year."

"They've got descriptions of both of you, your ID photo, and copies of Tony's security picture from the Historical Society. I'd reach for the sky anyway, and try to look in-nocent."

"Who came up with 'decaffeinated'?"

"Me. It's one of those words you can't mistake for something else."

"What's wrong with 'Geronimo'?"

"It's been used recently; Tony might

tumble. Also it's hard to work into a conversation."

"Okay. Let me do my homework."

He left while I scanned the floor plan. It was the size of a road map, drawn to scale, and smelled mildewed, with brown spots like an old man's skin. The warehouse was a huge square cavern partitioned with open wood framing into rooms, each the size of a ten-bedroom house. The automobiles in storage would be parked in rows like in an underground garage. Why Tony Pirandello had chosen it for the meet was easy to figure out. The echo factor would alert him if anything more than a single pair of feet entered the building. He could duck in and out among the cars and avoid an army of cops for hours. He knew all the exits, all the nooks and crawl spaces; it would be like stalking a flea in a horse barn. Sooner or later, boredom and slowed reflexes would open a hole in the net and the flea would slip through.

The layout didn't need much memorizing: All the rooms were identical in shape and square footage and accessed either through broad framed openings or simply by stepping between the uprights, provided they weren't spaced too close together. I concentrated on the exits. The windows, which would be the factory type, gridded into square panes by iron frames, were set too high to climb through. I hoped none of the doors leading outside had been boarded up or bricked in; the date of the plan preceded Pearl Harbor.

When Alderdyce came back through the door I was putting on my suitcoat, which gave me an idea. "Tell the boys with grappling hooks I'll be in shirtsleeves, white. If Tony learned anything from his cousin, he'll be dressed in dark clothes."

"Freeze your ass off."

"Keep me alert, and maybe out of friendly fire. Anyway, it'll be climate-controlled. In this town we treat cars better than we treat people."

He stared at me a moment, fists balled at his sides — at ease, for him. "How's your bad leg?"

"We've got rain or snow coming tomorrow. That answer your question?"

"I should've asked how your running game is. It might come to that, if he's as spooky as he sounded."

"I popped a couple of pills on my way in. Prescription ibuprofen," I said, when his brows went up. "I sent the Vicodin packing a year ago."

"Going in armed?"

"You're damn right I am. Amateur fugitives have twitchy trigger fingers."

"Say that three times fast," he said.

I drove my own car, past the armored bread truck parked nose-out with no lights showing where Summit dead-ended on West Jefferson, men in night goggles and Kevlar presumably crouched inside. I didn't turn my head for a better look; I'd had my mind read too many times to direct attention to my backup parachute. To my left, a ragged hangnail moon cast multiple scalloped reflections on the Detroit River, charging hell-bent for leather toward Lake Erie. It was the mildest night of the spring so far, flirting with forty degrees, and the warm-up had created a low fog that rolled along the choppy surface and soft-filtered the lights of Windsor on the Canadian side. Dense in patches, it threw my headlights back at me like a gray wall. I slowed down to watch for deer and the occasional wandering homeless.

At such times, a route you've traveled nearly every day for years becomes foreign territory. Distances seem greater and nothing looks familiar. Noises travel, as across flat water: The shrill hoarse bugling-elk siren of an emergency vehicle clearing traffic

303

sounded so close I automatically started drifting toward the shoulder to make way, but there were no flashers in sight. It could have come from Highland Park, five miles north.

After an hour on the road — it was probably ten minutes — I came within view of the Fort Wayne barracks, sitting on what was left of sixty-two acres of well-armed garrison, now roughly six blocks square. I saw its six chimneys first, then the elongated building itself, four stories high including a gabled attic, with tall windows arranged in rows like regiments. With the moon glimmering on its whitewashed brick and its foundation appearing to float on a layer of ground fog it looked as peaceful as a cemetery at midnight, and why not? It had stood on that spot since 1851, and so far no shot had ever been fired in its defense or in siege.

It had been commissioned partly to defend the border against raiders from Canada, but mostly to put pork in some congressmen's cellars: The old-fashioned square nails had cost as much as a dollar apiece in the ledgers. Soldiers had drilled there for nearly a century, but not even the Civil War put it to use for its original purpose. During World War II it had served as a recruitment center and storage for tanks built by Chrysler. Now it was a military museum maintained by the Detroit Historical Society, with armaments and uniforms on display dating back to before the War of 1812, and its grounds were routinely swept of partiers and vagrants. There were more of those than history buffs these days. Because its mettle has never been challenged, some locals believe that as long as Fort Wayne remains standing, no outside invader will ever threaten the city.

Which leaves us with only the people inside to worry about.

Beyond the building, a darker construction carved a black hole out of the lights across the river. At first it looked dark inside, but as I crept closer, the speedometer barely registering, I saw low-level security bulbs glowing feebly behind high-placed windows.

I found a three-cornered niche on the edge of the roadway, a speed-trap feature, and backed into it. The clock on the dash read 10:38. I switched off the ignition and listened to the engine clicking as it cooled in the damp air. I was breathing shallowly. I sucked in deep to break the seal. Then I ditched my suitcoat and grabbed my flashlight, a big one encased in black rubber I'd bought at a police auction after the Malice

305

Green killing had banned them from the equipment room; it was as long as my forearm and heavier than a blackjack. I pointed it at the floor under the dash and snapped it on for a second to check the bulb and batteries. It was bright enough to double as a flare in case I needed backup, illuminating the underbellies of clouds when pointed skyward.

Getting out, I hung it on my belt by its clip, clamped the Chief's Special in its holster into place so its grip nestled in its permanent hollow to the right of my spine, and dropped my shirttail over it. A sharp little breeze from Ontario chilled me to the bone. I thought of putting my coat back on, but it was too late to tell the Early Response Team of the change; I didn't want to use the wire in case Tony Pirandello was within earshot.

I hoped the wire was working. Modern technology was moving so fast it had passed the problems inherent in skin-to-ear transmission right by.

I rotated my arms to boost circulation — carefully, to avoid dislodging the tape on my chest. After that I couldn't think of anything else to keep me from going into the heart of darkness, so I stepped away from the friendly shelter of my automobile and went looking for a chain-link fence to scale. I wasn't too old for that yet, no sir.

# THIRTY

The fence was eight feet high, the gate secured with a chain and padlock. Security had the only key to that one, and there'd been no time to locate the personnel in charge of it. A local recession that predated the national one by ten years had made continuous on-foot surveillance impractical, so the guards rotated on an alternating schedule, leaving regular patrols to the squad-car cops assigned to the neighborhood. This was an off night, as Tony would know, even if the schedule had changed since his time; few people leave their inside friendships behind when they leave a job. I assumed there were cameras, but they're only as good as their blind spots, and he'd know about those too.

Locks aren't my strong suit. I can pop a latch with a credit card, but then so can a high school freshman. Picking them is a special skill. Even then they don't slip as easily as they do in movies. Straight from the factory no two are alike, same as snowflakes and fingerprints, and the longer they're in use the more the tumblers and keys wear into grooves unique to them. In any case I hadn't the time to fool with it. I started climbing.

From bottom to top took longer than it would have ordinarily; I was carrying extra weight and that damn wire had me worried. Letting myself down on the other side went a little faster, but I didn't want to leap the last three feet because of all of the above and a bullet I'd taken through a leg years ago, gone but not forgotten. The cold and the climb already had it throbbing. Even hospital-grade ibuprofen is no substitute for addictive painkillers.

Back at ground level I waited another minute for my eyes to adjust to the darkness inside the compound, then started toward the warehouse at an easy walk, as if I were strolling around the block in my own neighborhood. If Tony was watching, I didn't want to skulk like an uninvited guest.

The building had been pale brick before dark paint was added — red, probably, by daylight, to bring it up to colonial code. But there'd been no room in the budget for a fresh coat, so it had peeled away in leprous patches. A steel fire door, painted once also in a wood-grain pattern that wouldn't fool anyone after seasons of sun and rain and snow and ice and lead-based auto exhaust, had a modern brass lock. Just for fun I tried the thumb latch, and when it opened the door without resistance I put away the key the curator had provided, stepped inside, and yanked it shut behind me to keep from silhouetting myself against the pale moonlight. I crab-walked to one side to get away from the door. Doors attract bullets, and Tony might have changed his mind about turning himself in.

Canister lamps recessed in the ceiling twenty feet overhead shed light that didn't quite reach the floor, a single slab of concrete with a smooth surface, sealed with something that made it easier to sweep. But it reflected off curved enameled fenders, the rims and glass of bulbous headlights, and great plastic blisters that protected the historic automobiles from dust and moisture like the boy in the bubble. Bug-eyed, perched high on their chassis, their narrow tires the only thing connecting them to a natural element, they looked like prehistoric insects preserved in amber.

There was light enough to proceed without using the flash, but I was glad I had it.

Its heavy butt inside its steel-and-rubber skin bumped comfortingly against my thigh, the next best thing to an encouraging pat on the shoulder. If the .38 failed me, I had a bludgeon for backup. I walked down a wide center aisle, my feet on the cement making scraping sounds that whispered in the rafters. As I walked I glanced to right and left, not to admire the artifacts of the Industrial Age, but to look for someone crouching between their rear and front bumpers. The place couldn't have been furnished better for ambush if they'd put a renegade Apache in charge.

"Tony?" I used my indoor voice, but it bounded around the room like the sounds from a lively game of basketball. I stopped until it quit, listening for others, but no one answered. I moved on.

Past a phaeton that looked as if someone had slapped a motor on a frontier buck-board, with a spring seat and wooden-spoked wheels. Past an experimental model Ford Mustang, shaped like a dinghy, with a candy apple–red finish and white leather seats. Past a square bottle-green Model T sedan, painted before Henry Ford discovered that Japan black dried faster, speeding up the assembly line. Past the inverted fishbowl of an AMC Pacer. Past Dodges,

Pierce-Arrows, curved-dash Oldsmobiles, Buick Super 8s, Willys Jeeps, Terraplanes, tortoise-shaped Nashes, torpedo-nosed Studebakers, cracker-box Edisons; Kaiser-Frazers, Hudson Hornets, Stutz Bearcats; concept cars that had never touched pavement, *Titanic*-size disasters that never should have, a black '49 Mercury shaped like Buck Rogers' spaceship. Those were the ones I could identify. Fleets of makes and models I couldn't. I suppose there was just one of each, but the wildly contrasting body shapes and unfamiliar insignia and kaleidoscope colors and the intoxicating smell of Turtle Wax and immaculate rubber had me dizzy and seeing everything in multiples. All put up in plastic, like giant Matchbox toys in FAO Schwartz.

In the heart of Detroit, just minutes from the sprawling Ford River Rouge plant, the Fisher Building, the Renaissance Center, and Grand Circus Park, where I'd spent most of my adolescence and all of my adulthood. I couldn't believe I hadn't known the place existed. Some swell detective.

"Walker?"

Even as it echoed throughout that barn, that tight shallow voice might have been a hallucination. The place was that unreal.

I stopped. I couldn't tell where the call

had come from. "Yeah, Tony."

"You alone?"

"Cut the small talk. You've got ears."

"You packing?"

I'd slid my hand under my shirttail to rest on the butt of the revolver. "No. You?"

"No. I never mess with 'em."

Couple of liars talking in the gloom. "Come out and let's stop shouting," I said. "All this river air is giving me a sore throat."

There was a long stretch of silence. Then air stirred ahead and to my left and Anthony Pirandello stepped out of the shadows between a pair of wooden uprights and stopped with a ragtop seven-passenger Lincoln on one side of him and a fin-tailed Chevy on the other.

In the dusky light he resembled his cousin less than he had in the apartment. He hadn't Yummy's belly or of course the facial surgical scar, and it struck me then that without it the family features had no character at all. Both men needed haircuts; Tony's showed no gray yet. He wore a dirty gray sweatshirt, baggy slacks, some kind of sneakers, and a zip-front jacket two sizes shy of closing in front. I figured he'd snatched it from someone's basket in a Laundromat. He hadn't had time to grab outerwear when he'd fled his place and Alison Garland's corpse on the bed. Shadows lay in the folds of his face like dust on old bunting.

He stood half-turned my way with his left arm out of sight. I was standing the same way, only it was my right hand hidden behind my back. Mirror images, both heeled.

"You look beat, Tony. Been sleeping?"

"Now who's making the small talk? How many cops you got surrounding the place?"

"Oh, pretty much all of 'em. You're the flavor of the month on every bulletin board in the jurisdiction."

Another quiet stretch. "You wearing a wire?"

"Uh-huh." I could almost hear the ERT on the other end grinding his teeth. "You didn't say I couldn't, so I just figured."

"It's okay. I got nothing to say I wouldn't say in court. Where they keeping Marty?"

"County jail." I watched my breath curl in the weak shaft of light from the canister above my head. The place wasn't as warm as I'd expected, but I wasn't feeling the cold. Adrenaline's as good as a Union Suit in a pinch. "He rolled over on you, Tony. Yummy did. Tagged you for the Garland girl's murder."

"Bullshit. I don't know no Garlands."

"It doesn't matter if you didn't know her name. He says you shot her and put her in the apartment so he'd go down for it. He's the one with the record."

"*Bull*shit!" It ricocheted off every hard surface like a bullet. I tightened my grip on the Chief's Special.

"It checks, Tony. The inspector and I were up to our chins in uniforms almost before he could call it in. Anonymous tip, Dispatch said. He'd have had just enough time to slip out on some excuse before they came and put the collar on you."

"When'd he make the call, smart guy? We went to a bar and came back together. We were never more'n two feet apart the whole time we was out."

"Which bar?"

"How the hell should I know? Who looks at the sign? The one on the corner, where I always go. It might not even have a name. You might've noticed I don't live in Bloomfield Hills."

"The cops'll check it out. The bartender or someone might remember if you were the Siamese twins you say you were. Yummy's crowding fifty. The bladder wouldn't be what it used to be. Maybe he stepped down the hall to squirt. This one of those places with a pay phone near the toilets?"

"Who uses pay phones anymore? He's got a —" He stopped himself.

"So he had a cell. Even better. Tony, he sold you out. The cops have his statement on paper and on DVD: available soon in a store near you."

"It's a lie either way. You know what he said when he saw that stiff laying there? 'That bitch!'; that's what. That sound like a man that expected to find what he found?"

That one stopped the conversation for a moment. It was becoming surreal.

"What bitch was that, the dead girl? He blamed her for getting herself killed and landing in his apartment?"

"*My* apartment. How the hell should I know? Maybe it was another bitch. The one that put her there."

I felt the cold then.

For a space I couldn't remember the go word. Then it came back. "Your story doesn't mean anything here, Tony. It'll tell better downtown, where the cops can sort it out. Your record's better than Yummy's; that counts for something. Isn't that what we're here for, so you can come out of the woods?"

"My sheet's clean. Unlawful driving away of an automobile, that's what they tagged me for, twenty years ago, when I was a kid. I did my probation. Then five hundred hours of community service for laying out my foreman at Chrysler a couple of years later. Not even a littering beef since. That sound like a killer to you?"

"Not to me, and not to them either. Isn't that what I said? Give me the piece, Tony. You don't want to be holding it when the cops come. They might get the wrong idea."

"I told you I'm unarmed."

"Me, too. We didn't know each other so well then."

"Drop yours first. Then we'll see."

The inside of a cheek got chewed. It was mine.

"Okay, I'm easy." If he'd brought me there to kill me there'd have been smoke in the air already. I slid out the .38, slow as the tide. Holding it awkwardly by the middle, I bent down, laid it on the slick floor, and slid it shuttle-fashion a couple of yards up the aisle. I straightened up and waited.

A couple of seconds went past, tricked out as minutes. Then he stirred. Out came a .32 semiautomatic, a pawnshop piece with black plastic grips. It came to rest a moment later, nearly touching the revolver. He rose from his crouch.

"Better, no?" I said. "Cold in here. Let's

go down to the precinct and grab a cup of coffee. What do you like, regular or — ?"

I can't remember if I said the word. If I did, it was drowned out by a report that rang off the sheet metal on both sides of the aisle like a cherry bomb. The plastic bubble shielding the gangster-type touring car to Pirandello's left collapsed slowly, with a whistle of escaping air; the bullet had clipped it on its way into Tony's heart.

# THIRTY-ONE

I was on the floor between the shot and the echo, rolling toward our guns. The one my hand found first was Tony's little Saturday night special, but there was no time to shop around. I reversed directions, rolled onto my left shoulder, and fired at nothing: In that echo chamber I had no idea where the slug had come from, but it's only polite to answer, especially when the shooter has the range down pat and you need to keep him busy between shots. The little .32 made a sharp little bark like a terrier, hurting my ears even worse than the first report, loud as it was, and as unexpected.

A little inquisitive squeak of air brought my attention back to Tony. He was just beginning to fall, with his hand halfway to his chest and his knees bending and turning; descending, like a dancer sinking to the bottom of Swan Lake. I thought he'd've been horizontal long before that, but time slows when you're scrambling for your life. I figured less than three seconds had elapsed since we were standing facing each other.

A guy like Tony couldn't maintain that kind of grace all the way to the finish. One of his shoes slipped on the glazed surface of the concrete and he flopped the remaining two feet like a sack of mail. Something rattled like a broken fan blade and then he was quiet, as quiet as the ancient automobiles resting in their cocoons.

Something struck the floor near my right knee, followed instantly by the roar of the discharge. It was close enough to pepper my pants with bits of cement. I got my knees under me and pushed off, chest down, sliding into home base in the shadow of a Chrysler truck with bloated fenders. There I managed to push against the resistance of the inflated bubble and lay flat under the broad running board, using it as a shield as I tried to pin down the source of the shooting. I couldn't rely on my hearing to separate the noise from its echo, so I concentrated on my vision.

I unclipped the big flashlight from my belt and flung it into the aisle between the rows of cars. It struck down at the halfway point and rolled in the direction of Tony's corpse. A bullet kicked up dust an inch short of the flash. I saw the muzzle flare then, in the same instant I heard the shot, high up the wall at the end of the aisle nearest the entrance. The shooter had chosen higher ground, like any good pro. Not on top of a car; the rounded air-filled protective wrapping would've made the footing dicey at best. A platform of some kind.

I had the little pistol leveled already, propped on my elbow on the floor with only my arm and my head poking out from under the running board. I sighted in on the fading phosphorescence of the flare, fired. Someone yelped, something clattered to the floor. Something heavier hit just behind that, a body falling or someone leaping off his shooting stand.

It was a leap, because then I heard rapid footsteps. I tightened my grip on the .32, leveling it parallel with the floor, but then the footsteps got quieter and I knew they were going away. After that I didn't hear anything, because the world was a confusion of sirens.

I'd forgotten about the wire, which had picked up the gunshots. I never got the chance to say "Decaffeinated."

*"It's a lie either way. You know what he said when he saw that stiff laying there? 'That*

321

*bitch!'; that's what. That sound like a man that expected to find what he found?"*

*"What bitch was that, the dead girl?"*

We were in the curator's office in the military museum, which smelled of mildewed wool and dry rot. Alderdyce had gotten keys to the barracks and the office along with the one he'd given me to get into the warehouse; how he'd anticipated needing the room was his secret. If he'd missed a step in thirty years on the job, I wasn't around to see it. He stood, I sat, in a folding metal chair someone had borrowed from high school band. I smoked a contraband cigarette and enjoyed the heat, even if the thermostat was set low for evening. I was still in shirtsleeves. I scratched my chest where the tape had been removed, along with a clump of hair.

The room looked as if someone was either moving in or moving out. Cardboard cartons were stacked in every corner and the chipboard desk was empty of everything except the .32 popgun and the gizmo replaying Anthony Pirandello's words and mine. Hearing a dead man speak is always unsettling, even in a place not already overpopulated with the ghosts of minutemen and Yankee volunteers.

We listened through the first gunshots,

then he replayed it all for the third time, his big fingers fumbling with the little buttons on the MP3 player or whatever it was. A tech with the Early Response Team had recorded it straight from my wire onto a disc or chip you could lose in a belly button. Smaller and tinnier is the new bigger and better.

"Do I really sound like that?" I asked when he finally turned it off. "I'm a baritone in my head."

"You didn't see anything. Maybe something in the muzzle flare? Black? White? Male? Female?"

"I was lucky to see the flare. Whatever it was, I think I winged it."

"Sounded like it. We'll know when the flack-jacket boys report. I'm not waiting for the weasels from the lab to finish their chow mein and ride in on their Segways."

He hated CSIs for some reason. Maybe he'd get over it when he had his own TV show.

He stared at the window. Only his reflection showed against the blackness outside. " 'That bitch!' What do you think he meant?"

"Maybe Alison Garland. You can get mad at a nail when it won't hammer in straight."

"You believe that?"

"The part about the nail."

"Who, then?"

I had a theory, but I didn't want to say it aloud and make it real. "That's what Yummy should have said: 'Who?' It's what anyone would say if he didn't recognize the corpse. He was surprised, all right, but that was because it didn't belong in that bed. He knew who it was, all right, and he knew who put her there."

"A partner?"

"Or an employer. The woman I'm thinking of doesn't go fifty-fifty with anyone."

"That again. You're turning into a conspiracy nut."

"I hope I am."

He picked up the little semiautomatic, popped out the magazine, ejected the cartridge from the barrel, and put it all back together. He paid as much attention to the operation as brushing his teeth; when you've spent most of your life around guns you make them as safe to handle as possible without thinking. He let it rest on his palm like a compass. "Not bad shooting, if you did hit anything. Tony wasn't the best judge of firearms."

"He was an amateur, like I said. That's why the trick worked. He didn't know Yummy well enough in his working life to know he didn't spill his guts easily."

"Not that you got anything out of him we can use."

"We got the one thing. There was more, which is why somebody followed him to the warehouse and took him out."

"Maybe they followed you. Maybe that Town Car crowd."

I still hadn't told him about the Israelis. "If they did, they changed vehicles. I don't think I was followed. It would've been hard to penetrate the place without being heard. The place echoed like Lou Gehrig's farewell speech. If anything, whoever it was was already in place when Tony showed up."

"Are you saying the police line was tapped?"

"It isn't impossible, but not necessarily. Any kid with a scanner can pick up a cell phone transmission. Or it could have been an educated guess. Tony's ties to the warehouse weren't a state secret. They might have had a plant in all the likely places he'd choose for a meet."

"How'd they know he wanted a meet?"

"He was scared. Of the two, he was the one most likely to strike a deal. They'd go after the bird in the bush and take out the one in hand at their leisure. I guess you've got the Swiss Guard surrounding Yummy by now."

He stretched, cracking every bone in his body. Since he was made mostly of bone it sounded like the skeleton dance. "We're calling it twenty-four-hour suicide surveillance, to keep the press from catching wind of a possible lead story. He sneezes, he'll get a gesundheit from five sides."

One of the ancient floorboards creaked outside the door. He asked who it was before the visitor could knock.

"Lieutenant Halley, Inspector. ERT."

He came in at Alderdyce's invitation, six-four in khakis and a vest that covered him from neck to groin. The long bill of his baseball cap cast a shadow past the tip of his nose in the overhead light. "Shooter fired from a staircase leading to the roof," he said, holding out a plastic snack bag containing three brass shells.

The inspector took it, held it so the light fell on the numbers stamped on the flanged ends. "What the hell fires a thirty caliber?"

"Walther P-38 comes to mind. Muzzle velocity trumps some larger rounds. Vic took one in the pump, looks like. Some bully shot in that light."

"Okay, *True Grit*. What else?" Alderdyce handed back the evidence.

"Your civilian nicked the shooter. Some

blood spots, but the pattern petered out after a few yards."

"What, no compliment to the civilian?" I asked. "I was firing at an upward angle, and the light was even worse for me. It didn't reach the walls."

But I wasn't in the room for Lieutenant Halley. "He went out a rear exit, scaled a chain-link on the river side. Gravel there, no footprints. But we got these between the warehouse and the fence." He stashed the bag of shells and came up with a digital camera from another pocket, a red Canon the size of a business-card case. Alderdyce and I huddled around the tiny screen as Halley pushed a button. Waffled tracks in loose sand diagonaled across the screen, spaced out in a running pattern. Halley or someone had thought to place a new yellow pencil next to one of the footprints.

"Size four?" The inspector's question went up on the end like the uncertain answer to a tough question.

"Maybe four and a half. Boy's-size sneakers."

"Or a small woman's," I said.

Both men looked at me, lighting a fresh cigarette with a flame I couldn't keep steady.

Alderdyce dismissed the lieutenant. When

the floorboards outside stopped complaining, he said, "Charlotte Sing's not the only petite person in the world. Anyway, she doesn't do her own heavy lifting."

"She would if she's running out of help. The world police agencies have her hemmed in from three sides. If she chooses the fourth, any one of the Asian nations would execute her without trial."

He drew out another folding chair, sat, and rested his forearms on the desk. "Fire away. What's her game?"

"I'm guessing, so don't tank me for withholding evidence. Suppose she was planning to use Elysian Fields for another drug-fueled plan to destroy the West, but before she could get it up and running, the manager she'd hired got his fingers into the medical marijuana scam, drawing official attention. So she kills him, or has him killed. Then I showed up, asking questions about one of Elysian's customers. She puts Yummy Mondadori on my trail to find out what I'm after. He finds out, I don't know how yet. Then she brings in a ringer for the customer to end my interest. But Detroit cops raid the place, which spoils it for her uses once and for all. The plan's on autopilot by this time, the ringer, Alison Garland, can't be recalled. When Alison reports it didn't work,

Yummy kills her, probably leaving her where she fell, or the body wouldn't have been so easy for Sing to scoop it up and dump it in his cousin's apartment where he's staying, then make an anonymous call to the cops so he'll be tagged."

"Why take the chance he'd talk? Why not just drop the hammer on him?"

"I said I'm guessing, filling in the holes after I stumble into them." I put out the cigarette against the metal seat of my chair. "Her picture's in every police station in the free world, and there are surveillance cameras all over the city. Maybe she can't move during the day, but she couldn't wait for sundown. If it made perfect sense it wouldn't be a hunch. She knows Yummy's reputation or she wouldn't have recruited him. She could be reasonably certain he'd keep his mouth shut even if he knew he'd been betrayed, and take his pound of flesh on his own after he made bail or a good mob attorney got him off scot-free. Clearly he doesn't know who he's dealing with. But meanwhile he's on ice, so she can move to Square Two."

"What's that?"

"Who knows? Intellectually speaking, she's out of my league, and I don't know anyone loony enough to predict what crackpot plan B she's got in mind."

"I don't like it," he said. "I'm always suspicious when a theory fits the facts. All we need now is evidence."

I almost said, *I think I know where we can get it.* I was tired, and I have a bad habit of talking in my sleep.

# THIRTY-TWO

I woke up famished, rare event. All that talk
about breakfast being the most important
meal of the day clashes with all the talk
about not eating when you're not hungry.
But there's nothing like surviving a gun
battle for jacking up the appetite. My
stomach was doing cartwheels, happy to be
secreting all its juices instead of spilling
them out through a hole.

I'd slept, after a fashion. I kept hearing
gunshots ringing off bare brick walls, seeing
muzzle flashes and trying to return fire, but
when the trigger didn't pull I looked down
at the gun in my hand, and it was a museum
piece, like the flintlocks and Springfield
rifles in the military museum; the parts were
all fused solid. I kept waking up from that
one, then sliding right back in, and then I
didn't want to go back to sleep, so I thought
a hole into the bedroom ceiling until there
was enough light to show me the little

hairline cracks in the plaster.

The telephone rang while I was frying eggs in bacon grease. I slid them onto a plate to finish cooking on their own and picked up in the living room.

"You didn't call, so I thought I'd call you. This is the postfeminist era, right?" It was Smoke.

"Been boning up on the Mesozoic, I see." I yawned it.

"Am I calling too early?"

"No, I'm just shot." I chuckled.

"What's funny?"

"Nothing at all. I'm giddy. I was up late." My stomach growled. "Hang on a minute."

I laid down the receiver, went back into the kitchen, topped off my cup from the pot, came back carrying it and the eggs, and sat in the armchair, cradling the receiver between my head and my shoulder as I ate.

"What's for breakfast?" she asked.

"Unborn chickens stewed in cholesterol. You?"

"I never eat before noon."

"Good for you."

"What are you doing today?"

"Working."

"Oh." Pouty word. "I thought I might talk you into playing hooky and spending the day with me."

"Maybe this afternoon."

"What's so important you're up at the butt-crack of dawn?"

"I need to check something."

"Come with?"

"Sorry."

"Dangerous?"

"God, I hope not. But the less people know about it, the better it is for everyone all around."

"Now you've piqued my interest. I'll be quiet, I promise. You won't even know I'm there."

"Like hell I won't."

She made a throaty sound I felt in my testicles. "Well, maybe part of the time."

"Rain check."

"Hey, mister, I'm —"

"Lay off, Amber Dawn."

"Whoa! Serious crap."

"Call me after you eat." I said good-bye through a mouthful and hung up. Shaving later after my shower, I looked at my reflection above the sink. "Stud."

Before I went out I gave the .38 a good cleaning, turned the cylinder and dry-fired it to make sure all the moving parts worked. It had had some rough handling the night before, and the thing about nightmares is they come true more often than sweet dreams. I put in fresh loads and went out into what promised to be the first decent day of spring, with the sun turning the frost on the winter-killed lawn into dew. I thought I heard a bird singing, but it turned out to be a sanitation truck backing up in the next block.

It was still too early for guest activity at the Book-Cadillac Hotel. A vacuum whined in the lobby and the clerk behind the desk was doing his morning organizing in slo-mo. He didn't look up as I crossed to the elevators.

There were four of them, three standing open. I didn't think anything of it at the time. Even in the Motor City there's always an early riser getting set to go out for a run.

I got out on the floor where the agents from GOLEM had brought me from the car wash. Their room was to the left, but I turned right. A sharp stubborn stench clung to the constantly recirculating air in the hallway. It was like a burnt match held close to the nostrils, only not quite. It's not quite like anything but what it is.

The elevator next to the one I'd used stood with its doors open; they have electric eyes now to keep them from closing when there's an obstruction. I recognized the tan suitcoat on the back of the man who lay between them with one arm outside the car. A carton of unfiltered Camels lay just outside his reach, one end sticking out of the plastic drugstore bag in his hand.

The sulphur smell was stronger as I approached. Captain Asa Leibowitz lay on his chest with his head turned to one side, a tired, baggy profile against the sculptured carpet. His other hand was nowhere near his revolver, an Israeli knock-off similar to my Smith & Wesson but chambered for nine-millimeter, stuck in a clip on his belt where his coattail had fallen away from it. It was much smaller than his partner's Desert Eagle, but it packed plenty of punch, when you had the chance to use it.

He hadn't. The car had stopped, the doors had opened, and someone had been standing there waiting. There were no stains on the back of his coat. No exit wound meant a relatively small caliber. Well, it had been effective against Tony Pirandello at much greater range.

The skin of his neck was still warm. I thought at first I'd found something going on in the carotid, but that was just my own rapid pulse bouncing off dead tissue.

# THIRTY-THREE

I frisked him and found his key card tucked between U.S. and Israeli currency in a square wallet he carried in his hip pocket.

There was no time to waste. I didn't know who might have heard the shot or how long it would take him to decide he hadn't dreamed it and call the desk, and the hotel was too respectable to put off calling the law after security investigated. I'd missed the killer by minutes, or I'd be hearing sirens already. We'd passed each other while I was on the way up.

Stepping lively, I turned the corner — and stopped in front of the Israelis' door with the key card pointed at the slot. The smell of burnt powder was nearly as strong as it had been in front of the elevator. Instinctively I looked at my feet. Something yellow glittered between fibers in the carpet; an empty brass shell. I didn't pick it up to look at it. I knew it would belong to a .30-caliber weapon.

Something was wrong with the glass peephole. All the others on that floor reflected light from the sconces in the hallway, but this one was dark. I settled the point by sticking my finger through it. No glass.

I knew what had happened then. I could map it out. I drew the Chief's Special, knowing I wouldn't need it but glad to feel its solid grip, tripped the lock with the card, and wheeled inside with the door to avoid being framed in the opening, just like swinging on a garden gate.

All the lamps were on. I smelled the humidity of the shower; that pair was strong on personal hygiene. But Major Lazara Dorn was fully dressed, in what I assume was the same suit she'd worn when she got the drop on me in the car wash, a smaller number than Leibowitz's but from the same lot. She'd had it cleaned and pressed, but it did no justice to the graceful lines of her slender body. She lay on her back, in her stockinged feet, her coat and blouse rucked up to expose a narrow navel in a flat belly, her big semiautomatic lying two feet from her hand where it had landed when she let go. She'd been cautious enough to bring it along when she answered a knock at the door, but unwise enough to look through the peephole to see who was on the other side, just as she had when room service came my first time there. This time the visitor had fired through the hole, straight into her right eye. Her head was turned that direction so I didn't see the empty socket. I let it stay that way. I thought of her eyes, gray-blue with no mascara on the lashes.

I didn't hang around long enough to look around. I hadn't time, and there wasn't any point. The killer wouldn't have entered the room, but gone directly to the elevator and waited for Leibowitz to return with Dorn's cigarettes. It had to have been in that order. An ejected shell meant a semiautomatic, a self-contained firearm, unlike a leaky revolver; all the noise would come out the end of the barrel, therefore inside the room, where it would be muffled from the neighbors. Assuming a suppressor wasn't used, the second report, in an open hallway, might have drawn attention, requiring a quick exit on the part of the shooter.

That part was confirmed when I opened the door and heard the elevator bell ring on that floor. Whoever had called the desk had taken a few moments to decide the noise he'd heard was real, then several more to decide to do something about it. I eased the door into its frame until the latch caught, then went the other direction and took the stairs to the lobby, following the same escape route as the killer. At ground level I wiped both sides of the key card against my pants and flipped it through the hole in the bullet-shaped trash container next to the fire door. The cops could make what they liked of that, if the search was thorough.

Driving away from there, nicking lights and ignoring horns, I shook out my cell and called a number I'd recently committed to memory.

"Hi, you've got Smoke. Well, her disembodied voice. You know the drill."

I waited for the beep, then told her to barricade herself in her apartment and not answer her door for anyone but me. When she didn't pick up, I feared the worst, a tactic that's worked for me over the years. I ended the call and speed-dialed Alderdyce's cell.

When he came on I gave him as much as I could on the fly. There wasn't anything to be gained by throwing wraps over the Israelis anymore. He was professional enough to take in the information and defer the usual threats about withholding evidence for another time.

"So you think these spooks had Elysian

Fields under surveillance when the manager was murdered?" he asked when I finished.

"It doesn't make sense any other way. Somehow Sing found out about Dorn and Leibowitz and now she's cleaning up after herself. She's getting ready to light out, or she wouldn't be working so fast: First Tony, now the Israelis. You'd better jack up the security around Yummy. He may be next."

"More likely you. You're the easier mark. She just missed a twofer last night, and she's past cute tricks like ringing in a phony Cecelia Wynn to take you off the case."

"I'm still not sure why she went to the trouble. Maybe she thought I'd be one murder too many at that early stage. But there's an easier mark yet." I told him about Smoke Wygonik.

"What makes you think she can turn Sing? If it's Sing. Unless you let her sign a false statement about her boss's killing."

"I didn't coach her. I don't think she knows anything. But somehow Sing found out about my interest in Cecelia Wynn; I think Smoke told her, or someone sent by her, and Sing needs to close that loophole. I'm on my way there now, but —"

"I'll send a car. What's her address?"

I gave it to him and punched off. My phone chirped then. I had a message.

"Hey, it's Smoke. I just got in with a rotisserie chicken and a bottle of wine. Nice day for an indoor picnic, don't you think? What's this about locking myself in?"

Just then I was turning the corner onto Orleans, so I didn't call her back. I left the Cutlass rocking on its springs by the curb and climbed the steps to the converted warehouse where she lived. There was no police cruiser in sight yet, but I'd had a head start on the fleet.

She buzzed me into the building and I rode the elevator up, revolver in hand; that might be the way I would ride them from now on. When the doors opened and no one shot at me I trotted between the unfinished walls to her door.

She opened it without asking who'd knocked. She wasn't even holding her homemade bludgeon with the nail sticking out of the end.

I holstered the .38. "I told you to make sure —"

She swung the door wide, turning away from the opening in the same movement. Charlotte Sing was sitting in one of the unmatching armchairs. Her stockinged legs were crossed and a slim P-38 rested on her knee with her tiny hand wrapped around the butt.

# Thirty-Four

"Come in, Mr. Walker. Need I explain a gun in the hand is worth two on the hip?"

She looked like a porcelain doll in a Shanghai junk shop, but she didn't sound like anyone who might have modeled for it. Everyone who speaks English has an accent of some kind, depending on place of birth or environment; everyone but Madam Sing. She had inflections, there was nothing mechanical about her, but an army of coaches had worked on her speech, perfecting its shape, the way a master cabinetmaker hand-rubs mahogany until the surface is flawless. It had an eerie effect, on me at least. Just hearing it slowed my pulse and lowered my body temperature to ninety-seven.

Of course, the speaker herself might have had something to do with that. She was wanted for capital crimes in most of the countries of the world, and she'd never spent a moment in the backseat of a police car. Her fingerprints and DNA were in no one's file. The most recent photograph anyone had of her had been taken twenty years ago, when she'd applied for her passports: plural. She had more of them under different names than a deck has cards.

You could recognize her from that likeness, as old as it was. She was somewhere north of sixty, but cosmetic procedures, glandular injections, and a health regimen that made Cecelia Wynn's herbal pills seem like a triple cheeseburger kept her a well-preserved forty, always and forever.

I didn't wait for the order. I stepped inside far enough for Smoke to close the door, fished out the Chief's Special between the thumb and forefinger of my left hand, and laid it on a gateleg table, one of the items Smoke had furnished the place with from thrift stores. I stepped away from it.

"I'm sorry, Amos. She was here when I got back from the market. Who is she?"

"My poor manners." The Amerasian relaxed her grip on the Walther, but kept her hand resting on top of it. "The name I was born with is difficult for most Americans to pronounce. You may call me Charlotte Sing — a bastard combination of my two nationalities, but convenient. I'm usually addressed as Madam. I don't insist on it. My business is investments and imports."

Smoke jumped on it. "You're a smuggler?"

Sing smiled at me. "An intelligent young woman. You continue to impress me with your taste. A smuggler: Why not? It has a piratical ring I like."

She was wearing a tailored suit, a muted rose, with a blazer that buttoned in the middle and a skirt that caught her just above midcalf, red patent-leather heels on her feet. Her hair was shorter than I remembered, blue-black and swept to one side. Knowing her, it would all be up to the current fashion, and expensive enough to feed a village in her native South Korea. Being an international fugitive wasn't so hectic she couldn't keep abreast.

A gauze patch made a triangular interruption above her left temple where the hair was shaved. Had I fired two inches to her right the night before, this meeting would never have taken place.

"It was heroin, last time," I said. "Before that, it was human organs on the black market. Dope again, now. You're repeating yourself in your dotage."

If that hit home — and it should have, considering how much she'd spent in the war on gravity — she didn't show it. "You should know by now I never do exactly the same thing twice. When we spoke most recently, the drugs were a weapon, to undermine your precious society. They're still a means to an end, a pedestrian one this time. I need cash."

Smoke made an unladylike noise. She was dressed for the street, in a blue V-neck blouse, artfully faded jeans, and ankle boots. A green parka with a fake-fur lining lay across one arm of the sofa, next to a table holding up a woven cotton grocery sack. The neck of a bottle of white wine stuck out above the top. Her hair was loose, a little flyaway from static electricity. I couldn't see what color her eyes had chosen that moment. She was looking at her uninvited guest. "So you're a mule. I expected something more exotic."

"The young are so cynical. They haven't earned that privilege." She was talking for her, but not to her. "Every campaign needs funding from time to time. At the moment I'm down to my last hundred million. It doesn't go as far as it used to."

"Don't knock it, Charlotte," I said. "You've come a long way from the hook shop."

Now she looked at Smoke. "Mr. Walker's referring to my unpaid internship. I came to this country to join my father; not one of the Few Good Men, I'm sorry to say. He sold me into slavery. By the time I was fourteen, I knew every way there was to please a man. I should be grateful, I suppose. I used what I'd learned to make a profitable match, which I parlayed."

"You ran a good string," I said. "Right up until the World Bank froze all your accounts."

"Fortunately, I had the foresight to put a little aside. Enough, anyway, to buy my way into my current partnership."

Monomaniacs can't resist talking about themselves. I encouraged it. I'd been there less than five minutes, although it seemed longer. I didn't know what time to expect the squad car Alderdyce was sending. "What happened at Elysian Fields?" I asked.

"Petty greed, and a mistake on my part. It's not always good policy to keep the help in the dark. If I'd told him a portion of my plan, cut him in for a share of what he thought were the profits, he might have reconsidered selling so-called medical marijuana to pad his paycheck. I don't live in the past, however. I took steps."

"Lady, you've lived in the past so long you could use it as your voting address. Anybody else would've moved on after he made a billion off gambling and prostitution and human trafficking. You had to throw in with every crackpot who thinks the Statue of Liberty's a middle finger to the rest of the world. So you had the manager killed — or maybe you did it yourself, like you did Tony Pirandello — but before you could dispose of the body, the cops raided the place and found him. That burned your plan to use the health-food store as your base of North American operations. That was kind of too bad, because that little deal you pulled, substituting Alison Garland for Cecelia Wynn to get my nose out of your business, that was sweet. More like the old Madam Sing."

At the mention of the Pirandello shooting, she touched the bandage on her head with her free hand. "I underestimated your marksmanship in the dark. But the wound was slight enough to pass off as a minor accident, sparing the trouble of finding a doctor who wouldn't report it.

"By the time the situation changed, the Garland plan was too late to call off. I couldn't get in touch with her. She was an employee of mine, by the way: a computer filer with a credit bureau I use for money recycling, what you would call laundering. Not that she knew it; it's a subsidiary of a

347

subsidiary, and difficult to trace back to MacArthur Industries; or Pacific Rim, as it's now called. The photo in her personnel file was a close match with the one you —"

She stopped herself. She wouldn't have talked herself into a trap only a year ago. Life on the lam had sharpened certain reflexes, dulled others.

I pretended I hadn't heard. Everything depended on keeping her off the defensive. If time slowed any further, the clock would be running backwards. That cop was taking the scenic route. "It was pretty fancy stitching just to keep me from drawing attention to the place," I said. "Why not just do me like you did the manager?"

"Unlike him, you might have been missed. Your friend in the police department might have pursued the matter. Remember, when I made the plan there was still hope of reversing my blunder."

"Which was when you put Yummy on my tail, to make sure I took the bait."

"Yummy? Oh, yes, Mr. Mondadori. You once accused me of living in a pulp magazine, but the colorful nicknames you choose for your petty criminals tells me I'm not alone. He was useful, until he wasn't. You gave Miss Garland quite a fright in that restaurant, made her silence doubtful. After

Mr. Mondadori disposed of that problem, he thought committing a second murder so soon after the first entitled him to a bonus."

"He tried to blackmail you?"

"In his defense, he thought I was one of those white-collar women driven by desperation to break the law. I let him go on thinking that while I called in a favor from one of his associates, a more reliable man altogether."

"It would've been a lot less complicated if you'd gone to him first."

"In hindsight, yes. He was the man I had in mind for the disposal problem at Elysian Fields. That's his specialty, which is why I didn't think of him. Killing is Mondadori's. He'd killed the manager and been paid well for it, so I assumed he'd be as efficient in the case of Miss Garland. I could have paid him, of course, and never missed the amount: He had no idea of the size of my resources. I don't mind being taken advantage of — it goes with great wealth — but when is the bill paid in full?"

"That's easy," I said. "When you go to your body guy and have him dump Yummy's handiwork in the house he's living in. Then you tipped off the cops. What if he talked?"

"People in his line of work have a built-in

resistance to police interrogations. It's that charming underworld notion of honor among thieves."

"Not one of the delusions you suffer from."

"If I learned nothing else from my apprenticeship, it's that life has no value. I considered the situation worth the risk, if all it bought me was time to close up my operation and leave. I —" She turned her head a fraction of an inch, listening.

I'd heard it, too: A powerful engine rumbling into the block, tires crunching on broken asphalt as it braked. Cops don't use sirens on babysitting assignments. I spoke quickly to take her mind off it, shifting my weight onto the balls of my feet. I was out of reach of my .38, but there was another weapon within range.

"You lied when you said you never do anything the same way twice," I said. "You learned not to trust anyone with your killings but yourself, which is why you shot Pirandello in the car warehouse, just in case Yummy had told him who hired him for two murders. Then you did the same with the two Israeli agents who could place Yummy at the scene of the murder in Elysian Fields. He might talk his way out of the Garland rap, but connecting him with *two* homicides might turn him into a snitch before you could finish closing out those operations of yours. How'd you find out about them, by the way?"

"I have someone in Tel Aviv. He wasn't as punctual with the information as I would have liked. I won't use him again soon. Struggling to live within his means will make him more dependable next time."

"He must be someone high up."

"Not at all. Minor functionaries are privy to far more information than their high-profile superiors, and they're poorly paid. They're a bargain, really. And so eager to please."

Smoke put in an oar. She was standing by a window with the shade pulled down, methodically rubbing an arm with her other hand. "Why are you here?"

Sing looked at her as if she'd forgotten she was there. She hadn't, though. I jumped in before she could answer. I felt the vibration of the heavy-duty elevator rumbling up the shaft; I was standing on bare floor and Madam Sing was seated with a rug at her feet, so she might not have been aware of it, but I remembered how much noise it made as it slowed, and especially when it came to a stop. I spoke loudly to cover it. "She's here to do exactly the same thing for the fourth time. You're the only one still running around loose who can definitely tie Sing to the Cecelia Wynn case, and through that to five murders connected to it."

"Me? How can I — ?"

"Because you showed her Cecelia's picture."

The elevator stopped on that floor with a clang. It sounded as loud as someone using a pair of manhole covers for cymbals. The P-38 came up. I lunged, snatched the wine bottle from the sack on the end table, and swung, aiming for the hand holding the pistol.

Not fast enough, though. Not nearly fast enough to beat a .30-caliber slug.

# THIRTY-FIVE

The P-38 barked, a short savage yelp, just as the barrel of the bottle made contact with the hand holding the pistol. She'd aimed it at me, but the blow deflected the trajectory. I had the satisfaction of feeling bones snap, and hearing the same intake of breath I'd heard when I grazed her in the car warehouse, but even as the gun struck the floor and I kicked it away, dropping the bottle in favor of the Smith & Wesson behind my back, I turned Smoke's way just in time to see her knees give out. One hand was splayed on her blouse just above the waist. Blood leaked between the fingers.

Charlotte Sing was on her own knees, reaching for the Walther with her uninjured left hand. I hooked a foot under her midriff and heaved, flipping her over onto her side. She cried out when her broken hand struck the chair she'd been sitting in, shoving it crooked. I started toward where Smoke had fallen.

Then the door flew open, bringing the shattered jamb in with it, and also a man wearing the midnight-blue uniform of the Detroit Police Department with a Sig-Sauer semiautomatic clasped in both hands.

"Drop the weapon!" he roared. *"Now!"*

I dropped the weapon. Now. Exposition could wait.

"What a cocked-up mess."

Alderdyce was behind his desk, reading the report from the first officer on the scene.

I was standing on the other side, waiting for the telephone to ring. The cops he'd sent to Detroit Receiving had orders to call the moment there was news from the room where surgeons were operating on Smoke Wygonik. "If you're looking for an argument, I can't help you."

"You got two foreign nationals killed. If we'd known they were involved, we might've nabbed Sing outside their hotel room."

"They made a good case for keeping my mouth shut. They knew the risks. I sort of liked Dorn, but she said herself GOLEM agents have the life expectancy of the common housefly. And we can add Israel to the list of countries waiting in line to extradite."

I'd seen something you don't see every

day, Charlotte Sing cuffed to a DPD officer. He hadn't been able to shackle both wrists with shards of bone sticking out of her right hand, but she'd been pale with pain and in no mood to resist.

Smack behind the patrol car that took her away had come the EMS unit for Smoke. The girl had lost a lot of blood, despite my best efforts and those of Officer Winthrop of the Tactical Mobile Unit. As the attendants rolled her out she smiled wanly at me through the oxygen mask and was barely able to squeeze my hand.

Alderdyce said, "I never realized Sing was so small."

"So is a brown recluse," I said.

"What I mean is she must have climbed onto a stool to fire through that peephole."

"Not really. She could have stood on tiptoe and stretched her arm. If her timing was right she didn't have to see just when Dorn put her eye to it after she knocked. She must've been watching the hotel ever since she got herself patched up from the thing at Fort Wayne. She knew sooner or later one of them had to go out on some errand. When Leibowitz went for cigarettes, she got the one inside the room, then staked out the elevators."

"Five murders on top of a drug conspiracy. Yummy'll trade state's evidence for a twenty-year pop and call it Christmas."

"You'd better double his guard. She still has people on the outside."

"Is it okay if I already did that?"

The phone rang on his desk. He looked at caller ID. "Receiving." He picked up. "Alderdyce. Yes. When? Okay, thanks. I know." He hung up, his face bleak.

"Yeah." I let myself out.

The police located Smoke's parents in Madrid, New Mexico. They came in to bring the body back. Alderdyce, who'd supervised the details, stopped by my office on his way back to Homicide. He'd put on a sober black suit and knitted black tie for the occasion.

"Everything go all right?" I filled two glasses from the working bottle.

"Oh, we've got it down to a science now." He drank, swallowed, made the appropriate face. "I thought I should tell you in person what we found in a backpack in Smoke's loft."

"How much?"

"Just under ten thousand. I guess she spent some of it on incidentals."

"A rotisserie chicken and a bottle of wine."

"You're not surprised."

"I almost got it straight from Sing, but she caught herself. I'd figured it out by then; I just didn't know how deep Smoke was in. That morning she pressed me a little too hard to take her along when I went to the hotel — although she didn't know it was the hotel I was going to and I doubt she knew anything about it. It hadn't happened yet. I'd left a picture with her after I asked about Cecelia Wynn, the first time we met. Someone had to have told Sing what my interest was, and given her a photo so she could match it with a ringer. Ten thousand seems pretty steep, but there was more to the job.

"Yummy got the assignment to tail me around town and report to Sing, but after he blew his cover in the foyer of my building, and especially after he tried to jack her up for more money, Smoke inherited it. I didn't tell her much, but it was enough for Sing to track my progress. She knew I was spending quality time with Homicide, so she or one of her people staked out the precinct with a high-tech scanner. That's speculation, but it still makes as much sense as the first time I suggested it. She probably trusted that job to herself, just like when she followed up on it at Fort Wayne. Her organization's running low on employees she can rely on. Now that I think of it, that's why she stopped herself before outing Smoke. She never intended to kill her. She'd proven herself in my case."

"Moot point, if Sing killed you."

"She wasn't there for that, just to find out how much I knew. She isn't one to abandon a plan if it can be salvaged."

"We found a shopping list of herbs in the Dumpster behind the Wolverine Hotel, in a hand like Alison Garland used when she was impersonating Cecelia Wynn. Cecelia must have left it at the store. Sing gave it to Garland for practice. Do you think Smoke knew she was an accomplice to drug-dealing and murder?"

"I like to think not."

"She really got to you, didn't she?"

"Well, you know what they say." I drained my glass.

"Yeah. The bitch is dead."

# THIRTY-SIX

Charlotte Sing never stood trial in the United States. Israel filed for extradition, followed closely by China, both Koreas, Sweden, Denmark, and several emerging nations in Africa. There would be others as the news worked its way around the world, but the State Department gave China the first crack, as a gesture of good faith against Washington's monetary debt to Beijing. Detroit hollered loudest of all. No one was listening, as usual.

No footage appeared on TV and no pictures appeared in the papers of Sing, with a cast on her hand and her arm in a sling, boarding a Delta jet at Detroit Metropolitan Airport between two burly U.S. Marshals. That's because it was done by way of the underground sometime in the puny hours of the morning, to avoid any attempt to rescue her or on her life. An Islamic cleric in Syria had issued a fatwa against her for misappropriation of funds intended for the destruction of Israel; and as for Israel itself, what had happened to Eichmann in 1962 is considered current history there, and sound political policy.

So Madam Sing vanished behind the Bamboo Curtain, to face execution or life in some hole like the one Major Lazara Dorn had described to me. Not knowing which has aged me a little.

Meanwhile I had a case to put to rest.

The window-studded façade of the big house on Lake Shore Drive reflected itself in a fresh puddle of water in the courtyard. As often as William the chauffeur washed Alec Wynn's vehicles when he wasn't driving them, I still wasn't sure how he spent most of his day. I can operate a motor vehicle; anyone born within forty miles of Detroit can drive himself home from the maternity ward. It looked like a good job for catching up on my reading when I've had my fill of missing persons, international spies, dragon ladies, and lesbian bars. I don't mention corpses because I got my fill of them long ago.

Trina, the Brazilian maid, was expecting me. Her hair looked whiter and her eyes more dull, but that could have been projection on my part: I felt old enough and dull enough for both of us. She directed me to the morning room and returned to whatever her duties were. I was a fixture in the house now, requiring no escort.

Nothing had changed in the quiet room where Cecelia Wynn had sat writing invitations and notes of thanks at her desk; nothing, that is, except the stench of chlorine from the swimming pool outside. It seemed stronger, and this time the door was closed. The surface should have been littered with the carcasses of birds that had flown too close to the fumes. Maybe the pool man had taken care of that, working his miniature butterfly net at the end of a long staff. When Trina left I slid open the glass door and stepped onto the tiles, breathing through my mouth. It didn't keep my eyes from watering. I lit a cigarette, fighting poison with poison.

Wynn came out five minutes later. Today's gray suit was tailored as well as all the others, but he seemed to have shriveled inside it. The time that had passed still wasn't that long, but anyone can give a physical impression based on a mental state.

"I walked out of a meeting after you called," he said. "I wasn't really there

anyway. I hope this means you've found Cecelia."

"I've found her. I think."

"You *think*?"

"I haven't found her in all the places I've
looked, but negative evidence doesn't count.
That's why I came back here."

"You're babbling."

"Her note," I said. " 'Don't look for me.'
Of course she knew you would. You had to
prove you could fulfill at least one of the
duties of a husband."

"I told you of my shortcomings in confidence. Who else have you told?"

"Stop talking like an idiot. Don't you
watch television? These days you're not a
man until your little man lets you down." I
lit another cigarette, to fill my nostrils with
something besides chlorine, and flipped the
match toward the pool. It floated motion-
less for a moment, then drifted toward the
filter outlet, which sucked it in with a slurp.
"If it means anything, Debner couldn't keep
her happy either. No man could."

"Are you saying my wife's a nymphoma-
niac?"

"No. She's a homosexual."

"That's a damn lie." But it lacked conviction.

"Not a practicing one. It's possible she

didn't even realize what her problem was until five weeks ago, when she accidentally saw your former maid naked. The maid's a lesbian and recognized the reaction. They develop a sense for it after a while, like a blind man's hearing. Cecelia was proud, wasn't she?"

"Intensely. She didn't see it as a sin. Neither do I. Pride's responsible —"

"I know all about the pyramids and the Declaration of Independence. This isn't a PowerPoint presentation. When are you going to do something about this pool?"

The change of subject threw him for a moment, but he seemed to welcome it. "The man I consulted has a crew coming next week. He thinks it's methane gas causing the odor, from an old sewer line running under the yard. The city capped it off when the new one went in, before I bought this house, but he thinks it's developed a crack. It's a choice of digging up the yard or adding more and more chlorine to cover the smell. Have we talked enough about the damn pool?"

"Sure. I was just gathering my thoughts. I'm going to be a cockeyed psychologist, like everyone else who watches daytime TV." I waited for him to shoot that down or wave me on, but I couldn't tell if he was even listening. He stood staring at the fence that separated his house from his neighbor's, fists balled in his pants pockets. Maybe there was a long-standing feud over property lines. You never know what the rich are thinking.

"A lot of smoke gets blown about the male fear of loss of masculinity," I said. "No one talks about women's fears for their femininity, especially strong women who are often compared to men because they don't pull their aprons up over their faces when a problem needs a solution. For most women it's a lark, a little harmless experimentation in college or in the cloakroom at the nineteenth hole. You and I will never get it, because we're men, and ostensibly heterosexual. But Cecelia wouldn't either. She had a specific idea of the kind of woman she was and the kind she wanted to be. The herbal pills were all part of that: an ongoing campaign to improve herself according to the conventions. But the conventions threw her a curve.

"She'd fight it, of course," I went on. "She fired a servant out of hand, to get temptation out of the house, but that would just increase the pressure to look for it outside. I spent an hour in a bar established just for that purpose. When a woman like her faces

364

the truth, she can go one of three ways: ignore the situation, embrace it, or run away from it. The first one's a ticking time bomb. The second's thrilling to think about, but it means giving up on the plan you spent so much time building, just walking away from it, and that's frightening as hell, because you can't know what you're trading it in for. That leaves running away. But she'd already tried that with Lloyd Debner, back when she had no idea why she was so dissatisfied with her life. Now that she knew, there was only one other escape route.

"She would be too proud to spell it all out in her note."

Wynn's face matched his suit. He groped with one hand, grasped air, stretched his arm, felt the filigreed metal of a pool chair, shuffled over, and lowered himself into it. I'd never seen a man age so quickly outside of science fiction. He put his elbows on his knees and his face in his hands.

I almost threw my cigarette butt into the water, thought better of it, and crushed it underfoot on the tiles. Even that seemed like a blasphemy: Everything was hallowed ground. "I'm sorry I doubted you, Mr. Wynn, just because her note was undated. When you reach that point in your thinking, who cares what day it is?"

"Where is she, Walker? Where's Cecelia?"

I stepped over to the pool and looked at my reflection. A light steam rose from the heated water into the frosty spring air. I could see through to the bottom, but there was a recessed area under a shelf along the north edge, some contractor's idea of a helpful step to boost swimmers out of the pool. In practice it was a design flaw, creating a pocket that would trap leaves and twigs and other debris that would normally be sucked into the filter outlet or float to the surface. Shadows swirled in the pocket, thick and dark and full of secrets.

# ABOUT THE AUTHOR

**Loren D. Estleman** has written more than seventy novels and has won four Shamus Awards for detective fiction, five Spur Awards for Western fiction, and three Western Heritage Awards. The Western Writers of America also has awarded Estleman the Owen Wister Award for Lifetime Contribution to Western Literature. In 2013, the Private Eye Writers of America presented him with its lifetime achievement award, the Eye. *Don't Look for Me* is the twenty-third Amos Walker mystery, and it marks the final book of Walker's Charlotte Sing trilogy that began with *American Detective* and *Infernal Angels.* His recent novels include the third Valentino mystery, *Alive!,* and an epic historical fiction novel of an iconic American gangster, *The Confessions of Al Capone.* He lives with his wife, author Deborah Morgan, in Michigan.

Learn more at www.lorenestleman.com.